Dear Reader,

Welcome to the Daddy School! Some of you may have been reading my Daddy School books since the first one came out in November 1997. Some of you may never have read a Daddy School book before. Just to bring you up to speed: the Daddy School is a program founded by best friends Allison Winslow (a neonatal nurse) and Molly Saunders-Russo (a preschool director) in Arlington, Connecticut. In their work, they kept meeting men who wanted to be better fathers but weren't sure how to go about it. Not only did they set up a successful school for fathers, but they found true love in the first two books of the series.

The relationship between men and their children is so complex, so heart stirring. My father was a committed and enthusiastic caregiver in an era when most men would have preferred eating live worms to changing a dirty diaper, and my husband has been equally devoted to our two sons, serving on the front lines at mealtimes, cleaning up after them, bandaging their scrapes and cuts and explaining the mysteries of the universe to them. He taught them how to build model airplanes, how to pitch curve balls and how to deal with bullies. They're teenagers now, as big as he is, and the bonds he forged with each son the instant a midwife placed him in my husband's waiting hands have grown stronger every day.

For a man, opening one's heart to a child can be as risky as opening one's heart to a woman. Fortunately, for men like Brett Stockton, the hero of *Somebody's Dad,* the Daddy School can help a man find the courage to take that risk.

I hope you enjoy *Somebody's Dad.* Please feel free to visit my Web site, www.juditharnold.com, or write to me c/o Harlequin Books.

Judith Arnold

JUDITH ARNOLD

Somebody's Dad

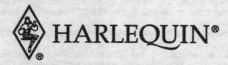

TORONTO • NEW YORK • LONDON
AMSTERDAM • PARIS • SYDNEY • HAMBURG
STOCKHOLM • ATHENS • TOKYO • MILAN • MADRID
PRAGUE • WARSAW • BUDAPEST • AUCKLAND

To my husband, Ted,
a fanatically proud and devoted daddy

ISBN 0-373-83499-3

SOMEBODY'S DAD

This edition published by arrangement with Harlequin Books S.A.

® and TM are trademarks of the publisher. Trademarks indicated with
® are registered in the United States Patent and Trademark Office, the
Canadian Trade Marks Office and in other countries.

Visit us at www.eHarlequin.com

Printed in U.S.A.

CHAPTER ONE

"I DON'T WANT to do this," Brett muttered.

"Am I supposed to care?" Janet adjusted his necktie, giving it a gratuitous tug, as if she wanted to strangle him into silence. "You don't have a choice, Brett."

"Who's the boss here?" he asked.

Her response was a snort. On paper, he was the boss. But in reality, Janet ruled the office with brutal precision. Short and lean, her silver hair brushed straight back from her face and her nose curved like a beak, she reminded him of a hawk—one that wouldn't hesitate to use her talons if necessary. As an assistant, she was invaluable. As a colleague, she was a pain in the ass.

He sighed, not an easy thing to do with the knot of his tie pressed snugly against his windpipe. She smoothed the collar of his jacket, then studied his hair with obvious disapproval. "You've got to do this. Arlington Financial Services needs a human face in its annual report. You're human and you've got a face. So—as my grandson would say—get over it."

"Get over what?" he argued. "I pose for a picture every damned year. No law says I've got to like it."

"I know you weren't satisfied with last year's photographer," Janet conceded.

"He made me look like Mr. Potato Head's mutant half brother."

"You didn't look that bad," Janet argued.

"I looked bad."

"Well, I hired a different photographer for this year. I met her when she arrived, and she's very nice."

"Great." Just what Brett needed: a nice photographer. It didn't matter how nice she was; he hated posing for photos. They always seemed so...*posed.* In his high school yearbook photo, he appeared to be suffering from terminal hay fever. In his college yearbook photo, his ailment must have descended from his sinuses to his gastrointestinal system; his grimace in the picture could as easily have arisen from acute heartburn as from his discomfort in sitting for a photographic portrait.

And now, as the founder and president of Arlington Financial Services, Brett had to pose for a photograph for the annual report every year. He didn't need Janet to explain to him that investors felt better when they had a picture of the man they were entrusting with their money—but for the life of him, he didn't know how year after year of awkward, self-conscious photos of him in the report could reassure anyone he was worthy of their trust. It was a miracle his clients didn't react to his pained smile and anguished eyes by withdrawing every last cent they had invested in his funds.

"You know what I should have done?" he asked as Janet whipped a comb from a pocket in her skirt and started fussing with his hair. "I should have hired a model to stand in for me. Someone rugged and confident."

"Rare is the male model who looks rugged and confident." She clicked her tongue, pocketed her comb and turned to inspect his desk. "The folder has to go," she declared.

"I need that folder. I'm working." At least, he'd been working until five minutes ago, when Janet had invaded his office to announce that the photographer had arrived and was currently taking pictures of assorted members of the Arlington Financial Services team.

"Your desk should be neat. Clients don't want to think they're handing their money over to someone whose desk is messy."

Brett's desk was anything but messy. The onyx pen stand, the modern, geometrically shaped lamp, the teak In and Out boxes and sleek computer were arranged with enough flair to resemble a layout from some high-end office supply catalog. The open folder was the only indication that someone actually toiled at that desk. "Maybe the photo should show me working. That would inspire confidence."

"I've seen you working, and the sight doesn't inspire confidence. You look like a slob when you work. You've always got your sleeves rolled up unevenly and your tie hanging loose and your hair all messy."

"Hey, come on! I'm a genius!"

"I'm not arguing," Janet said, gliding around his desk and shutting the folder. "But you don't look like you're working when you're working."

"Okay. I get it. I'm supposed to look nothing like the way I look when I'm actually working, so people who see my photo will think I'm working."

"Exactly." She slid the folder into the top drawer

of his desk. "Sit," she ordered him, gesturing toward his chair. "I'll go find that photographer and tell her you're ready."

"I'm not ready," Brett protested, but Janet ignored him, marching toward the door like a raptor in search of fresh prey. "Say I'm in a lousy mood!" he shouted after her.

Janet mumbled something unintelligible and probably profane as she disappeared down the hall.

Brett sighed again, then wedged his index finger beneath the knot of his tie and eased it down a couple of centimeters. Maybe if he could be photographed in a sweatshirt and jeans, sitting for a photographer wouldn't bother him so much.

No. His apparel wasn't the problem. Posing was. Something about staring into the cyclops lens of a camera unnerved him.

He couldn't imagine why getting shot—by a camera, for God's sake, not by a gun—rattled him so much. He ran a successful business, made plenty of money for his clients and himself, lived affluently and didn't resemble Mr. Potato Head's mutant half brother, except in last year's annual report. He played cutthroat tennis and dollar-ante poker, went head-to-head with Wall Street nabobs, and strong-armed friends and enemies alike into donating money to his pet causes.

But bring a photographer into the situation and he'd freeze up. His jaw would stiffen, his neck would ache and he'd feel clumsy, at the mercy of someone he didn't even know. He hated to be at anyone's mercy.

"He's in here," he heard Janet saying, her voice

growing louder as she neared his office door. "He's in a lousy mood."

Brett swore under his breath. He glanced at the open doorway, then focused on the empty desk in front of him. As much as he hated being at the mercy of others, he also hated being idle. He ought to be reviewing his file on Baro-Tech, Inc., so he could decide whether to invest money from his high-risk fund in the firm. He ought to be doing *anything*—picking the brains of his managers, checking out the new models on the Porsche web site, playing tic-tac-toe left hand against right—anything other than staring at his work-free desk, braced like a convict about to face a firing squad, about to get *shot*.

"Right in here," Janet continued, and he forced himself to rise from his chair and attempt a cordial welcome for the photographer his secretary led into the room. She appeared young, breezy, as relaxed as he was tense. Her smile was so natural he couldn't help returning it, even though in his case it was more a courtesy than a genuine show of pleasure.

She walked over to him, her right hand outstretched and her gaze steady. Straight, dark-blond hair framed the sort of face that could be called handsome: sharp chin, high forehead, long nose and large hazel eyes. She wore khakis, a white silk T-shirt and a lightweight moss-colored blazer that picked up the green in her eyes. In her left hand she gripped the handles of a bulky leather tote bag.

Her camera would be in that tote, he reminded himself, his smile fading.

"Well," she said cheerfully, "you're much better looking than I expected."

"I showed her last year's annual report," Janet

informed him. "Sharon Bartell, this is Brett Stockton. Brett, this is Sharon Bartell, and whether or not you want her taking your photo, she's going to do it. So be a big boy and eat your vegetables." With that, Janet glided from the room.

The photographer peered after her for a moment. When she turned back to Brett, she was grinning. "She's quite a character."

"That's one way of putting it." He let out a breath. "You're not going to make me eat my vegetables, are you?"

"No vegetables. I did bring lollipops." She ventured farther into the room, studying it from different perspectives. Adjusting the vertical blinds, she pondered the angle of the late-morning sunlight that filtered in, her lips pressed together and her expression thoughtful. A tiny scowl spanned the bridge of her nose as she contemplated her surroundings.

He wondered if he'd have to defend his office to her. It was a fine office. Not big, nothing ostentatious about it and it suited him. He'd be damned if he was going to let her put him on the defensive. He'd hired her, after all—well, technically, Janet had hired her, but Brett was the CEO of the company paying her fee—and it was her job to make him look human while he sat at his desk, not to inspect his office with such a critical eye.

"Okay." Apparently done analyzing the room, she strode to his desk and switched on the light. Then she set her bag on one of the visitors' chairs and rummaged through it. When she pulled out her camera he winced. She must have noticed, because she said, "Lots of people hate having their pictures taken, Mr. Stockton. I'll make it as painless as I can.''

''I appreciate that.''

''Why don't you sit.'' She pointed to his chair, then poked around some more in her bag and removed a flashgun and a light meter. She was slim and long limbed. Little makeup, no nail polish. When her hair fell in front of her face, she tucked it behind her ears. Her lack of elegance made her look like a teenager, but the faint lines at the outer corners of her eyes added a few years to her appearance. ''I've taken plenty of pictures of your staff already,'' she told him, her voice a rich alto, much too mature to belong to a teenager. Late twenties, he'd guess. ''A few candids, a few posed. Whoever publishes your annual report should have more than enough material to choose from.''

''That'll thrill them,'' Brett said dryly.

She smiled. Every time she smiled, he realized, her face transformed from handsome to pretty. Her cheeks arched, her thin lips spread wide and her eyes brightened.

He watched her as she pressed a button on her light meter and frowned. Frowning transformed her face, too, animating it. He hoped she wasn't a poker player, because her every thought played clearly across her face. ''Your office is kind of dark,'' she said. ''Doesn't it bother you, working in this dim light?''

''I was a vampire in a previous life,'' he confided.

She laughed, a throaty sound, and met his gaze. He allowed himself a brief smile, which slipped away once she resumed working with her light meter.

She pulled a white square of cardboard from her bag and affixed it to her flashgun with a rubber band.

"Last year the photographer really hated the light in this room," Brett told her. "He wound up bringing in one of those huge lamps that resemble umbrellas."

"I'll bet that made you feel like a celebrity." She flashed the gun while monitoring her light gauge.

The sudden explosion of light caused him to flinch. "It made me feel like an idiot," he said.

"I'll try not to make you feel like an idiot today." She sent him a quick smile. He wished she would laugh again. Or flick her hair back so he could observe the sleek line of her chin, the delicate curve of her ear, the small gold hoop adorning the lobe.

She glanced at him and he realized she'd caught him—well, not exactly ogling her, but staring. He averted his gaze, feeling very much like an idiot, after all.

"No, no—look at me. I won't bite, I promise," she teased. "You're the vampire, not me."

He turned back to her and she gave him a dazzling smile. He wished he could return it, but she was lifting the camera to her eye and he felt himself go rigid.

She hesitated, her brow dipping in a frown. "Oh, my. You look like you just swallowed something disgusting, Brett. Can I call you Brett?"

"Call me whatever you want," he grumbled.

"You know what I do when I'm photographing a child and the child starts to panic?"

"You give him a lollipop."

"I give him a toy." She lowered her camera and dug around in her tote. After a few seconds she pulled out a small stuffed bunny. "No, that won't do. What kind of toys do you like?"

"I don't like toys."

"No toys?"

"Unless you count high-performance cars."

She groped in her bag. "Nope—no cars in here. Do you like dancing girls?"

He couldn't tell if she was mocking him or just trying to loosen him up, but her question edged toward one of those illegal areas—sexual harassment or something. Before he could decide whether to act indignant, she pulled from her tote a doll dressed as a belly dancer. A flimsy square of cloth hung across the doll's mouth, and she wore a filmy vest and blousy trousers and lots of plastic beads around her neck. She perched the doll on his desk and pressed down on the doll's head. Apparently it contained some sort of spring mechanism, because the doll proceeded to bounce up and down and gyrate.

Brett guffawed.

She snapped a photo.

"Are you crazy?" he asked, still laughing. The doll was ridiculous, her Betty Boop eyes painted onto her plastic face, her midsection bouncing around. "You can't use that picture."

"Why not? It's great." Before he could object, she snapped another photo, and another.

"Seriously." He held up his hand to stop her. "If my clients see a photo of me with that—that *thing* on my desk, they're going to pull their money out of Arlington Financial Services and have me carted off to the nearest padded cell."

"She won't show up in the photo. Don't worry about that."

"She's grotesque."

"She made you smile. She usually works better than the bunny on kids, too." Sharon grinned at him, and this time he grinned back. "You look wonderful when you smile. I got some great shots of you."

"Are you sure you'll be able to cut her out of the picture?" he asked, gesturing toward the plastic belly dancer. Unable to resist, he reached out and pressed the doll's head. It launched into a fresh round of bouncing and gyrating, and he laughed again. The click of the shutter as she shot another picture eroded his amusement.

"You'd be amazed at what technology can do with a photograph. But if you'd really like, I'll take her away. Maybe we should get a few serious shots, anyway."

"Yeah, that would be useful. I don't think my clients want to see me grinning like a fool."

"You were grinning like a successful executive," she assured him, scooping up the doll and dropping it into her tote. Turning back to him, she lifted her camera, then hesitated. "And now, instead of a successful executive, you look like a successful executive who's overdosed on a laxative. I know I said serious—not panicked."

"Maybe my clients should be aware of how much panic is involved in high-stakes investing."

"Do you panic a lot?"

"No," he admitted, lowering his hands to his knees so she wouldn't see how tightly fisted they were. "I'm perfectly calm ninety-eight percent of the time. The other two percent of the time, I'm posing for pictures."

"Good thing you decided not to become a movie

star.'' As she talked she snapped photos. He heard the camera's motor, saw the flashgun fire in blinks of light, and tried to ignore the pressure of his tie against his Adam's apple. ''You're an extremely handsome man, you know,'' she said as she shifted a few steps to her left, took aim and snapped a few more shots.

''Are you making a pass at me?'' he asked, amused despite his anxiety.

''You've got me figured out, haven't you.'' *Click.* ''No, I'm not making a pass at you. Just stating a fact.'' *Click.* ''That's nice, Brett. If you could just…''

''Just what?''

''Nothing.'' *Click, click, click.* He had no idea what he'd done, what she'd wanted him to do, what she'd changed her mind about. All he heard were the clicks. His jaw cramped from his effort to hold it still. He tried to gaze past her but couldn't, not when the left half of her face was hidden by her camera and the right half looked so intent, her eye shut, her chin steady. ''You're doing great.''

''No, I'm not.''

''Ten bucks says you're going to win the Hunky Executive Award based on your annual report photo.'' *Click, click.*

He laughed and she clicked again. ''You *are* making a pass at me.''

''I make passes at everyone, especially if it gets them to look as good as you look right now.''

He knew she was playing him, but he was enjoying the game. Usually when a woman flirted with him, she had a specific, selfish goal in mind: to snag him. When Sharon Bartell flirted with him, it was for an utterly selfless reason: to improve his appearance in her viewfinder. He couldn't imagine why her flirting would work—and for all he knew, it *wasn't* working. She might be lying about his appearance in the hope that he'd believe her and uncoil a little.

Even if she was lying, he liked being complimented by her. He didn't have to try to guess what her angle was, whether she was hoping for a one-night stand or something more involved, whether she was more attracted to his personality, his wealth or his connections. He knew what Sharon wanted to get out of this encounter: a halfway decent photograph of him. Not having to figure out her motives, he could let down his guard a little.

Click, click. Click. "You ought to try wearing more colorful ties," she advised.

"Really?" His tie was subtle, quietly classy. He hated ties but recognized their necessity. If he was going to wear one, he didn't want it to trumpet its existence.

"Even hotshot executives wear colorful ties these days." *Click. Click.* "A blue tie would bring out the color in your eyes."

"Why would I want to do that?"

"Because your eyes are sexy." One final click and she lowered her camera. "I think I've got enough."

He exhaled, feeling the muscles along his spine unclench. Loosening his not-blue tie and unfastening his collar button were as refreshing as guzzling cold water after a hard-fought set on the court at the tennis club. "Does this mean you don't think my eyes are sexy anymore?" he asked.

She smiled. "I still think they're sexy." Before he could react, she swung her camera back up and shot a final, unposed picture of him. He felt ambushed. He hadn't had a chance to tense up and shape his mouth into its I-hate-posing grimace. His posture was slouchy, his tie dangling. God knew he wouldn't look like the competent founder and president of a highly profitable investment firm in that photo.

He wanted to ask her why she'd taken it, since it was certainly not going to appear in the annual report. He wanted, even more, to ask her whether she truly thought his eyes were sexy, whether she'd be flattered or upset if he'd said he thought her eyes were sexy, too. But she hunched over her tote, fastening a lens cap onto her camera and then carefully wedging it in, removing the cardboard from her flashgun and packing those items away. Her posture and actions warned him off. "Do you want a lollipop?" she asked. "I've got grape, orange and cherry—the kind with a blob of chocolate inside."

All the flirtatiousness had left her. She was closing up, shutting down, through with Brett Stockton and Arlington Financial. And yes, he realized, her eyes *were* sexy, tilting slightly up at the outer corners and fringed with thick golden lashes.

A lollipop was the last thing he wanted from her. He wasn't sure what the first thing was, though. A photo for the annual report, he told himself—but he wanted something more. Her attention, her wit, the mischievous smile she wore when she made her doll belly dance for him. Another, longer, look at her eyes.

Belatedly, he remembered to answer her. "No, thanks. I don't really like lollipops."

She hoisted her bag and turned to him, her expression cool and reserved, not a shred of playfulness in it. "You'll see all the proofs," she told him, "but I'll develop the half-dozen I think are the best. You can decide which one to use."

"Fine." He rose from his chair, aware that she was about to leave.

"I got some excellent shots of you," she assured him, although her smile seemed less certain than her words. She returned her gaze to her tote, denying him the chance to peer into her eyes. "You'll definitely have some good ones to work with."

"Thank you."

"I'll let Janet know when the proofs are ready. It should be within the week." She extended her hand to him.

He took it and held on for a moment. He felt overwhelmed by questions: *How sexy do you think I am? How colorful should my ties be? Did you mean anything you said in the past fifteen minutes, or was it all just a game to trick me into looking human for your camera? Why should I care if it was?*

But she was already sliding her hand from his grip and starting for the door. "Thanks again," he said.

With a wave and a nod, she was gone.

HE REALLY DID have sexy eyes.

Sharon's taste had never run to buttoned-down executive types, but Brett Stockton lingered in her mind long after she'd left his office. He was a man of intriguing contradictions: those soft blue eyes set in a face of hard angles, a face that radiated enormous warmth when he smiled and biting frost when he didn't. He'd worn an obviously expensive suit tailored to his trim body, but his apparel seemed to fit him better once he'd loosened his tie and opened his collar button. Maybe he'd looked more together when he'd been less buttoned-down because by the time he'd tugged his tie loose she was finished taking pictures of him.

That, of course, was his biggest contradiction: that a man as successful as Brett Stockton, the president of a multimillion dollar investment firm, a power broker in Arlington, a lord of the realm, could be so intimidated by a camera.

She would have liked to spend longer with him. Actually, she would have liked to take him out of his office and someplace where the light would be smoother and warmer, someplace where he could have focused on something other than her and her camera. A profile shot would not have been appropriate for his company's annual report, but she could have done wonders with one, capturing the harsh lines of his nose and chin, the sheer plane of his cheek, the dark waves of hair liberating themselves from the dictates of his comb. She would have kept his tie loose, the sign of a man who worked so hard he couldn't be bothered with impeccable grooming.

After assuring his secretary that the proofs would be ready in about a week, Sharon left the suite of offices that housed Arlington Financial Services, one of several companies that filled the floors of a swanky brick office building in downtown Arlington. Waiting for the elevator to arrive, she wondered whether she should distribute her business card to the other companies—a market research firm, a consulting firm, a law firm identified by a high-powered string of partner names. Maybe they published annual reports, too. Maybe creating those annual reports would require the services of a diligent, tal-

ented photographer with a small studio and a large
pile of bills.

She decided to wait until the photos for Arlington
Financial Services were ready, and then hand out her
card. If the photos came out well, she could suggest
Brett Stockton as a reference when she tried to drum
up business elsewhere.

Winning this job had been a coup. She'd never
been good at marketing her services. She'd always
preferred to concentrate on the artistic side of photography: getting the lighting right, composing the
photos well, playing with color, capturing scenes at
their most telling moments, making people look better than they expected. Advertising, promoting, bill-
ing and balancing the books—those were the aspects
of her job that she hated. Angie took care of the
bookkeeping for her and kept her ads up to date in
the local circulars. But the most important selling
tools Sharon had were the quality of the photos she
took, and herself. She was getting better at pressing
her cards into the hands of people who might hire
her, but it still wasn't easy for her.

Today had gone well, though. She'd gotten some
wonderful candids of Arlington's staff. A terrific shot
of two employees at the coffee machine, debating the
possible impact of the Federal Reserve's latest ad-
justment of the prime rate. A shot of a fund manager
alone in her office, staring out the window as if trying to divine economic trends from the pattern of the
traffic on Hauser Boulevard. And that final shot of
Brett Stockton, when he'd let down his guard.

She couldn't wait to see how that one came out.

The elevator carried her down to the basement garage, and as she entered the echoing expanse of cars

and concrete, she tried to put Stockton out of her mind. But his image seemed imprinted on her memory as if it were a negative.

She knew next to nothing about him. His funds were highly rated, but when it came to investments, she was lucky to be able to set aside a few dollars a week for her local savings account. Stock and bond funds were beyond her budget right now.

High-performance cars were also beyond her budget. As she strolled along the row of cars in the garage, she wondered which, if any, of the expensive models belonged to him. The BMW over there? That Infiniti? The metallic-silver Audi? The Porsche with the big spoiler swooping below the rear window?

Her Volvo was parked at the far end of the visitors' row. It was eleven years old and showing its age, but it still ran. Sharon treated it gently. She fed it the highest grade of gasoline, vacuumed its interior once a month and prayed a lot. Three years ago, she would not have imagined that she'd someday be pleading with God to keep her car alive and functioning, but life was full of surprises.

Fortunately, sometimes those surprises were good ones.

That she was still thinking about Brett Stockton's beautiful blue eyes as she steered out of the garage and into the traffic was a surprise. Whether a good or a bad one she couldn't say.

CHAPTER TWO

HE SPOTTED HER on the corner in front of the entrance to the YMCA. She stood gazing up at the
door's facade, camera in hand, her hair pale against
her blazer.

The YMCA was located in an old, bulky structure
that occupied most of the block. Built of brownstone,
it boasted towering front doors embellished by gothic
ornamentation. Brett had always considered it ostentatious for a building that housed a sweat-smelling
gym, a bunch of children's arts-and-crafts and swimming programs, and a few classrooms where adult
ed courses with titles like "Six Weeks to Working
Italian" and "Basic Carpentry Techniques" were
held. But despite the building's delusions of archi-
tectural grandeur, he occasionally made use of that
sweat-smelling gym when he and his friends got together to shoot hoops. The Italian and carpentry
classes didn't interest him, and as far as Brett was
concerned, the children's programs—full of paint-
smeared, noisy tykes racing up and down the halls,
their shrieks echoing off every hard surface—were
the best reason to avoid the YMCA during daylight
hours.

The late-afternoon sunlight washed the facade in
pink and gold, highlighting the rococo trim. Brett
stood in the doorway of his own office building half

a block down from the Y, observing Sharon Bartell as she lifted her camera, aimed at the doorway and fired. Watching a building get shot didn't bother him at all.

She appeared oblivious to the rush-hour cacophony around her. Pedestrians swarmed past her, most of them thoughtfully giving her a wide berth. Cars cruised through the intersection in four directions; the light at the corner switched from green to red to green again, causing engines to rumble as they slowed down and roar as they accelerated. Sharon stood isolated amid the traffic and noise, protected from it by an invisible shell of concentration.

He could never detach himself from his surroundings that way. When he was working he needed to be free of distraction. He liked the dim lighting of his office because it helped him to focus on the one illuminated area of the room—his desk. He put up with Janet's officiousness because she guarded his office door ferociously, saving him from unnecessary distractions. When he was playing he didn't care what was going on around him—and how loud it was. But at work he required silence and stillness.

Sharon didn't seem to have any problem creating her own silence and stillness in the midst of chaos. That had to be a talent at least as valuable as being able to take good photos—and being able to make an uptight subject of her photos laugh.

Spying on her from the doorway of his own building, he admitted that she'd been on his mind most of the afternoon. Not because she was ravishingly gorgeous but because… Well, he wasn't quite sure why. Partly it was her grace, the way she moved so efficiently, so smoothly, with such confidence. Partly it was her sense of humor, teasing him with that silly dancing doll and the promise of a lollipop. Partly it was the intelligence in her eyes, the animation lighting them. But mostly it was that final shot she'd taken of him, when his defenses had been down. He hadn't been able to stop thinking about that.

At the end of the day, he ordinarily would have gone from his office straight to the basement garage, but that evening he'd wanted to stop in at the Connecticut Bank and Trust branch at the opposite corner of the street to check on the deposits for that weekend's fund-raiser. He could have phoned the manager there and gotten the figures from her, but he'd been restless all afternoon, and the sky outside his window had been cloudless and shimmering as the sun spread late-summer warmth down to the horizon. And after the torment of posing for pictures earlier that day, a stroll through the fresh air of early evening in downtown Arlington might help him burn off some tension.

The moment he spotted Sharon snapping photos of the YMCA building, his errand at the bank evaporated from his mind.

She lowered her camera, and he took that as his cue to approach her. The pedestrians still detoured around her the way they might steer clear of a panhandler, but she didn't notice.

She didn't notice him, either. Even when he was just a few feet from her, she remained transfixed by the building before her, examining it as if searching for flaws in the elaborate relief work that framed the massive double door. "Hey," he called, quietly enough that she could pretend she hadn't heard him if she didn't want to talk.

She spun around and her face broke into a smile. Had he thought she wasn't ravishingly gorgeous?

She wasn't, not by the usual standards. Her nose and chin were too long, her cheeks too hollow, her eyebrows too pale. Yet the way her face lit up, the way it became infused with energy and spirit amazed him here just as it had in his office. She didn't need to trot out her little belly dancer doll to get past his defenses. A single smile did the trick.

"Hi! Give me a sec," she said, then turned back to the building, moved a few steps to the left and lifted her camera to her face once more. He saw that shell of intense concentration close around her again as she took a few more photos. Then she let out a long breath, snapped the lens cap onto the camera and faced him. "I just wanted to capture the building while the light was good. It changes so fast at this time of day." She glanced westward, and he looked, too. Even to his untrained eye, the sky appeared a little pinker than it had been just minutes ago.

"Does the YMCA publish an annual report?" he asked.

She chuckled. "If they do, they didn't hire me to do the photos. This is spec work." She packed her camera into her tote bag. "Buildings are easy. They don't get nervous when they see me." Satisfied that the camera was securely stored, she lifted the tote. "The light was just perfect. It really did gorgeous things to the building's facade. It made the brownstone look like copper. When you get that kind of light, not quite twilight but a sort of amber radiance..." She drifted off and her smile grew hesitant.

"An amber radiance," he repeated, curious to hear the rest of her thought.

She shrugged, obviously embarrassed. "I don't mean to rhapsodize. It was just a very nice lighting effect, that's all."

"Rhapsodize away." He realized that her description of the light was exactly what he would have expected from her. Anyone who'd passed her while she'd been photographing the building would have expected it. That was why they'd circled around her—out of respect for her work and her sensitivity to things like amber radiance and brownstone turning to copper.

He also realized that when she talked about the pictures she'd been taking, she radiated her own unusual light—a passion about what she was doing, what it meant, how much she enjoyed it.

Brett loved his work, too. He could relate to that kind of passion. "So, this was spec work?"

"I've been taking some pictures around town." She glanced at her watch, then returned her gaze to him.

"I'm sorry—I'm keeping you." But he wasn't ready to say goodbye to her yet. Even when he'd been suffering through the ordeal of having her photograph him, he hadn't been eager for her to leave. Sharon Bartell intrigued him. Especially when she smiled.

He ought to get her phone number, at least. She wasn't wearing a wedding band, and she'd said she thought he had sexy eyes, even if that had only been a professional tactic. There were possibilities here.

"It's okay. I mean, I do need to get home, but…"

"Are you free Saturday night?" he asked.

Her smile faltered. Maybe he should have been subtler, approached her more cautiously. But she hadn't been subtle and cautious when she'd told him his eyes were sexy, and he happened to be of the opinion that her eyes were also sexy. Why play games? They were both adults.

She studied his face, the fading daylight playing through her hair and making the strands glitter. "Why do you ask?"

"I thought you might like to join me at a benefit dinner at Reynaud," he said, naming the restaurant where the benefit was to be held. "It's for the Leukemia Foundation."

Her smile returned, but he read no in the way her eyes shifted, avoiding him. "That sounds lovely, Brett, but—a fund-raiser at Reynaud?" She shook her head. "I could write a check if you'd like."

"I meant that you'd come as my guest," he clarified.

"As your guest."

"I'm not asking for a donation. Just your company."

She had a lot of different smiles, he realized, a repertoire of them. The one she gave him now was surprised and hesitant, but the no had disappeared from her face. "Well, I—you're sure you don't want a donation? Because I could—"

"If you want to donate, that's fine. But I'm asking you to accompany me. So we could spend some time together."

"A date."

"Something like that, yeah." This time her smile demanded that he smile back.

But she still hadn't said yes. She didn't say anything. She seemed stunned into silence.

"It'll be fun," he promised. "Great food and a lot

of people parting with their money for a good cause. It starts at seven. I've got to be there from the start, since I'm hosting the thing, so I'd have to pick you up a little early. I need your address, of course." The hell with subtlety.

"Well." She fingered the handles of her tote for a moment as she collected her thoughts. "I'd like that, Brett. I'd like it a lot."

"Great."

"But first I have to make sure I can line up a baby-sitter."

Baby-sitter? She needed to line up a baby-sitter? She had a kid? Shit.

He didn't like kids. In fact, he hated them. Even if they weren't clamoring up and down the halls of the YMCA with paint on their noses and paste in their hair, he hated them. He didn't think they were adorable. He didn't get warm and mushy when he inhaled the fragrance of baby powder. He didn't grin indulgently when some pudgy munchkin with dimples in her cheeks and crust around her nostrils mispronounced a multisyllabic word. He didn't feel hopeful for the future when he passed a schoolyard and saw it filled with kids playing soccer or Little League baseball, screaming one another's names and cheering whenever someone on their team made a great play. His eyes didn't mist over when he saw scrappy youngsters in TV commercials pleading with their elders to buy sugary cereals or quit smoking. UNICEF cards did nothing for him.

He acknowledged that the human race needed to keep producing new generations in order to survive, and he appreciated the willingness of most people on the planet to do their share for the preservation of the species. But Brett had had his fill of children a long time ago, and he wanted nothing to do with them now.

It was too late: he'd already asked Sharon to join him at the leukemia dinner Saturday night. Although he had a policy of not dating women who had children, he couldn't retract his invitation just because Sharon turned out to be a mother. He'd get through the evening, make the best of it, and he'd cross her off his list of social companions as soon as he dropped her off at her front door.

"Okay," he said slowly, forcing his smile to remain in place. Maybe he'd get lucky and she wouldn't be able to find a sitter, and he'd go to the dinner alone, as he'd originally planned. Somehow, not having her accompany him didn't seem all that lucky to him, though. "Give me your number, and I'll call you in a couple of days and see if you've been able to find someone."

If she sensed the downturn in his spirits, she didn't comment on it. Groping through her tote, she located a small leather envelope, unfolded it and pulled out a business card. "Do you have a pen?"

He pulled one from an inner pocket of his jacket.

She jotted her home number on the back of the card and handed it to him. "I'll see what I can do," she said. "I'd really like to come. It sounds like fun." She looked so pleased he felt like a bastard for suffering second thoughts about having invited her. But it wasn't his fault. He liked her fine—what little he knew of her. He liked her enough to want to get to know more.

He just wished she wasn't the sort of woman who

needed a baby-sitter if she wanted to spend Saturday night with him.

WHAT A DAY, she thought as she steered the Volvo over the first speed bump on the drive that meandered through the Village Green condominium complex. What a day: she'd earned a nice paycheck that morning taking photos of the staff at Arlington Financial Services, she'd gotten some strong pictures of scenes around Arlington for her portfolio and she'd been asked out on a date by Brett Stockton.

A date. Good God. The last time she'd gone on a date had been in high school. She tried to remember if she and Steve had ever dated in college. They'd met, hit it off, hung out together, gone with groups of friends to concerts, movies and campus recitals and sat up into the wee hours listening to Pearl Jam and Mary Chapin Carpenter, drinking bad chablis and arguing about campaign finance reform. They'd become lovers, they'd become engaged and they'd become husband and wife. But she didn't think they'd ever actually gone on a date.

That Sharon would be going on a date was only half the shock, though. The other half revolved around whom she was going on the date with.

Brett Stockton. A tall, polished, knock-your-socks-off good-looking executive, a man who earned a fortune by earning fortunes for others. And he was going to escort her to a benefit dinner at the most elegant, most expensive restaurant in Arlington.

The whole thing was pretty hilarious.

She eased over another speed bump and turned left onto the lane that led to the row of town houses that contained her home. Someday she'd like to move into a detached house with a yard where Max could play, where she could erect a swing set for him and they could plant a garden. But for now, the condo was ideal. She didn't have to worry about maintenance, and she was fortunate to live next door to Deborah Jackson, whose daughter, Olivia, was going to marry Max someday. Deborah and Sharon had already worked it out. Olivia and Max played well together, and the mothers got along magnificently. Why not merge the families?

She pulled into her assigned space, hauled her tote out of the back seat and locked her car. Bypassing her own house, she headed directly to Deborah's front door. Deborah had picked the kids up from their preschool that afternoon. Tomorrow it would be Sharon's turn.

She heard squeals of laughter through the door before she even had a chance to ring the bell. That sound—children's laughter—was the sweetest music in the world. It depressed her to think that in ten or twelve years, Max's voice would change and she'd never hear his squeaky soprano giggle again.

She heard it now, in a raucous duet with Olivia. Heaven only knew what they were laughing about. Two-year-olds found the oddest things amusing.

Deborah swung the door open. Clad in shorts and a loose-fitting tank top, with her thick black hair gathered into a barrette to keep it off her neck, she made Sharon wish she, too, had stopped off at home to change out of her work clothes. At least she didn't have to wear dresses and stockings to work. Panty hose in August was her definition of hell.

Two shrieking, silly two-year-olds might also qualify as a definition of hell, but Sharon loved them—not just her own son but her future daughter-in-law—so she forgave them their rambunctiousness. "Are they making you crazy?" she asked, glancing past Deborah into the living room. The kids weren't there. They must be downstairs. Their shrill voices resonated through the floor.

Deborah laughed. "Nah, I was already crazy before they came along. Come on in."

Sharon stepped into the air-conditioned living room. When she was doing outdoor shoots she could seal herself off from her environment. Even if the air was heavy with the accumulated heat of a long, late-summer day, she wasn't uncomfortable as long as she was working. Once she was done, though, awareness of the world around her rushed in like a river breaking through a dam. Her conversation with Brett had held the world at bay, but as soon as he'd left her, the early evening heat had flooded her, forcing her back to hot humid reality. It didn't help that her car lacked air-conditioning.

She removed her blazer so the cool air could stroke her arms. "You want iced tea, lemonade or beer?" Deborah asked.

Sharon didn't have to think long. "Beer. Have you got a minute?"

"If I didn't I wouldn't have offered you a drink." She strode into the tiny kitchen.

Sharon veered to the top of the stairway leading to the finished playroom in the basement. "Max? Mommy's here."

"Mommy!"

She felt her mouth lift in a smile as her son clambered up the stairs, his feet already big enough to clomp and stomp. She couldn't help smiling when he raced to greet her. It was a reflex, as uncontrollable as the reflex that had made her breasts leak milk when he'd been an infant, crying. Max was her baby, her beloved, the heart of her life.

He reached the top of the stairs, Olivia close behind. For a moment, Sharon saw only Max, his hair falling in a shiny blond cap around his face, his cheeks still round with baby fat and his nose a shapeless button above his mouth. "Mommy, Mommy!" he shouted, so loudly people were probably scratching their heads three towns away, wondering what the ruckus drifting in on the evening breeze could be.

Sharon dropped to her knees and gathered Max into her arms. "How's my big boy today? Did you have a good day?"

"A good day," he reported, still at top volume. "We did clay."

"We played with clay," Olivia confirmed. They were in the same class at the Children's Garden Preschool. In fact, it was through the school that Sharon and Deborah had met. When Deborah and her husband had separated and she'd needed a place to live, Sharon had mentioned that the condo next door to her own was for sale. Standing with Deborah in the school's parking lot, commiserating with her over her marital woes, Sharon had recruited her as a neighbor.

Sharon widened her embrace so she could include Olivia in her hug. Olivia's hair shaped two puffy pigtails that looked like pompoms on either side of her head. The hairdo and the tiny gold hoops adorning her ears were her only feminine affectations. Her outfit was interchangeable with Max's: they both wore striped T-shirts, denim shorts and colorful sneakers.

"We made lots of things with clay," Max reported.

"I made a dog," Olivia boasted.

"I made a dog and a snake," Max said, topping her.

"I made a dog and a snake, too."

"Mine was long!"

"It sounds like lots of fun," Sharon cut them off, fearing that if she didn't, they'd compete over their ceramics projects until one or both of them burst into tears. "You guys can go back downstairs and play some more. I'm going to talk to Olivia's mommy."

"Okay," they chorused.

"Does anyone have to use the potty?" she asked.

They were already halfway down the stairs when they shouted, "No!"

Sharon grinned. They were both pretty close to potty-ready, but they couldn't be bothered with sitting on the little plastic seat and waiting for nature to take its course, when there were more exciting things to do. She'd get Max onto the potty that evening, when Olivia wasn't around to distract him.

She pushed herself to her feet and went into the kitchen, a compact room the mirror image of her own. Deborah had already opened two bottles of beer. She had one next to her on the counter, where she was fixing a salad. The other stood on the tiny breakfast table near the window, waiting for Sharon. Deborah turned at Sharon's entrance and eyed her quizzically. "Okay, honey—tell me why you needed a beer instead of an iced tea."

"All I *needed* was something cold and wet,"

Sharon said as she dropped onto one of the chairs and kicked off her shoes. "But beer has fizz. I guess I was in the mood for fizz."

"Uh-huh." Deborah clearly wasn't convinced.

Sharon sipped some beer and sighed. It was cold, wet, fizzy and yes, she'd needed it. "The strangest thing happened to me today, Deb," she said. "I got asked out on a date."

"A date!" Deborah pressed a hand to her bosom, as if the shock of Sharon's words was throwing her into cardiac arrest. "Oh, my God! You can't be serious!"

"Don't make fun of me," Sharon protested, although she couldn't help grinning at Deborah's melodramatic performance.

"All right, I won't make fun. Tell me everything. A date? With a man? Like for Saturday night?"

Sharon nodded. "Like for Saturday night. And not just a man. A rich executive."

"Now you're talking." Abandoning her salad, Deborah joined Sharon at the cozy table. "How rich?"

Sharon poked Deborah's arm. "You're married to a rich executive," she reminded her. "And you've been separated from him for a year. Maybe you ought to be warning me about all the pitfalls."

"My rich executive is an ass," Deborah argued. "And if I'm married to him it's only because we haven't gotten around to sitting down with the lawyers yet. And 'rich' is a bit of an overstatement. And anyway—" she drank some beer "—we're not talking about Raymond right now. We're talking about your date. What's his name?"

"Brett Stockton."

"Oh, yeah, that sounds rich. Where's he taking you?"

"He isn't taking me anywhere if I don't line up a baby-sitter."

"Don't you worry about that." Deborah dismissed Sharon's concern with a wave of her hand. "If you can't find someone, I'll watch Max for the night. I'm not going anywhere. So tell me—what's the plan? Where's this executive guy taking you on your big hot date?"

"It's not a big hot date," Sharon protested. To be sure, Brett's invitation chilled her slightly. It seemed so ritzy, so beyond her world. "We're attending a benefit dinner at Reynaud."

"Reynaud? Wow." Deborah's eyes grew round. "Raymond took me there on our first anniversary. Dinner for two set us back more than a hundred dollars. What kind of benefit?"

"For the Leukemia Foundation."

"Wow. This is upper-echelon stuff. Am I going to see your photo Sunday morning in the society pages of the *Arlington Gazette*?"

"God, I hope not." Sharon hadn't even thought of that. "I'm not a society type, Deb. I don't even know why he asked me."

Or why she'd said yes. Maybe it was because, despite her feeling rather outclassed by Brett Stockton, she'd seen him when he was unsure of himself. She could tell herself he was a hotshot executive, a mover and a shaker, one of Arlington's elite—but he'd been humbled by her camera, and that made him more accessible to her, more human.

Or maybe she'd said yes because he had such sexy eyes.

She hoped he hadn't asked her out because she'd told him his eyes were sexy. Flattering him that way had only been an attempt to loosen him up, to wrest a smile from him—or at least something better than the I've-been-sucking-lemons-all-day-and-my-dog-just-got-hit-by-a-car expression that had taken over his face every time she'd pointed her camera at him. Yes, she'd flirted with him—because flirting worked. Taking a photograph of someone was an intimate act. Flirting was a way to ease through that intimacy. She nearly always flirted with her subjects, whether they were children or high school seniors posing for yearbook photos or CEOs who needed updated head shots for their company's annual report.

Had Brett thought her flirting meant something more? How could he, when she'd trotted out the belly-dancing doll? And she'd joked about his tie and kept him talking and softened him up a little... What if he'd asked her out because he thought she'd been coming on to him? What if her use of the word *sexy* had given him ideas?

Well, he *did* have sexy eyes. She hadn't been lying when she'd told him that.

"So," Deborah asked, "what are you going to wear?"

"I have no idea. A benefit dinner at Reynaud? I need real clothes for that."

"Maybe you should buy something new."

"I'll think about it." She'd think about her budget, too. "I don't even know if it's formal. Do men wear tuxedos to these things?"

"Like I'm supposed to know?"

"Raymond would know," Sharon pointed out. Deborah's estranged husband was a rising executive

with an insurance company. He might not attend
many benefit dinners now, but he was being groomed
for what Deborah disdainfully referred to as "better
things." In fact, he was so busy scaling the corporate
mountain that he'd neglected his wife and baby,
which was why Deborah was currently living with
her daughter in the Village Green condominium
complex instead of with him.

"I'm not going to call him to discuss formal wear.
If you want to, be my guest." Deborah's nostrils narrowed—a sign of irritation—and she sipped some
beer.

"I'll figure it out without his input," Sharon said.
"When Brett phones me—assuming I find a baby-
sitter—"

"You've got one," Deborah reminded her, tapping her chest with her index finger.

"I'm going to try to find someone. Nothing personal, but Max will sleep better if he's in his own
room. And when Brett phones, I'll ask him just how
fancy this thing is."

"I think you should buy something new," Debo-
rah insisted. "Just for the thrill of it. It's not like you
go out on a date every day."

"It's not like I go out on a date every year,"
Sharon said with a laugh.

A shriek from downstairs jolted both women out
of their chairs. They raced down the steps to find
Olivia and Max both sobbing. "I want the truck!"
Max howled, clutching a plastic dump truck. "I want
it! It's mine!"

"It's mine!" Olivia insisted, tears streaking down
her cheeks. She raced to her mother, arms outstretched, reaching for comfort.

"Mine!" Max shouted. For the past six months, that had been his favorite word, or perhaps his second favorite, after *no*.

"Put down the truck, Max," Sharon ordered him, sounding to herself like a police officer trying to get a criminal to lay down his weapon and surrender peacefully.

"Mine," he whimpered, then hurled the truck onto the carpeted floor.

Sharon considered scolding him for throwing the toy but decided not to. He'd relinquished it; that was victory enough. She also decided not to make him apologize to Olivia. She believed that forcing a child to apologize when he wasn't sorry only taught him to be a hypocrite.

Of course, she could be wrong about that. She was winging it, doing her best to be a good mother yet never quite convinced she had the job mastered. If Steve were alive, she could ask him: Do you think I'm doing this right? Should I listen to Expert A or Expert B? Is it time to potty-train Max, or should I leave him in diapers a few more months? Should I make him tell Olivia he's sorry when I know he really isn't?

But Steve was gone and she was on her own. Deborah offered guidance, but she was on her own, too. The director of Max's preschool was a wonderful source of ideas and suggestions, as was Max's pediatrician, and Sharon read books on parenting. She hoped that she wasn't destroying her little boy's life with her ineptitude.

What she needed in her life was a grown-up. She was tired of being the family's only adult. Her parents weren't much help; they'd raised her with a hands-off attitude, loving but never quite dependable, and the fact that she'd somehow managed to stumble into a state of relative maturity was something of a miracle. She was determined to do better by her son.

But she really wished there were another adult she could count on, someone solid and dependable. The kind of person who worked at a desk and earned a steady, comfortable income, who understood the ways of the universe and took life seriously.

Maybe that was what had appealed to her about Brett Stockton: he was a grown-up. Not a show-off, not a lovable six-foot-tall boy like Steve, but someone with gravity. Someone who looked good in a suit and tie—even if the tie was just a bit too somber.

Maybe the reason she'd agreed to this date with him was that he seemed mature and responsible, that he would never fling a toy truck to the floor and wail, ''Mine!''

But his sexy eyes had something to do with it, too.

CHAPTER THREE

ON THE RARE occasions when Brett was impulsive, he usually wound up regretting it. The time he'd decided on a whim to drive with two college buddies to Fort Lauderdale for spring break had been a disaster: the car's radiator had broken somewhere in South Carolina, the repair had devoured two days and most of their money, forcing them to subsist on peanut-butter-and-raisin-bread sandwiches, and when they'd finally reached Florida, the skies had opened up, releasing torrents of nonstop rain the entire time they were there.

Or right after he'd finished business school, when he'd asked Michelle to marry him. He'd loved her, and he'd loved sleeping with her, and one night after some truly phenomenal sex, he'd recklessly proposed to her. She'd said yes—and he'd immediately suffered misgivings. Those misgivings had deepened over the next few weeks, when she'd refused to stop babbling about how many babies they would have.

He didn't want babies. He didn't like babies. He'd raised four siblings when he'd still been a child himself, and he'd hated the noise, the mess, the staggering responsibility.

Which was one reason he was still entertaining serious doubts about his impulsive decision to ask

Sharon Bartell to accompany him to the dinner at Reynaud tonight.

He'd phoned her a few days ago, as promised, and she'd happily reported that she'd been able to line up a baby-sitter. He'd actually contemplated calling the whole thing off when she'd said that. He could have been honest and told her it was his personal policy to avoid social entanglements with mothers. But he couldn't justify canceling the date once she'd gone to all the effort of hiring someone to watch her kid.

He would just have to get through it. The bottom line tonight was raising money for the Leukemia Foundation. Whatever happened between him and Sharon was irrelevant.

She'd given him her address—a town house in the Village Green condominium complex—and he drove in circles around the winding, artfully picturesque roads for a while before he found her unit, nestled among a row of identical units. A tricycle sat on the sidewalk outside one town house, and a small swarm of kids on scooters zoomed up and down the street. A child-friendly neighborhood, he thought, wondering how old Sharon's child was. Young enough to need a baby-sitter, obviously.

Sighing, he parked, strolled up the walk to her front door, rang the bell and tried to ward off his sense of impending dread. After a long minute, Sharon swung open the door. But her back was to him; she was busy addressing someone behind her. "Max, it's okay. You can watch the sing-along video."

"No!" a shrill voice resonated. "Wanna watch the video!"

"Then go watch the video," Sharon said.

"No!"

"You don't want to watch it?"

"Wanna watch it!"

"Then go ahead and watch it."

"No!"

Throughout this futile exchange, Brett had a view of Sharon's back—and that view made him wish she didn't have a child. She was wearing a simple, slim-fitting black dress, the neckline of which draped low to reveal the smooth, golden skin of her upper back, the shadowed contours of her spine and shoulder blades barely visible but exceptionally tempting. Her arms were bare, as long and slender as a ballerina's, and the dress ended at her knees, revealing long, slender ballerina legs. Her dress sandals added a couple of inches to her height. Her hips were curvy yet compact.

Then she turned to acknowledge him, and the view got even better. The dress was simpler in front than in back, but its plainness only emphasized the surprising beauty of the woman wearing it.

Yes, surprising. He'd thought she was a pleasant-looking woman when he'd met her, and she'd gone from pleasant-looking to pretty once she'd stopped aiming her camera at him, and from pretty to prettier whenever she smiled. But tonight she had her hair smoothed back from her face and held in place by a black satin headband. She'd applied her makeup with a light touch so it was barely visible, but somehow it enhanced the elegant hollows of her cheeks and the width of her lips. Pearl studs dotted her ears and a gold chain holding a pearl pendant circled her throat. "Hi," she said, giving him such a sweet, hesitant smile he almost forgot about the kid bellowing "No! No! No!" behind her.

"Hi," he said.

"Let me get my son settled down, and then we'll go." She beckoned him into the living room, a snug square of space furnished with a sturdy brown couch, matching chairs and rugged tables. The walls held a gallery of photographs—taken by her? he wondered—and he would have liked to study them. A few brightly colored plastic toys lay scattered across the rust-colored carpet.

When Sharon stepped aside he saw the kid hovering on the top step of a stairway leading down. About three feet tall, he had whitish-blond hair cut à la Moe Howard of the Three Stooges. His cheeks were ruddy and he wore pajamas with pictures of steam shovels and dump trucks printed on the fabric. He glared at Brett, then scampered to his mother's side and wrapped himself around her leg. "I wanna watch with *you!*" he shouted.

Sharon tried to bend down, but apparently such a maneuver was difficult with the twerp clinging to her leg. "You'll watch the video with Tracy," she told him, then gestured toward the stairs, where a teenage girl hovered, smiling eagerly, as if her enthusiasm would be enough to lure the kid away from his mother's ankle.

"Come on, Max—let's watch the video," the girl said, extending a hand.

He clamped himself more tightly around his mother's leg. "No!"

"He's two," Sharon told Brett, as if that explained everything. Her smile was apologetic. "Max, Mommy's going to leave now. You're going to stay here with Tracy. You can play, you can watch videos, you can have an apple later—''

''Apple*sauce*,'' he demanded.

''Fine. Applesauce.''

She exchanged a look with the teenager, who crossed the living room and knelt down next to the kid. ''Max, come on—let's watch the video. I want to watch it with you.''

''Watch it with Mommy,'' he grumbled, although his grip on Sharon's leg relented. He gave Brett a lethal stare. *The feeling's mutual,* Brett wanted to assure him.

''Try to get him to bed by eight-thirty,'' Sharon instructed the sitter in a soft, soothing voice. ''Have him sit on the potty before he goes to bed, just in case. And he'll need help brushing his teeth. I left the phone number of the restaurant on the kitchen table, along with Dr. Cole's number and my next-door neighbor's number. You know Deborah Jackson, don't you? She'll be home if you need anything.''

''That's all right,'' Tracy assured her. ''My mom's home, too—right across the street.''

''Great.'' Sharon glanced down at her son, who abruptly lost interest in her and was trotting back to the stairs. ''Goodbye, Max!''

''Bye,'' he said without turning around. Tracy followed him down the stairs, and the living room filled with blessed silence.

Brett wanted to say something, but he wasn't sure what: *That was irritating. Why did he say no when he meant yes? Does he put you through that kind of torture every time you go out without him?* Or: *Doesn't he know how to talk without screaming?*

*Why did he look at me as if I were Satan's spawn?
Is he always that obnoxious?* Or: *You look fantastic.*

Those were the words that came out. And thank
God—if he'd blurted out that he thought her kid was
obnoxious, their outing would be doomed.

It was doomed, anyway, because her kid *was* obnoxious. But he'd resolved to make the best of it.
And looking at Sharon was definitely going to be one
of the evening's highlights.

His compliment caused her cheeks to darken.
"Thank you. I see you're wearing a colorful tie."

He knew some of the men at tonight's dinner
would be wearing tuxedos and bow ties, but that
wasn't his style. Instead he wore a black suit, a blue
silk shirt and a Jerry Garcia tie featuring an abstract
pattern of blue, crimson, lemon yellow and slate
gray. He rarely wore the tie, which his sister had
given him for Christmas last year, but when he'd
searched his tie rack the colors had beckoned him.
Sharon would like it, he'd thought as he'd pulled it
off the rack.

He motioned toward the front door. "Shall we?"

"Yes, we should definitely clear out before Max
throws another tantrum," she said with a conspira-
torial smile. She lifted a small black purse from the
coffee table and headed for the door. Her steps
weren't quite as certain as they'd been the day she'd
photographed him. She looked as if she wasn't used
to walking in high heels.

One reason he was glad not to be a woman was
that he'd hate wearing the painful kinds of shoes they
so often subjected their feet to. Yet he loved the way
her sandals exposed her arches and emphasized the

narrowness of her ankles, the way the heels augmented her height so he didn't tower above her.

They paused on the porch so she could lock the door, and then he took her hand and tucked it into the bend of his elbow. Just so she wouldn't teeter and trip in those shoes, he told himself.

Because really, his finding her so damned attractive didn't change the fact that she had a kid. A loud-mouthed, foul-tempered kid who said "No" a lot.

Brett helped her into his car, then joined her. "Is this your toy?" she asked, buckling herself into the leather bucket seat.

"My toy?"

"When I was taking your picture, you said high-performance cars were your favorite toy."

His Infiniti was a decent car, but it was a little too practical to be a toy. "I was thinking more along the lines of Maseratis," he explained. "Ferraris. Lamborghinis." He pulled away from the curb, glimpsed her as he checked his side mirror and decided to forget about the brat for the rest of the evening.

Except to wonder about the brat's father. Was Sharon divorced? Brett dated a fair number of divorced women, and she didn't seem to have the edge they did, that veneer of sorrow or bitterness or pragmatism that layered over them, keeping them one step removed from whatever hurt they believed life and love and men might inflict upon them. If she wasn't divorced, then what? Widowed? Or a headstrong feminist who had decided to borrow someone's sperm and make herself a baby?

Curiosity got the better of him. "Your son's father...?"

"He died," she said.

Brett shot her a quick look to make sure she wasn't going to dissolve in tears. She appeared calm, accepting. No raw wounds, as far as he could tell.

"He was killed in a skiing accident when I was pregnant with Max," she told him.

"That must have been rough."

She shrugged. "We've managed. How about you, Brett? Any children?"

God, no, he almost blurted out. "No children, no ex-wives."

"A confirmed bachelor, huh?"

"If you're referring to that church ritual for teenagers, yes, I'm confirmed."

She was kind enough to laugh at his joke. In the dark confines of the car, her laughter sounded hushed and throaty. A pleasant buzz of sexual awareness vibrated through his body. He perceived it like a white noise, in the background but definitely there.

He wasn't going to act on that awareness. He'd enjoy it for the evening the way he might enjoy a song: he'd listen but he wouldn't sing along. Sharon was a mother—a young widow—and he knew better than to get involved.

"Tell me about this dinner we're going to," she said as he steered north toward downtown. "Are you active in the Leukemia Foundation?"

"Behind the scenes." The roads were busy, cars carrying people to their Saturday-night activities. "I know a lot of power people in Arlington. I invest a lot of their money for them. So I can put the touch on them if it's for a good cause."

"I'd better confess something, Brett," she said, lowering her voice, which made it sound even more alluring. "I've never been to a benefit dinner before.

Not this kind of thing, anyway. I recently attended a potluck supper to raise money for a new jungle gym at Max's preschool—but I wore jeans and sneakers to that."

He bet she'd look good in jeans and sneakers. Maybe not as good as she looked right now, though.

"Is there anything I should know?" she asked. "Anything you want to tell me before we get there?"

"The napkin goes on your lap," he teased. "The little fork is for the salad."

"Thanks," she said sarcastically, although he heard amusement in her voice.

"And you'd better not whip out your belly-dancing doll."

"Well, darn. I thought she'd fit right in."

He eyed her again. Her smile dazzled him. *Just for tonight,* he warned himself. He'd enjoy this for tonight, and then he'd put her out of his mind.

SHE HAD KNOWN the restaurant would be elegant, but she still felt a little disoriented by the silk wallpaper, the plush carpet, the army of obsequious waiters circulating through the private dining room. She and Brett had arrived early, since he was the host of this gala, and for a few minutes, while he'd gone off to discuss logistics with someone on the restaurant's staff, she'd stood alone, fingering one of the pale-peach tablecloths, examining the silverware—little salad fork and all—at the place setting before her and watching as waiters wandered from table to table, tweaking the elaborately folded napkins, lighting the candles and adjusting the chairs. But Brett had soon returned to her, and then more people arrived. In the corner of the room, near an area cleared of tables, a trio of musicians played mellow jazz.

Sharon observed the people around her like an anthropologist studying a tribe. The men were by and large dressed conservatively, but the women fluttered around like exotic birds, displaying their designer dresses and minaudières, flashing their expensive jewelry and looking a hell of a lot more comfortable in their high heels than she felt in hers.

Once the party kicked into gear, Brett rarely left her side. He seemed to know everyone in the room, and over and over again he introduced her: ''This is Sharon Bartell. She's a photographer here in Arlington.'' Whenever someone asked, she told them she ran Bartell Studios on Dudley Road and had met Brett taking his picture for his firm's annual report. People seemed to find this amusing.

If she were shrewd, she'd be passing out her business card. In a crowd like this, full of people who no doubt ran corporations that issued annual reports, she could drum up some business. But she wasn't shrewd, and even though she could use all the business that came her way, that wasn't what this evening was about.

''Hey, Murphy!'' Brett clasped hands with a good-looking man in a pale-gray suit and a stylish black shirt. ''Sharon, this is Dennis Murphy, an overpriced attorney and one of my poker buddies. Murphy, this is Sharon Bartell, a photographer friend of mine. Oh, and this is Murphy's wife, Gail,'' he added as a slim blond woman in a rose-hued dress turned toward them after snatching a glass of champagne from a passing waiter. ''Gail's a lawyer, too.''

"An underpaid one, unlike my husband," Gail told Sharon.

"I didn't know there was such a thing as an underpaid lawyer," Sharon joked.

"Oh, there are lots of us. We work in the Public Defender's Office."

"They may underpay you—but unlike some of us, you're guaranteed a queen-size bed in heaven when you die," Murphy pointed out, giving his wife an affectionate squeeze. "Plus, you get to hobnob with the mayor."

"Not because I'm a public defender. Because my boss stuck me on a stupid committee."

"What committee is that?" Sharon asked. Several of the people Brett had introduced her to served on different fund-raising committees. The benefit world of Arlington, Connecticut, was evidently a small one. Sharon imagined this same cast of characters would all be showing up next month at the auction to raise money for AIDS research, and in November for a party to collect Christmas gifts for needy children.

"The birthday committee," Gail told her. "Next year is the city's three hundredth birthday."

"I've heard a little about that," Sharon said.

Gail grinned. "You're going to be hearing a lot about it over the next year. You're going to be hearing so much about it you'll be sick of it by the time the festivities begin. Arlington is hyping this birthday as if it were the Second Coming. And I'm stuck on the committee—at no extra pay." She rolled her eyes.

"But a guaranteed seat on the express train to heaven," her husband promised.

"What is the city planning?" Sharon asked.

"You name it. A huge parade, of course. A carnival. Special vacation packages to bed-and-breakfasts in the area. All sorts of art programs. A couple of theater people from New York who have weekend houses out on the west side of town are writing a musical revue tracing Arlington's history, from the Native American settlements to today. I've seen a rough draft of the script, and it's awful."

"Really?" Sharon laughed.

"And we're going to be stuck watching it from front row seats, too, I bet," Murphy complained.

"The committee has asked for revisions, but they're New York *artistes,* so who knows what they'll do. Then there's the sculpture the mayor wants to install in the lobby of City Hall. We've already gotten bids on that. I've seen some of the submissions. One person came up with a statue of a Native American and a white settler shaking hands. Very trite. Someone else came up with an abstract design that looks like a bowling ball with spears sticking out of it."

"How much is the city going to pay for this thing?" Brett asked.

"Too much," Gail assured him. "Watch your mailbox. We'll be soliciting for contributions soon. And if you know what's good for you, Brett, you'll donate."

"Yes, ma'am."

"And then there's the commemorative book the city is going to publish."

"I've heard about the book," Sharon said. What she'd heard was that it would be filled with photos of Arlington and the surrounding region. Photographers from as far away as Boston were putting together proposals. Whoever won the commission would receive not just a generous fee but invaluable exposure for their work.

Sharon would love the exposure. And she needed that generous fee. When she and Steve had opened the studio, before Max was born, they'd had the time and energy to build their business into a profitable enterprise. It was still profitable—only now Sharon was running it by herself and raising a son at the same time. She lacked Steve's flair for promotion. He'd always been the one to sell their services, while she'd preferred working behind the camera.

Ever since she'd heard about the memorial book the town wanted to publish, she'd been building her portfolio in order to bid on the commission. If the photos she'd taken of the YMCA at sunset came out well, one would be included. She had taken a striking photo of City Hall at night, its dome a moonlit bell against the black sky; and the Old Town Hall at dawn, glazed in lavender light; and a gorgeous shot of an apple orchard in full bloom, which she'd taken during a drive east of town with Max last spring, before she'd heard anything about the commemorative birthday book. It had been a clear sunny day and the trees had been exploding with pink blossoms, so she'd pulled off the road, climbed onto the roof of the Volvo and snapped a few shots.

She needed more photos for her submission, but accumulating them was hard while she was so pressed for time. When she wasn't working in the studio or going out on paid jobs, she was with Max. And a part of her suspected that no matter how magnificent a portfolio she put together, the mayor would wind up choosing an insider to do the book. Some-

one he knew, quite possibly someone who attended
benefit dinners at restaurants like Reynaud, who hob-
nobbed with the folks here tonight, who traveled in
Brett Stockton's social circle.

She was traveling in that circle tonight. But she
was only a tourist, not a native. She hadn't bought
her seat at this dinner. And even if she was standing
with a glass of champagne in her hand, making small
talk with someone who might help to select the photographer for the book, she couldn't bring herself to
put her name forward. It wouldn't feel right, no matter how much she wanted that commission. Brett
might think she was taking advantage of him, and
she'd hate to have him think anything negative about
her.

He was so suave, so poised, so handsome—and he
was standing at her side, calling her his friend. She
could hardly believe this was occurring, but it *was,*
and she was determined not to screw up. She'd use
the correct fork for her salad, and she'd refrain from
promoting herself for the commission, no matter how
much she wanted it.

People began to gravitate toward the tables, and
Brett steered her to the table closest to a podium set
up in one corner of the room. ''I've got to do a few
host things,'' he whispered as he pulled out her chair
for her. His breath brushed her hair and danced
against her ear, and his hand left heat where he
touched her shoulder.

He was more than suave and poised. Much more
than handsome. She tried to recall the last time a man
had pulled out a chair for her, and drew a blank. It
had been so long since she'd been out with a man,
so long since she'd fixed herself up like this and been

treated with such courtesy. Courtesy was all Brett intended, she reminded herself—but that didn't lessen the dark thrill she felt when he touched her.

The Murphys sat at their table, along with someone with an impressive title affiliated with Arlington Memorial Hospital and the publisher of the *Arlington Gazette*. Sharon made chitchat with them until the room's noise level dwindled to near silence and everyone turned to the podium, where Brett loomed above the microphone. The recessed ceiling light cast stark shadows across his face, giving him a brooding, almost dangerous look.

What am I doing here? she wondered for the zillionth time that evening. Her first date since high school, her first time out with a man since Steve's death, and she was seated in an alien world of movers and shakers, wearing a dress she'd picked up off the clearance rack at Macy's and using the purse and shoes she'd bought for a cousin's wedding she and Steve had attended four years ago. And her escort for the evening was standing at a podium, eloquently thanking everyone who'd come to this gala. "A lot of you are here because leukemia has touched your lives personally," he said. "A lot of you are here because I twisted your arm. Either way, our money is being put to good use. It's saving lives. And helping to save lives keeps us honest. It keeps us human. It reminds us of how much we have, how fortunate we are and how much we need to do.

"Enjoy your dinners, folks."

Applause accompanied him back to his seat next to Sharon. "I hate giving those speeches," he admitted.

"Even more than you hate posing for pictures?"

"No. Pictures are much worse." He grinned. His elbow touched hers as he reached for his water glass. A fresh surge of heat flooded her body.

Maybe it was the champagne. Maybe it was the heady atmosphere, or the fact that she was far from Max, surrounded by adults, not having to think about potty time or lullabies. Or maybe she felt overly sensitive to Brett's every glance, his every accidental touch, because of who he was, how he looked, how it felt to be with a man like him. Maybe it was because of the *way* he gazed at her, his eyes the color of a clear autumn sky, his lips curved in a smile that expressed what he'd said when he'd picked her up that evening: "You look fantastic."

Waiters moved about the room in a smooth processional, bringing out course after course of gourmet cuisine. Sharon ate; she managed lucid conversations with the others at her table; she sipped the red wine the waiter had poured for her—but Brett's nearness pulsed inside her, a low constant beat. When he laughed, when he parried someone's caustic remark, when he twisted in his chair to confer with someone who'd wandered over from another table…she seemed almost painfully aware of everything about him. The way he angled his head when someone posed a question. The way he leaned back in his seat. The way he smiled at her every now and then, his eyes meeting hers and making her feel as if they were the only two people in the room.

She felt like a woman with him, an adult, someone desirable. Not a harried, loving, stressed-out single mother. More than an hour had passed without her thinking about Max. The realization made her feel both liberated and guilty.

The waiters glided around once more, clearing plates and filling cups with coffee. Brett patted her hand, murmured, "I'm on again," and asked everyone else at the table to excuse him, before he rose and returned to the podium once more. He turned on the microphone and his warm, resonant voice filled the room. "I want to introduce Dr. Mark Scheffer so he can tell you about the research he's been directing at Arlington Memorial Hospital—experimental treatments that have shown great promise and that have been funded, in part, by your generosity." More applause, and the fellow seated across the table from her stood and joined Brett at the podium. When he began to speak, Brett stepped back into the shadows, allowing him the spotlight.

Sharon picked at her dessert. She was full—from the food, from the experience, from the delight of being removed from her everyday world for a few precious hours. A part of her wished she could have spent this time alone with Brett, talking to him one on one and getting to know him better. But in a way, she *had* gotten to know him better this evening. Watching him preside over the room, seeing his confidence in the role of host, as comfortable tonight as he'd been uncomfortable the day she'd taken his photograph, gave her a clearer sense of who he was. She lacked all the details she might have learned if they'd had dinner by themselves: where he'd grown up, what his hobbies were, what kind of music he listened to, all those bits of trivia that, when gathered together, created the mosaic of a personality. But she felt as if she knew him in another, less specific but deeper, way.

The doctor finished describing his research. More

applause. Brett stepped back up to the microphone and said, "Now that we've all stuffed our faces, I think we ought to burn off some calories by dancing. So cram your feet back into your shoes and let's have some fun."

Dancing! The only dancing Sharon had done in years had been with Max in her arms. She'd spin him around and sing "All She Wants To Do Is Dance," changing *she* to *he* for Max's sake. Dancing with Brett was going to be quite a different experience.

The band sparked into an up-tempo tune. Brett walked toward the table, grinning at Sharon. "I'm not a great dancer," he warned, extending his hand to her, "but somebody's got to set an example here."

"It's your responsibility as the host," Sharon agreed, sliding her hand into his and standing.

"Are you having a good time?" he asked as he walked her toward the clearing at the other end of the room.

"Oh, yes," she assured him. "I feel like Cinderella."

"Well, I'm no prince," he warned, grinning mischievously. He pulled her into a loose embrace and proceeded to prove that he was, in fact, not a bad dancer at all. "You aren't going to turn into a pumpkin at midnight, are you?"

"Cinderella didn't turn into a pumpkin. She turned into a working slob with dishpan hands—which I'll probably turn into tomorrow, but not tonight."

"Hey, we'll all turn into working slobs tomorrow. Or maybe Monday. No one should have to be a working slob on a Sunday."

"All right," she conceded. "I'll wait till Monday to turn into a slob."

He let one hand rest at her waist. The other swallowed her much smaller hand. He kept a respectable distance between them, which she appreciated because it enabled her to see his face—and because it was hard not to respond to his nearness, the seductive beauty of his eyes, the sheer male warmth of him. Feeling like an appealing woman after two long years as an overtaxed mommy was as intoxicating as drinking a glass of champagne on an empty stomach. She loved the sensation, but she didn't trust it.

"Earlier," she said, "when you were up at the microphone—you said a lot of people in this room have had their lives personally touched by leukemia."

He leaned back. His smile faded slightly, but his gaze remained on her, cool and blue. "I lost my father to the disease."

"I'm sorry."

"It was a long time ago." He pulled her a little closer. The dance floor had gotten pretty crowded.

She wished she didn't like being in his embrace so much. She wished it didn't feel so wonderful, so natural, to have a man's arms around her. *Brett's* arms. She wished he would draw her even closer.

She reminded herself that she hardly knew him. As attractive as he was, as enchanted as she felt as their bodies brushed and pressed lightly and moved to the rhythm of the music, he was a near stranger to her. His father had died a long time ago. How long? Had the loss scarred him permanently? Could he offer her some insight into how she could help Max come to terms with the loss of his father? Max had never even known his father—did that make the loss easier or harder?

This wasn't the time to ask. The band segued into a slow soulful tune, and Brett did draw her closer. She shouldn't let herself relish his embrace so much, not when she knew so little about him. But she was Cinderella tonight, and his arms were strong and possessive.

She would go back to reality tomorrow, she promised herself. Tonight, she would enjoy the fairy tale.

As THE HOST, Brett had to be the last to leave. Sharon stood quietly by while he thanked his guests and waved them off. He conferred for a few minutes with the restaurant's manager, then took her hand and led her from the private room through the main dining room and outside.

"I can't remember the last time I stayed up this late," she said as they ventured out into the balmy quiet night.

"It's not that late. I was thinking maybe we could go out for a nightcap." He was actually thinking that they could spend a little time talking, just the two of them. She'd been a good sport about the evening— and maybe one reason he'd invited her to join him tonight was that he'd sensed she would be a good sport. But he owed her a little undivided attention. And he owed himself a few more minutes alone with her, before he put her out of his mind for good.

Dancing with her had been more fun than he would have liked. He hadn't forgotten what—*who*— was waiting for her at home. But he would have liked pretending, for a little while longer, that this spectacular woman who moved so well with him, whose hand felt so soft and delicate in his and whose eyes radiated such honesty, was someone he could really relate to.

"I'd love a nightcap," she said, "but I'm afraid I'd fall asleep and embarrass you with my snoring."

"Do you snore?"

She peered up at him, her eyes glinting wickedly. He could guess what she was thinking: that there was an easy way for him to find out if she snored. But it was one thing to flirt when they were safely in his office and she was wielding a camera, and quite another to flirt when the night lay still and mysterious around them and they'd just spent the last hour holding each other on the dance floor.

"No," she finally answered. "I don't snore." They reached his car and he unlocked it. He opened her door, but she hesitated before getting in. "Brett—what would you have done if I hadn't been able to come tonight? Who would you have danced with?"

"Everybody. I would have danced with all the women, taken turns, been a charming host."

"You *were* a charming host."

"Not once I started dancing with you. If everyone else had disappeared at that point, I wouldn't have even noticed."

He was standing close enough to smell her, a faint scent of vanilla and mint and wine. The half moon spilled light down on them, turning her hair silvery white. He had promised himself not to let this get personal, because she had a child.

But she'd been beautiful all night. More than beautiful—alluring. Enticing. That buzz he'd felt the moment he'd seen her had only grown more intense as the night progressed.

Against his better judgment, he stroked the edge of her chin with his index finger. Just to feel her skin, to see if it was as silky as it looked. He wanted to trace her lips with his finger, and then with his tongue. But a kiss would only make him long for more than kisses. And she wasn't the sort of woman a man could kiss—let alone do more with—without getting involved.

She was a mother, he reminded himself. She had a life he wanted no part of. If he had half a brain in his head, he would take her home and forget about her.

He gazed at her for a minute longer, then stepped back. Once she was settled in her seat, he closed the door behind her.

And cursed, because Sharon Bartell was one hell of a woman—and she was the wrong woman for him.

But Brett had backed off. He'd driven her home, stood with her on the front porch as they both watched the overhead porch light and let his gaze travel to where Sharon...

CHAPTER FOUR

"I DON'T KNOW what went wrong," Sharon said, then sighed and leaned back against the wood-slat bench on the edge of the Village Green playground. Max and Olivia were a shout's distance from the bench, conquering a complex climbing apparatus that incorporated ladders, slides, passageways and crossbars. They scampered from platform to platform, raced along a wobbly suspension bridge and slid down a curving plastic chute, giggling and bellowing. Sharon sat with Deborah, her vision fixed on the children while her mind wandered back to last night.

"Why do you think something went wrong?" Deborah asked.

"He was going to kiss me," Sharon said, genuinely bewildered. She and Brett had stood beside his car, surrounded by the night's stillness, and he'd stroked her face with his fingertips—and she'd been certain he would kiss her. It might have been her first date in years and Brett Stockton might have been a man unlike any she'd ever spent time with before, but she wasn't an idiot. She knew that when a man touched a woman a certain way, when he looked at her a certain way, when he danced with her a certain way and words became extraneous because so much was said with their movements, their eyes, their smiles… It meant he desired her.

But Brett had backed off. He'd driven her home, stood with her on the front porch so they could watch Tracy cross the street and let herself safely into her town house, and then he'd said good-night and left. As if that moment by his car outside the restaurant, his gentle caress and his longing gaze had never occurred.

"Maybe he was being a gentleman," Deborah suggested. "I know that's a rare breed, but maybe he thought kissing you on your first date would be pushing things."

Maybe it would have been, but last night Sharon wouldn't have cared if he'd pushed. She'd wanted his kiss.

"I don't think it was that," she argued. "Nothing about him indicated that he was a gentleman." She laughed sadly, then slapped a mosquito off her thigh and shifted on the bench, edging into the patch of shade cast by a leafy oak tree. "I mean, he was certainly very polite and all—" he knew which fork to use with the salad, didn't he? "—but he didn't seem prudish." He'd enjoyed her flirting at his office, even if her ulterior motive then hadn't been romance. And he'd touched her last night—more than once—deliberately. He'd patted her shoulder whenever he'd had to leave the table. He'd held her hand on the dance floor and wrapped his arm around her, not forcefully but with a definite purpose. "I was so sure...so positive he was going to kiss me. I must have misread the whole thing. It's been such a long time I don't even know how to interpret a man's signals anymore."

"You interpret signals all the time," Deborah reminded her. "Body language is practically your profession."

"I hardly think taking photos of high school seniors qualifies me as an expert on body language."

"High school seniors and company presidents. Honey, he was sending you mixed messages. He was playing head games with you. You don't need that."

"You're right. I don't." But saying so didn't make Sharon feel better. Her inability to judge Brett's intentions was puzzling, but what really troubled her was how much she'd wanted him. Their first date, an almost fantasylike outing for her, nothing to build a relationship on... But she'd ached for him to kiss her, yearned for it so much she'd spent the rest of the night thinking about it, worrying about it, and was still thinking and worrying about it Sunday afternoon.

"I don't know, Sharon," Deborah said after taking a swig from her bottle of iced tea. "Maybe I'm jaded or something, down on men and all that. But it pisses me off when they send you mixed messages. They want one thing until you think you know what they want, and then they change their minds and want something else. And all you can do is make guesses, because they can't bring themselves to open their damned mouths and tell you what's on their mind. Passive-aggressive crap, that's what it is."

"You're an expert," Sharon muttered, her tone heavy with sarcasm.

"I am," Deborah retorted. "I was married to Raymond for four years. That makes me an expert in all kinds of male stupidity."

Sharon smiled and sipped her own iced tea. It had

lost its chill, but it was still sweet and wet and welcome.

The few times she'd met Raymond, he'd seemed much nicer than Deborah had led her to expect. Of course she could sympathize with Deborah's anger when Raymond missed appointments with their marriage counselor because of his business obligations. He could be a bonehead. But Sharon sensed a melancholy about him, a regret that made her feel a little sorry for him, even if he was mostly to blame for his current plight.

She'd already gotten an earful from Deborah about his failure to stop by that morning to pick Olivia up for their weekly outing. He'd phoned ten minutes after he was supposed to arrive and explained that he'd gotten home late from a business trip and had overslept. "What kind of business trip lasts until late Saturday night?" Deborah had asked when she'd called Sharon and suggested they take their kids to the playground. "I don't want to be here if he stops by later. Let's go somewhere."

Sharon had been happy to get out of the house, too—and even happier to have the chance to tell Deborah about last night: the magic of the party, the elegance, the satisfaction of raising money for a good cause—and the kiss that should have been but never was.

"Mommy! Look!" Max hollered. Sharon smiled and waved as he climbed to the top of a rope mesh. "Look, Mommy! I'm big!"

"You're very high up," she agreed.

"Me, too!" Olivia shouted, scampering up the ropes next to him. "Look at me!"

"You're doing great, baby!" Deborah encouraged

her, then turned to Sharon. "Promise me that when they get married, Max won't play any head games with her."

"He's a boy," Sharon pointed out. "I don't think most men realize when they're doing something that drives us crazy. They're just being guys. They can't help themselves."

"Maybe." Deborah sighed. "So is it better to be an unintentional ass than an intentional one?"

"Hard to say. It's like the difference between manslaughter and first-degree murder. Either way, the victim winds up dead."

Deborah grunted in agreement. "Do you think your ass was intentional or unintentional last night?"

Sharon had no idea. "It doesn't matter," she said grimly. "I'm never going to hear from him again."

"You know that for a fact?"

She reviewed once more her evening with Brett, from his joke about finding out if she snored to his tentative smile and his final, wistful goodbye. Somehow they had journeyed from bashful hesitancy to close dancing, to that intense moment beside his car, to his departure while she'd stood on the porch, watching his car vanish down the street and feeling painfully alone.

"Yeah," she said with a sigh. "I know it for a fact."

"Hey," a soft male voice interrupted them.

They both spun on the bench to see Deborah's husband approaching. Tall and polished, clad in khaki trousers, boat shoes and a lime-green polo shirt with a tiny insignia stitched onto the breast pocket, Raymond might have been on his way to a golf course or a prep school reunion. He stared at Deborah, seeming to devour her with his eyes—until a shriek from the playground distracted him. "Daddy! Daddy!"

"Hey, Livie!" Bypassing the bench, he hunkered down and opened his arms to Olivia, who charged across the grass and hurled herself at him. "How's my baby? How's my little sweetheart?"

Deborah pursed her lips, obviously displeased.

"At least he showed up," Sharon whispered.

"Three hours late," Deborah whispered back.

"Better late than never."

"I can outcliché you, so don't even try." Deborah took a long drink of iced tea and capped the bottle. "He thinks he can show up whenever it's convenient for him, and Olivia's just so happy to see him it makes his irresponsibility all right. Well, in my book it's *not* all right."

"You go on and play with your friend," Raymond was saying to his daughter. "I've got to talk to your mama a bit, and then we'll do something together, okay?"

"No! I wanna be with you, Daddy!"

"Okay. Then we'll talk to your mama together," Raymond suggested, straightening up and lifting Olivia as he stood. He reminded Sharon of a young Billy Dee Williams, handsome and charismatic. She could understand why Deborah had fallen for him— even if he wasn't always as responsible as she would like.

Sharon screwed the top onto her iced tea bottle and stood. "Don't go," Deborah murmured, but Sharon had no intention of remaining on the bench, trapped in the no-man's-land between an estranged husband and wife. If Deborah needed her later, she'd be available. But right now, what Deborah needed was to talk to Raymond.

Sharon crossed the scruffy, summer-baked grass to the climbing apparatus. Max stood on a high platform, his eyes level with hers. He watched Olivia, his expression vaguely worried. Sharon doubted he had any concept of the Jackson family's problems. His worry was more likely due to Olivia's failure to come back and play with him.

"Who's that?" he asked Sharon.

"Olivia's daddy."

"I want a daddy," Max said.

She suspected he wanted a daddy the way he wanted Olivia's dump truck when she was playing with it, or the way he wanted a cookie when he saw her with one. What Olivia had, he wanted. His words meant nothing more than that.

But they resonated deeply inside Sharon. She wanted him to have a daddy, too. She wanted Steve to be here, witnessing the miracle of his son. She wanted him to scoop his baby into his arms the way Raymond had scooped Olivia. She wanted her son to know the security of a man's shoulder beneath his head, the loving rumble of a man's voice.

"I wish I could give you a daddy," she told Max, reaching over the railing and squeezing his shoulder.

"Olivia got a daddy."

"I know."

Max watched as Raymond lowered himself onto the bench next to Deborah and settled Olivia in his lap. Abruptly, Max reached his arms out to Sharon, as if the truth of his fatherlessness overwhelmed him and he needed his mother to comfort him with a hug.

She lifted him over the railing and held him tightly. Max's lower lip poked out in a pout.

"How about you and me taking a drive?" she suggested. He would probably fall asleep within minutes; the car's vibrations almost always lulled him into a stupor, and it was getting close to his nap time, anyway. A drive would distract him from Olivia's dad and get him to rest—and maybe she could scout some new locations to take photos for her submission for the Arlington commemorative book.

"I want a daddy," Max complained in a wavering voice. He rubbed a fist into his eye. He was already halfway to dreamland.

"I know you do. But we're going to go for a ride." As if cruising around town in a car was a valid substitute for a father.

Max whimpered slightly, as if to remind her that he was not satisfied. "I know," she whispered into his silky hair as she carried him past the bench. Deborah shot her a quick look, then nodded. She clearly saw no reason for Sharon and Max to stick around while she and Raymond quarreled about his failure to show up on time for his day with Olivia.

Sharon slid Max into his stroller, strapped the belt around his belly over his teary protests, and followed the sidewalk back to her row of houses. He kicked his feet against the chrome bars of the stroller, wailed a bit, then forgot how irritated he was when he spotted a large orange butterfly hovering above a cluster of dandelions. He was still chattering happily about the butterfly when they entered the house.

She changed his diaper, packed a few snacks for him—pretzels, cubes of cheese and a lidded cup of apple juice—and grabbed her camera tote. Max seemed to have forgotten his disappointment completely. He raced ahead of her to the door, and as soon as she opened it, he bounded down the steps, heading for the street. She sprinted after him, grabbed him before he got to the curb and carried him back up to the porch so she could lock the door. "Don't run into the street, Max," she scolded. "That's very dangerous."

"I go to the car," he explained.

"You have to wait for Mommy. You have to hold my hand."

"I go to the car."

"We'll go to the car together." After locking the front door, she lowered him to his feet, this time keeping a firm hold on him. His hand felt like a tiny animal in hers, warm and squirming, trying to break free. She clung to him until they reached her car, then buckled him into his car seat in back.

"Open the windows!" he screeched. The car's interior was scorching. She kept a towel spread across his seat to keep the plastic surface cool, but the air had baked all morning.

"I'll open all the windows," she promised, getting in behind the wheel, revving the engine and hitting all the automatic window buttons, which allowed the hot air from outside to mingle with the hot air inside. "Once we start driving, it'll cool down." One of these days, she imagined, Max might start whining for an air-conditioned car instead of a daddy. For now, "daddy" was probably a simpler concept for him to grasp than "air-conditioning."

They drove out of Village Green and the car's motion did cause the air to lose a little of its searing heat—but not much. Arlington wore summer heavily.

The pavement shimmered before her eyes, and people moved slowly. Hers was the only car on the road with its windows open; all the rest undoubtedly had air-conditioning.

For the first few minutes, Max yammered in the back seat, providing a running narration on everything he saw. "There's a tree! There's a big truck! There's a doggie!" But eventually he wound down, and when Sharon glanced into her rearview mirror, she saw that he had dozed off.

She sighed. She wished she could give him a daddy. She wished she could give him anything he wanted. She wished she could give herself what she wanted, too. She wished she knew what that might be.

Not a kiss from Brett Stockton. Deborah was right; the man's inconsistency last night hadn't been fair, it hadn't made sense and he wasn't worth wasting another thought on. Sharon had desired him only because he was the first man she'd spared a thought for since Steve's death. She was a healthy woman, she was lonely, she was horny—whatever the reason, she'd responded to Brett because he happened to be the first man to come along. There would be others.

For some reason, that thought didn't cheer her. She didn't want others. Horny and lonely she might be, but she wasn't on the prowl, desperate for male companionship. Once she'd recovered from the shock and grief of Steve's death, she'd actually come to admit that there were a few advantages to not having a man around: a lot less laundry, the toilet seat was always in the right position and she didn't have to battle anyone over the remote control. The house was hers to arrange as she wished. She chose her own decor and set her own rules. Her life belonged to her—and to Max, of course.

She missed Steve. At first, she'd missed him most at night, when she'd lain alone in their broad bed and heard the hum of the clock instead of the steady tempo of his breathing. She'd missed the way he always slung one arm around her and bunched his pillow up against the back of her head. She'd missed waking up with him, their legs tangled and his cheeks scratchy with a bristle of beard.

Now, though, she missed him most during the day—when she felt overwhelmed by the labor of keeping the studio profitable, or when she wanted to discuss current events with an intelligent adult, or when she watched a funny movie or TV show and longed to share it with him, to laugh with him. Sex...she'd like it, sure. But it wasn't something she thought about very often.

She was thinking about it today, thanks to Brett Stockton.

Who hadn't kissed her and whom, she was sure, she would never hear from again.

"I'LL GO," Brett said.

Janet glowered at him. "You'll go where? We can send anyone over there to pick up the photos. They're open until five today, the lady said—"

"What lady?" he asked, trying to keep his tone noncommittal. Janet loomed in his doorway, as effectively as a woman who stood barely five foot one inch could loom. She'd just informed him that someone from Bartell Studios had phoned to let them know Arlington Financial's order was ready. For some inexplicable reason, Brett wanted to be the one to pick it up. "Was it the photographer?"

"No, some other lady."

He hoped his face didn't betray his feelings. In truth, he wasn't sure what those feelings were. He really didn't want to see Sharon again.

Except that he did.

Which was really, really stupid, because he was too old to find anything exciting in a fling, but he couldn't imagine what, beyond a fling, could exist between him and her. A friendship? Not the way she looked, the way his body hummed with arousal in her presence. No, he couldn't picture himself getting together with her on a regular basis for coffee and deep conversation and nothing more.

He'd told himself to forget about her—but he wasn't listening to himself. He hadn't forgotten about her all day yesterday, while he'd puttered around his house in a sour mood, plowing through the Sunday paper without absorbing much of it, grumbling through a televised Red Sox game and sucking down a couple of beers while he watched an inane movie on cable about alien space invaders. He'd grilled himself a steak for dinner, discovered he didn't have much appetite and wished he owned a dog so he could feed it his ample leftovers.

He didn't want a dog. A dog was a creature that had to be taken care of—fed, walked, bathed, trained. Almost as bad as a baby.

Damn it, why did Sharon have to have that kid?

The fault lay with him, not her. He had no right to resent her for being a mother. He was the one out of whack, out of step. Somewhere in this world there had to be a woman who didn't want children, and someday he'd meet her.

He just hoped she felt as good in his arms as Sharon did.

"I'll pick up the photos," he said again.

"You don't have anything more important to do?" Janet asked.

"As a matter of fact, no." Nothing as important as seeing Sharon one more time—if she was even at her studio. If she wasn't, it would probably be just as well. "Where's the studio located?"

"On Dudley—255 Dudley. You should send someone else, Brett. You've got a business to run."

"The business isn't going to collapse if I take a ten-minute break." He shoved away from his desk, grabbed his jacket from the back of his chair and sauntered past Janet and out the door. His hair was mussed, his tie dangling, and he realized, once he'd entered the elevator down the hall from his office suite, that his jacket was extraneous. August had spread another sticky, steamy day across northwestern Connecticut. Even if he thought he'd look better donning the jacket, he wasn't going to. He had no need to make a good impression on Sharon.

He had no need to make any impression on her at all. He was a fool to be running this errand. He ought to press the Up button, return to his office and send someone else to pick up the photos. He was the damned CEO of the company, after all. He paid people to take care of the trivial stuff.

The midday heat assaulted him as he stepped out of the building. The pedestrians strolling along the sidewalk looked wilted and weary, and as he crossed the street the asphalt felt spongy against the soles of

his shoes. Sweat gathered under the loosened collar
of his shirt, and the shoulder over which he'd flung
his jacket felt as if it was in an oven, roasting its way
to well done.

He didn't turn around, though. He couldn't. He
was on some sort of masochistic mission: hiking
through heat and humidity so thick he could practically swim in it, to reach a studio where, if he was
either lucky or unlucky, he'd get to see a woman he
wanted to see but didn't want to see. Surely people
had been committed to insane asylums for less.

Her studio was a few long blocks down Dudley,
and by the time he reached the awninged front door
he had to use his handkerchief to wipe his face. Step-
ping inside, he sighed with deep relief as cool air
swarmed around him. He closed his eyes and savored
the rippling chill of perspiration evaporating from his
forehead and the back of his neck. Then he opened
his eyes and looked around.

The small front room contained a few chairs, a
reception counter and walls of photos: sappy bridal
shots, earnest yearbook pictures, the sort of glossy
black-and-white photos he associated with showbiz
personalities, sentimental portraits of elders, and
cloying photos of babies, children and toddlers, a few
of them augmented by fuzzy kittens or puppies so
adorable his stomach rebelled. Some of the photos
were huge, with museum-quality frames. Others were
small, gathered collagelike in frames designed to
hold an assortment of pictures. On a table in front of
the chairs sat an array of photo albums.

A woman stood behind the counter. Not Sharon.
Brett tried to convince himself he'd just dodged a
bullet, but disappointment overruled pragmatism.

"Can I help you?" the woman asked cheerfully. She wore a sleeveless cotton shirt and shorts, and she looked about forty degrees cooler than Brett felt.

"I'm here to pick up an order," he told her. "Arlington Financial Services. We got word that it was ready."

"Sure. I'll be right back," she said, then departed through a doorway. Her steps were so bouncy he wondered if she had springs embedded in her sneakers.

He sighed again, this time not in relief but in frustration—with Sharon for not being there, and with himself for caring. He could have sent Janet over to pick these photos up. No, not Janet—she was in her sixties, and this kind of heat could wreak havoc on an older woman, even one as tough as she was. Someone else from his staff, though. Bill spent his days off scaling mountains and portaging canoes. He probably would have viewed the walk to Sharon's studio on a hotter-than-hell day as a minivacation.

He saw activity beyond the doorway, a shadow moving, and then he got lucky—or unlucky. Sharon Bartell emerged, carrying a pastel-blue box. "Hello," she said, giving him a level stare.

She obviously wasn't thrilled to see him. Her mouth sat like a horizontal stripe above her chin, not even the tiniest hint of a smile tweaking its corners upward. Her jaw was set in a way that made her chin look pointier than he remembered it, and her cheeks hollower. Her eyes were a swirl of color, green and amber and overcast gray.

"You phoned my office," he said, as if informing his secretary that his order was ready was tantamount to inviting him to pay a social call.

"Yes. Your pictures came in."

"Came in? You don't develop them yourself?"

"I can develop them, but I usually have a lab take care of it. The lab I use does high-quality work." She set the box on the counter and lifted the lid. "Why don't you check them out. If you're not satisfied…"

· She didn't finish the sentence. Just as well, since at the moment he wasn't satisfied at all. He wanted her to smile the way she'd smiled Saturday night, when her entire face had radiated unadulterated pleasure. He wanted her to smile and tell him she felt like Cinderella.

Right now, she probably felt like a studio owner impatient with a client. He knew he should look at the prints in the box, but he wanted only to look at her, to will her to smile for him. Until she did, he didn't think he could motivate himself to deal with the box. He didn't think he could do anything but wait, and hope.

For what? She had no reason to smile. He'd shut down on her Saturday night, and she was probably insulted. She should be. He'd shared a lovely evening with her and then fled before she could even thank him.

"Look, I—" He drew in a breath, using the time to figure out what he was going to say. The truth, maybe? At least part of the truth. "I had a really good time Saturday night."

"You did?" She sounded genuinely surprised.

"You didn't think I did?"

"Well…I wasn't sure."

She was sure. Only someone blind, deaf and dim-witted would have viewed his behavior at the end of their evening as a sign that he'd had a good time.

"Okay." He drew in another breath. He wished his tie were neat, and he wished it had blue in it to match his eyes—eyes she'd once described as sexy. He wished Janet had nagged him to comb his hair and straighten his shirt. He wished he had the guts to tell Sharon more than part of the truth. "I didn't handle things as well as I should have Saturday. I guess I was having second thoughts."

"Second thoughts?"

About your bratty son. About how close I could get to you without the kid becoming a part of it. "I had a terrific time, and I should have said so."

"Okay." Her eyes softened a little, but she still wasn't smiling.

"I'd like to see you again." There was a nice fat chunk of truth for her.

"Really?"

He wished she didn't sound so surprised. "Yes, really. If you're free on Saturday…"

She didn't respond right away. Her fingers moved restlessly on the box, tracing the edges, tapping the corners. "I'm planning to spend Saturday taking photos around town. I've got a spec project I'm working on."

"The way you were photographing the YMCA building last week?"

"Exactly. So that's going to take up most of the day."

He'd been thinking about seeing her in the evening, after she'd dumped the kid on a baby-sitter. He'd been thinking they could have a nice, adult evening and he could forget, as he had for long stretches last Saturday, that she had a kid at all.

But he was aiming for the truth, and the truth was, if he was going to continue seeing her, he ought to see her as she was: a mother. "What were you going to do with your son while you took these photos on spec?"

"Bring him with me, of course."

He wasn't sure there was any "of course" about her answer. But maybe the kid acted better during the day. Maybe she'd trained him to carry her camera around for her like a caddy and give her pointers on the angle of the sun. "How about if I join you?" he asked.

She studied him. A tiny line deepened at the bridge of her nose, not quite a frown but close. "Do you really want to?"

No. He must have been crazy to suggest it. "Sure."

"Okay." Her face remained still, but her fingers bristled with nervous energy. She lifted the lid of the box, then set it back in place. "I'd like to get an early start."

"I can call you Friday to work out the times," he said.

"Okay. Fine." She jiggled the lid of the box again, then pulled it off and removed an order form. "Why don't you look this over."

She was nervous. *He* made her nervous. Big deal. He was nervous, too. He'd just done something he'd sworn his whole life he would never do: pursue a relationship with a woman who had a child. When he'd asked her to join him at the Leukemia Foundation dinner last week, he hadn't known she was a mother, but he knew now, and he was arranging a date with her anyway.

If roaming around town with her and her kid while she took photos qualified as a date.

He lowered his gaze to the box. The order form looked correct. The top two photos scored about a seven on a scale of one to ten, where one was appealing and ten was the stuff of nightmares. The third photo was one in which he was laughing. He squinted but saw no trace of her belly dancer doll, or even the doll's shadow, in the photo. He didn't look quite so ghastly when he was laughing.

He flipped hastily through the other photos and proofs. The ones of his staff members all scored ones and twos on his scale. In one picture, Janet looked deceptively benign, like the kind of grandmother who'd bake chocolate chip cookies on her day off.

"Great," he said, closing the box. "Do you have an invoice?"

"Your secretary said she'd prefer to have me mail the invoice."

"Then you'd better do that. Her word is law."

Sharon smiled. Just a glimmer of a smile, but it vanquished his nervousness. That was all he'd needed to see. Her smile was almost enough to convince him that spending a few hours with her kid on Saturday would be worth the torture. If he survived it, if he tolerated the little monster, maybe she'd smile again, a bigger, warmer smile.

He truly was insane. He'd trudged through air that felt as thick and searing as lava and agreed to an outing with a woman he should steer clear of. Even worse, he'd agreed to it knowing her kid would be part of the deal. Maybe the heat had melted his brain. Or maybe Sharon had melted it.

It wasn't until he'd returned to his office, cooled off and flipped through the photos again that he realized one was missing: that last picture she'd shot of him, the one he hadn't been prepared for.

CHAPTER FIVE

THEY SHOULD HAVE taken his car. He should have insisted on it. The air-conditioning in her car was apparently nonfunctional, the engine emitted an angry snarl whenever she accelerated, and worst of all, the back seat of her car contained one of those bulky padded infant seats—which was currently occupied by a screeching toddler.

Brett had no objection to loudness in the proper context: when listening to Aerosmith, for instance, or watching the Thunderbirds perform high-speed jet maneuvers at an air show. But noise created by a child was different. It abraded his nerves and made him remember why he hated kids—as if he needed a reminder.

"It's very nice of you to offer the use of your car," Sharon had said when he'd suggested it, "but I've got Max's child seat all set up in my car. And if he spills something or drops something—well, if he's going to make a mess, I'd prefer that he make it in my car than in yours."

Brett would prefer that, too. He'd prefer not even to think about the kinds of messes little Max could make.

Right now, as they pulled away from Sharon's town house, Max was seated in his chair, which was positioned in the center of the back seat. Sharon's camera bag was to his left, and another tote to his right. As Sharon had loaded up the car she'd informed Brett that this other tote was filled almost exclusively with items for Max: diapers, apple juice, crackers shaped like fish, cubes of cheddar cheese, a Ziploc bag containing grapes, a teddy bear, a book about choo-choo trains, a change of clothing, a tot-size baseball cap, and no doubt several other essentials that she hadn't mentioned and that weren't in sight at the top of the bag.

The kid was babbling, a running narration: "We go in the car. We got to go now. We go on a drive. I wave at the trees! Lots of trees! There's a birdie in the tree. Look at birdie!" Brett risked a glance backward and observed that Max was explaining these salient facts to the teddy bear, which he'd hauled out of the tote bag and was clutching in his pudgy hands.

"Does your son talk all the time?" he asked Sharon.

She was dressed for the heat, in a pair of khaki shorts and a sleeveless blouse of pleasantly faded plaid cotton. Her legs were long and golden, and he decided she looked better in shorts than she had in the cocktail dress she'd worn to the dinner last week, because the shorts exposed more of her. Her legs would have to be pretty damned terrific to compensate for the incessantly yakking tyke in the back seat. Fortunately, they were pretty damned terrific.

"Not all the time, no," Sharon said, shooting Brett a smile that was still right up there on his list of spectacular sights. "Sometimes he refuses to say a word. Usually that's when I need him to say something. And he talks nonstop when I need him to be quiet. He loves being contrary."

"And they call children blessings," he muttered.

Sharon must have thought he was joking, because she laughed. "I want to get some shots of the park down near the Oak Hill School," she told him. "That's where we'll start."

"You're just taking these photos for yourself?" he asked. If they talked about her work, maybe he could ignore the din of toddler commentary arising from the back seat.

She glanced at him, a faint frown denting her forehead. "No. What makes you think that?"

"You said something...." He tried to recall exactly what. He'd been befuddled when he'd gone to the studio to pick up his pictures, distracted by her presence and by the undertow of attraction that dragged him off course like a dangerous tide. She'd been talking to him, and he'd been thinking he ought to get the hell out of there and head back to safe, solid ground. Instead, he'd said he wanted to spend Saturday with her. She'd said she was planning to spend the day taking pictures... "On spec," he recollected. "You're doing this on spec."

She hooked her pinkie over the directional switch to turn on the signal. While Brett didn't like her car, he did like watching her drive. She drove more cautiously than he did, but he supposed that was what mothers did when their children were in the back seat. Her movements flowed, her hands climbing the circumference of the steering wheel as she turned it, then relaxing as the wheel straightened out on its own. Her sunglasses hid her eyes from him, but he could see the smooth contour of her cheek in profile.

Just as she took her time making the turn, she took

her time answering. "Yes," she finally said, her curt answer a letdown after he'd waited so long for it.

"You're doing this just for fun? Working on a Saturday for no pay?"

She shrugged. He wished he could see past the dark lenses of her glasses; her eyes might provide more information than her words. "I see birdies," Max announced from the back seat. "I waving to the birdies. Hello, birdies!"

Brett tried not to grit his teeth. He wondered why Sharon would want to kill a Saturday morning photographing a park near an elementary school just for her own gratification. There had to be more to it, but she seemed reluctant to explain, as if she didn't trust him.

And why should she trust him? She hardly knew him. They'd spent all of a few hours together one week ago.

Still, her reticence irked him. "If you don't want to tell me, that's fine," he said. "But I'm a little confused about why you'd ask me to join you if you don't want me to know what you were doing."

"It's not that I don't want you to know." She steered into the parking lot beside the park and yanked the parking brake. Then she sighed. "I'm putting together a proposal to submit for the commemorative book for Arlington's birthday."

"You want to do the photos?"

She nodded. "I'd like to win the commission. The money would be nice, and the exposure would be phenomenal."

"You should have told me sooner." He grinned, relieved that she wasn't hiding some dire secret from him. "I know a lot of people on the city's celebration committee. I could—"

"I don't want you to."

Behind them, Max launched into a monologue about the grass, the big rock, his ravenous hunger and his teddy bear's nose. Brett studied Sharon's face, wishing he had X-ray vision so he could see past those damned sunglasses. "You don't want me to what?" he asked.

She did him the favor of lifting her sunglasses onto the crown of her head. Her eyes were intense, earnest, almost pleading. "I don't want you to convince them to choose me for the commission."

"Convince whom?"

"The people you know on the birthday celebration committee. That nice woman, the lawyer, who sat at our table—"

"Gail Murphy?"

"Yes. And whoever else you know. I'm aware you're well connected, Brett, but I'd like to win the commission fairly."

He nearly guffawed. Cripes, how old was she? How could a woman who ran her own business, who'd been married and widowed and was currently raising a son single-handedly be so naïve? "People rarely win these things fairly," he pointed out. "Life isn't fair. If you want the commission, I can make it happen."

She shook her head so emphatically he suspected she was trying to refute herself more than him. "I've been putting together a portfolio of photos taken in Arlington and the vicinity. They're good. If I win the commission, it will be because I'm talented and I deserve it, not because someone I knew twisted arms for me."

"I wouldn't twist arms. All I'd do is tell the people I know on the committee that you're talented and you deserve it."

"And they'd say, 'Oh, you're right, Brett—thanks for that insight! If you think she deserves it, we'll hire her right away.'"

"I doubt I've got that much juice."

From the back seat came a strident voice: "Let's go! Out of the car! I wanna get out!"

It figured that the kid would interrupt with shrill demands while Brett and Sharon were discussing something important. She twisted to look at her son, but Brett caught her chin with his thumb and steered her gaze to him. "Other people are going to use their connections. Why won't you?"

"Because..." She sighed. Her eyes shifted from him. Her chin moved slightly, and he took that to mean she wanted him to remove his hand from her. He did, reluctantly. "Brett, I—I know this is going to sound silly, but I'm not like you. I don't have influence. I don't know people who have influence. I trust in hard work and talent to get me where I need to go, because that's what I've got going for me."

"Time to get out now!" the kid shrieked. "Now, Mommy! I wanna go now!"

"You do know people who have influence. You know me," Brett pointed out.

"And I—" She sighed. "I'd feel funny taking advantage of you."

He laughed. "You can take advantage of me any time you want. I won't mind."

"Maybe not, but *I* would."

"Now, Mommy!" The kid sounded outraged at her failure to obey. "I go out *now!*"

"All right, Max. We'll get out of the car now."

"Out of the car now," he repeated, his voice bristling with indignation.

Sharon turned from Brett and swung open her door. The warm air smelled of grass and dust and sunshine. She opened the back door and her son greeted her with a bleat of pleasure, his misery magically gone. "I get out now," he said cheerfully, scrambling out of his seat as soon as she released the clips that held him in place. "I have to play."

Brett remained in his seat a moment longer, wondering at what age a person could no longer assert that he *had* to play. Had he ever believed he had to play? He couldn't remember. Even as a child, he'd rarely believed play was an entitlement or a necessity. His sister and brothers had played—he knew, because he'd witnessed them hard at it—but he'd been older, and his responsibility had been to watch them, not to join in. He'd been Brett, in charge of everyone else. Playing had never been an option for him.

He got out of the car in time to see Sharon swing Max from the back seat and set him down on the park's scruffy lawn. As soon as she let go, the kid charged forward, his stubby legs carrying him with surprising speed toward a huge, rounded outcrop of granite, which he proceeded to scale. Sharon managed to collect her camera bag and lock the car without shifting her gaze from her child.

Brett shook off the pensiveness that had embraced him. He had the freedom to play now. Outside of work, he was responsible for no one, in charge of no one. He could do whatever he wanted, within reason and the law.

For one brief, strange minute, the only thing he wanted to do was climb that magnificent bulge of granite, just like Max.

SHE MIGHT HAVE BEEN startled by how handsome Brett was if she hadn't kept the photo.

She knew he was handsome, of course. She'd spent last Saturday night with him, far too aware of how attractive he was. But her soul wasn't a strip of film; it didn't preserve every image it encountered. All that had remained vivid in her mind was his mysterious behavior as their time together drew to an end. He'd wanted her; he hadn't wanted her; she'd wanted him and he'd cut and run.

But then the photos had come back from the lab, picture after picture of him at his desk, smiling hesitantly, smiling warmly, looking grim, smiling again, looking pained and then smiling once more. All right, she'd thought: he was a great-looking guy, but still not worth wasting mental energy over.

Until she'd seen the last proof and known she would never be able to stop thinking about him.

His face was so open in that photograph, the last one she'd taken. His eyes were naked, his starchy tension gone. He was neither smiling nor frowning, but instead wore an enigmatic look, one part curiosity, one part fatigue, one part longing. Whenever she gazed at the photo, she found herself trying to imagine what he longed for.

Things seemed to be going smoothly enough between them today. They'd been together only a half hour, but they hadn't hit any snags so far. He'd sent no mixed signals, no signals at all. His offer to promote her for the town book commission was generous and not entirely unexpected, but it didn't represent anything personal. It was just the sort of thing people who knew people who knew people did.

For some reason, though, she didn't want to accept intervention from Brett. If anything was going to develop between them, it wasn't going to be based on favors and debts.

Max was scaling his favorite boulder with all the fervor of a trained rock climber, although with considerably less finesse. Once he was done climbing on it, she intended to photograph it. At this time of year, bleached from summer sunlight, it broke stark and pale out of the earth. She wanted her portfolio to include a nice mix of Arlington's man-made and natural wonders: the YMCA building, the city hall, the hilariously sleek art deco liquor store on the south end of Hauser, the geometry of her own condominium complex with its staggered rows of triangular roofs—but also the apple orchards, the swells of the hills north of town, the dense forests of fir trees rich and green against a gray sky, and this rock. Once Max was done conquering it, of course.

Brett strode over to the rock, looking as if he wanted to join Max on it. What undoubtedly appeared mountainous to Max would be quite manageable to Brett. Maybe he'd climb to the top and help Max up. They could be a team.

The thought made her smile, even though she knew she should avoid such notions. She shouldn't be hoping for a friendship between Brett and Max when the friendship between Brett and herself was so tenuous.

"That's quite a rock," he said as she approached.

"A souvenir left by the glaciers." She popped the lens cap off her camera and took a picture of Max, his little face screwed in concentration as his sneakered feet skidded on the rock's curved surface.

"Is he safe doing that?"

"The worst that could happen is maybe a scraped knee or a bruise. The worst that could happen if I *didn't* let him climb is that he'd grow up afraid and supercautious." She sighed. "The hardest thing about motherhood is swallowing your fear and letting your kid take risks."

"I always thought it was trying to line up a babysitter."

She smiled and shook her head. "It's the sleepless nights. When they're young, you're up all night because they're crying and need to be nursed. When they're older, you're up all night because you're thinking of the perils lying in wait for them."

"But then they grow up and leave?" He sounded oddly hopeful.

"I don't know for sure, but I bet I'll still be lying awake, worrying about Max, until the day I die. The trick is to keep him from finding out how worried I am."

Brett propped a foot on the edge of the rock. His sneaker looked enormous, almost as long as Max's entire leg. Brett wore shorts, and for a moment she was transfixed by the hair along his shin and calf. There wasn't much, just enough to enhance the hard contours of his muscles and remind her of how long it had been since she'd seen a man's naked leg, since she'd seen a man naked.

She felt her cheeks bloom with a heat that had

nothing to do with the August morning. Fortunately, her camera hid half her face. She'd brought her Leica, which she preferred for outdoor shots. It seemed to capture natural light better than her Pentax. While Max labored his way to the top of the boulder, she took some shots of a cloud formation above the dense foliage of an oak tree, and the grid of concrete paths that cut through the park. Finally, Max reached the crest of the rock and stood, as proud as any climber who'd reached the summit of Everest. "Look at me, Mommy!" he crowed. "Look! I'm all the way up!"

She gave him a cheer and took a picture of him. "Do you need help getting down?" she asked.

"I can get down," he said, squatting and gazing anxiously at the grass below, as if it were miles away. He eyed Brett, who took a giant step backward. Tottering slightly, he bit his lip. "I can get down," he said a little less certainly.

Sharon's heart clutched in sympathy for him. He really wanted to climb down by himself, but he didn't know how and he was too proud to ask for help. She groped for a way to assist him without threatening his fragile ego. "Look, Max, your sneaker is untied. You can't climb down with an untied shoelace."

He scowled at the dangling laces on his left foot. "Tie it, Mommy."

She put down her camera and closed in. "You know, it's really hard for me to tie when you're up there. I'm going to have to get you down so I can tie it."

"I can get down," he said, extending his arms to her. She lifted him, planted a quick kiss in the warm hollow of his neck, and swung him to the ground. The instant she finished double-knotting his lace, he trotted off down the sidewalk.

"Could you keep an eye on him for a minute?" she asked Brett as she retrieved her camera. The sun hit the rock, washing over its nooks and etching its textured surface with light. She took several photos quickly, before a cottony wad of clouds could drift across the sun and alter the light. Concentrating on her shots, she lost track of everything around her—the crows poking through the grass in search of a stray seed, the dog barking adamantly at a threatening squirrel, the elderly couple enjoying a brisk power walk.

Once she had her shots, she capped the lens and searched the park for Max and Brett. They stood facing each other on one of the walkways, hands on hips, squaring off like gunslingers poised to shoot each other.

Laughing, she jogged over. "I'm all done," she announced. "Do you guys want to hang out here a little longer, or can we move on?"

Max broke free and dove into her arms. He looked concerned and a bit disgruntled, not quite on the verge of tears but getting there.

"What's wrong, sweetie?"

"We go now," he said, shooting Brett a dubious look.

Sharon glanced at Brett, trying to figure out what had occurred between them that would have rattled her son. His expression told her nothing. It was almost eerily noncommittal, his jaw set, his eyes squinting slightly from the sun's glare. "Is everything all right?" she asked him.

"Everything's fine," he said tersely, falling into step beside her and lifting her tote from her hand so she could carry Max in both arms.

Everything wasn't fine. Something had happened between Brett and Max, not traumatic enough to reduce Max to tears but unsettling enough to make them both very wary of each other.

So much for any magical bonding between her son and her— Her friend? Her escort? Her potential lover? The only man in her life at the moment.

Whatever Brett was to her, he and Max obviously hadn't discovered love at first sight.

THEY STOPPED at the Dairy Queen for ice cream. Seated across from the Bartells at a picnic table under the awning outside the snack stand, Brett watched Sharon wipe a dribble of ice cream from Max's chin with a napkin from the inch-thick pile she'd pulled out of the dispenser. Before hitting this oasis, they'd stopped to take photos at the pond near the library, and at the library itself, and at the athletic fields behind the high school, where two American Legion teams were battling for dominance on one of the well-groomed diamonds. At the library, Max had gorged on cheese and crackers, but two hours later he'd complained that he was starving again.

Brett and Sharon joined him in this snack. Brett had purchased a cup of chocolate soft serve for her and a vanilla-chocolate double twist in a cone for himself.

"The big question," she said as Max spooned another messy blob of ice cream into his mouth, smearing a significant portion onto his lips and chin, "is whether he'll fall asleep before he finishes his ice cream.''

"Not tired," Max insisted, his mouth so full the words came out garbled.

Sharon ate her ice cream daintily. Brett observed her as she slid the plastic spoon between her lips, as her tongue darted out to capture a tiny drip of chocolate at the corner of her mouth, and thought he'd never felt so ambivalent in his life. Witnessing Sharon eating ice cream was a sublimely sensuous experience. Witnessing her son eating ice cream was a complete turnoff—not because he was such a slob but because he was a child.

Licking his ice cream cooled Brett, making the afternoon heat more tolerable. Once the kid fell asleep, what would happen? Could Sharon tuck him into his little car seat in back, and then they could neck in the front seat? Brett would like that.

He'd like even more returning to her house, dumping the kid in his crib and necking with Sharon on her bed.

For every moment the brat had irritated him, he could account for a moment when Sharon had captivated him. Watching her take pictures was like watching a dancer, an artisan and a visionary all rolled into one. Sometimes he'd wanted to applaud her performance. More often he'd wanted to haul her into his arms and kiss her silly. The awareness he'd felt with her last Saturday hadn't been an aberration. Sharon Bartell got to him in a big way.

But just as he'd sink deep into a mental image of what Sharon looked like under that thin cotton shirt, or how she would sigh when he kissed her throat, when he glided his hands over her skin, when he found her body with his, the kid would pipe up, making an obvious and totally unnecessary observation about a dandelion, an insect or a vehicle—bicycles and pickup trucks seemed to play a prominent role in his world. Or he'd announce some essential fact about his physical state: that he was hungry, that he was wet, that he was running—as if everyone in the world couldn't see him pumping his little feet and swinging his fisted hands as he sped down the sidewalk. And Brett would think, *Am I supposed to care that your diaper is full? Am I supposed to do something about it?*

Of course he wasn't. Sharon was the parent on duty; she was the one who had to march into the library with her kid to use the bathroom for a diaper change. By the time they emerged, Brett was hard-pressed to imagine Sharon naked and sighing. She was just a mother then, not a woman. A mother with a demanding child.

He took some more ice cream into his mouth and let it let it slide down his throat, cold and sweet. He was in trouble. He wanted Sharon, but he couldn't have what he wanted with her, not as long as Max was in the picture.

"Not tired," Max declared, lowering his spoon into the soupy ice cream in his cup. "No, no. Not tired." At least he wasn't broadcasting the condition of his diaper this time. "Not tired, Mommy," he insisted, though he seemed to lack the energy to lift his spoon.

Sharon wiped off his mouth and one sticky hand. "Why don't you just lie down for a minute," she suggested.

"Not tired! No!" But he lay down, resting his

head in her lap. From his side of the table, Brett
could no longer see the kid. He liked that. But he
didn't like thinking of Max's head in her lap—a
place where Brett would like to rest his own head.
He could tell from the motion of Sharon's arm that
she was stroking her boy's hair, and he found himself
wishing she would run her fingers through his own
hair.

"Five minutes and he'll be dead to the world,"
Sharon predicted in a whisper.

Brett nodded. He supposed he ought to pretend he
was interested, but he wasn't. The only good news
about Max's becoming dead to the world was that
until he came back to life, he wouldn't be interrupt-
ing and imposing himself.

Brett ate his ice cream and tried not to stare at
Sharon. Her face troubled him. She looked so peaceful, so blissful, so attuned to her son's state. The kid
was tranquil and so was she.

She was a mother, and Brett had made a huge
mistake.

"What?" she asked, evidently reading his mood.

He forced a smile. "What?"

"I know this hasn't been the easiest day in the
world for you," she said, keeping one hand on Max's
head in her lap while she resumed eating her ice
cream. "Max can wear you out if you're not used to
him."

"I noticed." His cheeks were beginning to cramp.
He devoured a large dollop of ice cream so he
wouldn't have to smile anymore.

"What's perfectly acceptable to a parent might not
be quite so darling to someone who isn't related to

the child," she continued, as if she were offering him an alibi.

It was a good one, but it wasn't quite accurate. If he was impatient with Max, it wasn't because he didn't share blood with Max. It was because Max was a child, period.

He should tell her. If he was fantasizing about making love to her, the least he could do was tell her the truth. "I..." He couldn't come right out and say he hated children. It sounded so...*hateful.* "I don't like kids much," he admitted.

"Oh?" Her eyebrows arched in curiosity. Not revulsion, not condemnation, but what appeared to be fascination laced with mild disappointment. "I guess not everyone is crazy about them."

"There's noting wrong with your son. He hasn't done anything in particular. He's fine, as far as kids go. It's me. I don't like kids."

Apparently she could think of nothing to say to that. She lowered her spoon and swirled it through the melting ice cream in her cup.

He reached across the table and touched her hand. Her spoon fell into the cup and he closed his fingers around her, recalling how smooth and soft her hand had felt when he'd danced with her, when he'd held her. "It's a problem, Sharon," he said. "I like you. A lot. But you've got a kid."

"Yes, I do." A statement of fact, nothing more.

"So maybe we could just...you know, keep Max out of it?"

"Out of what?"

"Anything that happens between us?"

She smiled pensively but didn't pull her hand from his. Her fingers moved against his palm, igniting a totally unwelcome surge of heat in his groin. "Max is a part of me, Brett. How am I going to keep him out of anything important in my life?"

"I don't know."

"I thought—I mean, I've been having a great time today. I assumed you were, too."

"There have been some very nice moments." Like now, he pondered. With the kid unconscious and Sharon's hand in his own, and her eyes so luminous in the shade of the awning.

Without letting go of her, he slid down to the end of his bench, stood, and circled the table to her side. "Come here," he murmured, easing Max's head off her lap and gently down onto the smooth wood slats. Then he pulled Sharon to her feet.

She glanced over her shoulder at Max, as if afraid Brett was going to drag her away from her child. He was, but not the way she thought. She could remain standing beside the picnic table if she wanted, just a few feet from the kid.

Dragging her away had nothing to do with distance. It had to do with thought and imagination, with focus and need. It had to do with figuring out which pull was stronger: his attraction to her or his aversion to her son.

It had to do with his wanting to kiss her, *having* to kiss her, so he could figure out what the hell he was going to do about her.

CHAPTER SIX

LAST WEEK she'd expected him to kiss her. Today, in the early afternoon, in a public place, with cars cruising past the Dairy Queen and her son sleeping not five feet away, she didn't expect it—which made its impact all the more profound.

She tasted sweetness on his lips, hints of vanilla and chocolate. She tasted heat and passion, even though his kiss was restrained, a brush against her mouth, a moment of pressure, a soft graze. Her entire body resonated with it, ripples of pleasure and panic pulsing through her. She'd been missing this, a man, a smart, handsome, sexy man. God, she'd missed this.

She felt like Cinderella again—not dressed for the ball and escaping her everyday responsibilities for a night, but simply a woman swept into another reality for a few magical minutes, transported by the kiss of Prince Charming. She wanted to open her mouth to him, to open herself, to take him in.

But he didn't like children.

What kind of man didn't like children?

His mouth covered hers for one final, lingering moment, and then he drew back. The magic dissipated, depositing her back into reality. The afternoon warmth settled around her, teenage laughter from a picnic table on the other side of the building reached her and a truck rumbled down the street, its engine groaning. She smelled auto exhausts and the greasy scent of French fries and grilled hot dogs.

On the bench her son slept, an angel in repose. He was truly a beautiful child. Sometimes Sharon was shocked by his exquisite features, his long lashes, his delicate little mouth. After Steve's death, Max had been her reason for living. He'd kept her going, kept her on track, motivated her, refused to let her give up or slack off. For nearly three long years, he'd been everything to her.

But now she'd found something more, something Max could never give her. For the first time in those nearly three years, she'd kissed a man.

A man who didn't like children.

Brett trailed his fingers through her hair, sending another ripple of desire through her. She ducked her head, wishing she didn't respond to him, wishing she could change just one thing about him. Wishing, foolishly, that he hadn't told her the truth about himself and had simply let her believe he was crazy about children.

But when she lifted her gaze to him, she saw the truth in his eyes. He wanted her—but he didn't want a woman who happened to have a child.

"I should probably get Max home," she murmured, as if mentioning Max's name would force her to accept what was going on here. "It's been a long day for him."

Brett seemed to understand her message: he couldn't kiss her without acknowledging Max. Max was a part of her. Her attraction to Brett didn't change that.

"Do you want me to carry him to the car?" he

offered, eyeing her slumbering son with an obvious lack of enthusiasm.

Sharon didn't want him touching her son. If he didn't like children, he ought to keep his distance from the boy she considered the most magnificent child in the world. But Max asleep was a heavy load, almost too much for her. She shouldn't stand on principle at the risk of buckling under her son's weight. "Okay," she said, her voice a little rusty. "Thank you."

Instead of moving toward the bench where Max dozed, Brett remained where he was, studying her. "I'm sorry," he said. "I just…" He drifted off, apparently unsure.

"No need to apologize."

"I'm not apologizing. I'm just sorry things are the way they are." He ran his fingers through her hair again, slowly, tenderly. She could imagine what he'd be like as a lover, slow and tender. The thought filled her with regret, and then a pang of guilt for still wanting him. Max was her life. If Brett couldn't accept that, he wasn't someone she should want.

She avoided eye contact with him as she gathered up their cups, spoons and napkins and carried the trash to the garbage pail near the window where they'd ordered their treats. By the time she'd returned, Brett had hoisted her unconscious son onto his shoulder. For someone who didn't like children, he seemed to have mastered the technique of carrying a limp, sleeping child.

She lifted her tote and led the way across the outdoor eating area to her car, tucked between a minivan and an SUV in the gravel parking lot. She unlocked the doors, and Brett lowered Max into his seat with such caution and care she was hard-pressed to believe he didn't like at least this one precious child.

But if he liked Max, he would have said so. He was obviously as attracted to Sharon as she was to him. If he could have tolerated Max, he wouldn't have said he was sorry.

Whatever could have been would not be. If she was ever going to fall in love again, it would have to be with someone who adored Max. No matter how carefully he laid her child into his car seat, Brett wasn't that someone.

POKER WAS AT Levi Holt's house that week. The Tuesday night game always used to be at Evan's house before Evan, who had two children, got married. But now Evan had a wife and Levi had a child, so the rest of the players did what they could to accommodate the fathers in their group.

The five men, who'd been meeting every Tuesday night for years, sat around Levi's kitchen table, each of them armed with a cold bottle of beer. Levi's baby was almost asleep; Levi had planted a microphone near the kid's crib and a receiver on the kitchen counter, providing the game with a soundtrack of muted infant babbling. Brett had no idea what the kid was saying—it all sounded like gibberish to him—but he felt chastened by the sound, as if Levi's baby was saying, "Normal men like children. You're not normal."

"I'm in," Tom announced, tossing a white chip into the center of the table.

Brett studied his hand. A pair of queens, nothing to write home about, but worth staying in for the round. "I'm in, too," he said, adding a white chip to the pile.

To his left, Murphy studied his hand for a long, intense minute, then folded. "So, how'd you make out last week?" he asked Brett.

"Make out?" He hadn't made out at all. He'd committed the grave error of kissing Sharon and realized something powerful existed between them. He'd thought that one kiss would decide things for him, and it had—it had proven to him that if he could get over his aversion to kids, he and Sharon could be incredible together. But it had also informed him that if he *couldn't* get over his aversion, he'd better forget her, because the kid was part of the deal.

"With that Leukemia dinner," Murphy clarified. "Did you pull in as much as last year?"

"We made fifteen percent more," Brett told him. The other men at the table cheered him in assorted ways, Levi raising his bottle in a toast, Evan beating a drum roll on the table with his fingertips, Tom socking him in the arm. "Yeah, it went well," Brett added with a modest smile.

"That lady with you—what was her name? Sharon?"

Brett's smile faded. "What about her?"

"Someone new?" Evan asked, his eyebrows twitching Groucho-style.

"She was terrific," Murphy reported to the others. "Smart, pretty—much higher quality than Brett deserves."

The other men laughed. Playing along, Brett forced a chuckle. Murphy's words stung, though. Sharon *was* better than he deserved.

"She's a photographer, isn't that right?" Murphy

went on as Levi lifted the deck and dealt Evan three fresh cards. "She took Brett's photos for his annual report. She must have liked what she saw in the viewfinder, huh?"

"Doubtful," Brett argued. He really didn't want to talk about Sharon. Not after last Saturday. Not after he'd recognized how much he'd be giving up by walking away from her—and nonetheless choosing, out of fairness to her and his own sense of self-preservation, to walk away. "I take lousy photos."

"I still have last year's annual report lying around," Levi said. He had money invested in Brett's funds, and all investors received a copy of the report each year. "He really does take lousy photos. You looked like someone who'd been on steroids, kind of puffy and distorted."

"This year's photos came out better," Brett admitted.

"Because you had Sharon take them," Murphy pointed out. "She must be talented."

"She should get the commission for the Arlington book," Brett remarked. He knew she'd asked him not to intervene on her behalf, but mentioning her over a casual poker game wasn't intervening. He hadn't requested any favors or twisted any arms. He'd only made a comment to Murphy, whose wife just happened to be on the city's birthday committee.

That was how business was done. People made comments during poker games on Tuesday nights. If Sharon didn't like it, she could turn down the commission—if she happened to win it. Which she ought to. Murphy was right: anyone who could make Brett look halfway decent in a photograph was definitely talented.

"Is she submitting a proposal for it?" Murphy asked.

Brett pulled the three cards that weren't queens out of his hand and replaced them with the three Levi had dealt him. A jack, a four and another queen. He recalled an old saying his mother used to recite: "Unlucky in cards means lucky in love." He wondered if the opposite was true. He'd won quite a few hands tonight, but he wasn't feeling lucky.

"As far as I know, she's submitting," he said, waiting for the betting to resume.

"You want me to talk to Gail about her?" Murphy asked.

"Sure," Brett said. Evan tossed in a blue chip, Tom folded and Brett raised.

"This one's special, huh?" Evan asked. For a moment, Brett thought he was commenting on Brett's hand. Then he comprehended that Evan was referring to Sharon.

Yeah, she was special, damn it. Kissing her had only confirmed what he'd already felt about her. The way she moved, the way she composed her shots, the way she shut out the world when she was concentrating, the way she laughed... Special. Absolutely.

"So, what's the problem?" Levi asked, adding a blue chip to the kitty.

Brett's three queens won the hand over Levi's two pairs and Evan's bluff. Brett scooped in the chips and added them to his stacks, seeing each added chip as one more bit of proof that his love life was doomed. "What problem?" he asked, faking ignorance. "What makes you think I've got a problem?"

"Gentlemen," Murphy announced, "I saw this woman. She's the one. Brett's been bit."

"She's not the one," Brett snapped. Ordinarily, he didn't mind being ribbed, especially by his poker pals. Teasing was part of what bound these men together as friends.

But insisting that Sharon was the one touched a particularly sensitive nerve, one that had never been exposed before.

Murphy looked perplexed. "How can you say she's not the one? Even Gail liked her—and Gail's the toughest judge of character I ever met. Look how long it took her to figure out she liked me!"

Brett sighed. To remain churlish when he had such a huge heap of chips in front of him would not go over well with his friends. "All right," he conceded. "She's a fantastic woman. She's everything Murphy says she is. But she's not the one. She's got a kid."

His statement was greeted with groans and guffaws. The guys knew how Brett felt about children.

"Just one?" Evan asked. "How old?"

"I don't know—two, two-and-a-half, something around there."

"That's a sucky age," Evan reassured him. "Things improve when kids pass their third birthday."

"It's not his age," Brett argued. "Any age would be a problem. You know me."

"If the woman is really the one," Levi observed, "you might try to get past the kid thing."

Levi wouldn't understand. With the arrival of his baby, he'd discovered he had a knack for child rearing, and a taste for it. The other fathers at the table—Murphy and Evan—were insanely in love with their children. Tom had been married three times and was determined never to marry again, which meant the likelihood of his becoming a father was pretty slim. But even he wouldn't understand the antipathy Brett felt toward children. He hadn't lived Brett's life. None of them had.

"I'm serious, Brett," Levi added. "When you love a woman, you figure out ways to accommodate her."

"First of all, I don't *love* this woman," Brett said. He wished he could introduce a new topic—the Red Sox traditional late-season fade, for instance, or the governor's new tax proposal. "And second of all, if I *did* love her—" a totally preposterous notion; they had lots of chemistry going for them, but that was hardly the same thing as love "—the most loving thing I could do would be to clear out. The way I feel about kids, I don't belong with her."

"Have you ever considered changing the way you feel about kids?" Levi asked.

Brett muttered an obscenity, which made Levi laugh. "I am who I am," Brett reminded him. "Why should I change?"

"Because this woman may be the one," Murphy noted.

Brett swung his gaze around the table. His buddies were ganging up on him. If he didn't have the damned mountain of chips in front of him, he would leave. But the group had an unspoken rule about not leaving early when you were ahead. It was bad sportsmanship, and bad sportsmanship was a far greater sin than tormenting one of the players about his hang-ups.

"I think," Murphy addressed the other men, "that our friend Brett here needs a few lessons at the Daddy School."

"Lessons?" What the hell was Daddy School? Whatever it was, its name made Brett want to run as fast as he could in the opposite direction.

"It's a great program," Levi told him.

"My sister-in-law is one of the founders," Murphy said. "She's the director of the preschool Evan's daughter's been attending."

"And the other founder is the wife of a client of mine," Levi added. "They teach classes in how to become a better father."

"I don't want to become a father at all," Brett said defensively. "I sure don't want to become a better one." He punctuated that assertion by taking a long pull of beer.

"Forget about becoming a father," Evan explained. "They teach you how to get along with kids, how to get them to open up to you, how to build a stronger relationship with them."

Brett didn't want Max Bartell to open up to him. He didn't want to build a stronger relationship with the whiny blond imp. With the imp's mother, sure, but not with him.

Of course, the only way he could build a stronger relationship with her was through her kid. Max was the gatekeeper. Brett would have to get past him to reach her.

He didn't want to get past Max. But...damn. He wanted to reach Sharon. He did.

"Why don't you just give it a try?" Murphy suggested. "I met the woman in question, Brett. She's worth putting yourself out a little."

"I don't want to attend classes with a bunch of gaga dads," Brett objected. "I can just imagine them all sitting around, boasting about how wonderful their kids are, how much money they spent on their kids and how their kids pitch better than Pedro Martinez. I'd need a motion-disturbance bag to get through that kind of thing.''

''It's not like that,'' Evan assured him. ''Most of the fathers are insecure about their abilities. They're there because they want to learn how to be better at it.''

''Except for me,'' Murphy bragged. ''I attended it a few times and discovered they had nothing to teach me. I was already the perfect father.''

Levi aimed a red chip at Murphy's nose and fired. Murphy ducked, and the chip bounced off the refrigerator.

Brett didn't share his friends' laughter. He was already feeling queasy. The mere name of the program caused his stomach to buck. *Daddy School.* Brett didn't belong there. He'd hate it. He'd get nothing out of it.

Closing his eyes, he pictured Sharon. And it occurred to him that maybe he'd get something out of it after all—her.

But he didn't want to go. He was happy with himself; he saw no need to transform his life. Classes on how to connect with kids? No way.

''So, where does this Daddy School meet?'' he asked.

SHARON HEARD the bell above the door ring, signaling that someone had entered the studio. She'd sent Angie down to the bank with the previous day's receipts, so she had to go out to the front counter to deal with the customer herself.

Ordinarily, this would not be a problem. Ordinarily, she was not in such a sour mood.

She'd never been a temperamental person. Even after Steve's death, she'd maintained an even disposition, afraid that mood swings would make her pregnancy and the first months of her baby's life more difficult. Back then, surviving each day had been challenging enough without her turning into a grouch.

It was all Brett's fault that she was a grouch now. She'd been doing fine before she'd met him. She hadn't spent all her free time mourning over what her life lacked, yearning for a man to come along and fill in the missing pieces and hollow places. No man could do that—certainly not Brett. He didn't have what it took to be Sharon's lover.

She wanted to get beyond him, to move on. To forget the warmth and texture of his lips on hers, to eradicate her image of him carrying Max to her car, so strong, so protective of a child he apparently loathed. She wanted to regain her optimistic outlook, to fall asleep at night without first enduring hour after hour of restlessness over how empty her bed was. She wanted to get over him.

She might have a chance of doing that if she didn't keep staring at that one photo of him, the one she'd saved for herself. Like a masochist poking a bruise to see if it still hurt, she kept pulling the photo out of the envelope in which she'd stashed it and staring at it, resenting him for not being the man she needed him to be, hating him for having been so honest with her, wishing he didn't matter to her.

She plastered a fake smile on her face and marched into the front room, determined to keep her crabby, cranky state hidden from her customer. Her smile faltered when she saw the man lurking by the front counter. "Raymond?" she blurted out.

Deborah's husband had obviously come to her studio directly from work, since he was dressed in a debonair suit that was not the least bit wilted from the heat outside. His shirt was crisp, his hair neat, his tie even and snug against his throat.

Whenever she glimpsed him at Deborah's house, or at parents' meetings at the Children's Garden Preschool, Raymond Jackson appeared confident to the point of arrogance. But today he looked uncertain, his eyes troubled, his smile hesitant. "I hope you don't mind my stopping in," he said.

"Why should I mind? This is a public business."

"I'm not here on business," he informed her.

She stood straighter. "Is everything okay with Deborah? Is Olivia—?"

"Olivia's fine," he assured her. "So is Deborah. I guess," he added, then abandoned her to gaze at the walls, which held displays of the studio's assorted offerings. After scrutinizing some of the arty bridal portraits, he turned back to Sharon. "I was hoping... I know, I have no right to put you in the middle of anything, but—" he sighed "—she won't talk to me. She won't listen to me. I don't see how we're going to fix things if she refuses to deal with me. You're her closest friend, so I was hoping..." He left her to complete the thought.

Sharon had no idea how to help him repair his marriage with Deborah. As Deborah's confidante, she'd heard plenty about what was wrong between the Jacksons but little about how to make things right. In fact, the way Deborah talked, Sharon was almost convinced that Deborah didn't want to make things right at all.

"Aren't you working with a marriage counselor?" she asked gently. "That would probably be the best person to talk to."

"I missed last week's session. I had to be in New York City on business. And now Deborah's saying she doesn't want to see the counselor anymore, because I missed this one session."

According to Deborah, that week's session hadn't been the only one he'd missed—and there was much more to it than his missing sessions with the counselor. But Raymond looked so defeated Sharon couldn't send him away, not even out of loyalty to Deborah. Sharon wanted what was best for her friend. For all she knew, hearing Raymond out right now might be the best thing for Deborah.

"I know we can work this out," Raymond insisted. "I love Deborah. I want to be back in her life—and in my daughter's life, too. But Deborah refuses to even talk to me now."

"She's not talking to you at all?" Sharon hadn't realized things had deteriorated to such an extent.

"I call, I leave messages—she doesn't return them. I phoned her at work and she hung up on me. I thought about sending flowers, but she'd just think that was an empty gesture. If she really doesn't want to talk to me, flowers aren't going to change her mind." He sighed again, his pitiable expression belying his dapper grooming. "She says I spend too much time working. But why does she think I'm working so hard? It's all for her and Olivia. They're the reason I'm putting in all those hours at the office and traveling to Boston and New York. She wants it all—a full-time father for Livie, and someone with a fancy title and a big income.''

Sharon held up her hand to silence him. She preferred not to hear his tirade. ''I really think the marriage counselor—''

''No, listen. Here's what I was hoping you'd do. Just help me to get some time alone with Deborah, so she'd have to talk to me. If you could take Livie out of the house for a while—because Deborah hides behind Livie, she uses her as a shield. I try to talk to her about *us,* and she goes on and on about Livie. So I thought, maybe you could take her to the movies or something, maybe bowling—''

''Bowling?'' Sharon laughed. ''She's not even three years old! The bowling balls probably weigh more than she does.''

''All right. Forget bowling. A movie, then. Or some other outing for a couple of hours. Then I could have Deborah's full attention, and maybe she'd listen to me. Would you do that?''

He looked so plaintive she felt her resistance crack. Allowing herself even a sliver of sympathy for him struck her as a betrayal of Deborah, as if she were collaborating with the enemy—but really, what would be the harm of giving Deborah and Raymond a couple of hours alone? ''I don't like the idea of tricking Deborah,'' she hedged.

''You wouldn't be tricking her. You'd just be taking Olivia for an afternoon. You'd do that if Deborah had a doctor's appointment, wouldn't you?''

Of course Sharon would. And the fate of Deborah's marriage might be as important as anything a doctor could do for her. ''All right. I suppose I can take Olivia for a few hours this weekend.'' She wouldn't be able to drive around town taking pictures for her portfolio—as difficult as that was with one toddler in tow, it would be impossible with two—but maybe she could bring the kids here to the studio, arm them with crayons and paper and spend a little time developing the photos she'd already taken. Unlike her portrait work, these were photos she wanted to develop herself, so she could experiment with the tone and color and get them just right. Afterward, she could drive the kids to the playground, or to the park where Max's favorite rock was.

Where she'd gone with Brett last weekend. Where he'd watched Max climb the rock and wandered the paths with Max—and evidently despised every minute he'd had to spend with the boy. She suppressed a grimace at the memory.

Deborah might be furious with her husband. But at least he loved his daughter. At least he didn't detest children. How bad could he be?

"If you want to make a plan with Deborah for Saturday, I'll take Livie," she promised.

His smile was hesitant, flickering with hope. Sharon didn't know him well enough to interpret that smile, but she wanted to believe in it. She'd seen him open his arms to his daughter; she knew he loved Olivia. A man who loved children deserved a few extra points.

A man who hated children wound up with a negative rating. She was going to have to remember that—even when she was staring at that unposed photo of Brett, and remembering the heat of his lips on hers. A man who hated children deserved no points at all.

CHAPTER SEVEN

DEBORAH WAS STILL simmering when Sharon rang her doorbell Saturday morning. "I don't know why you let Raymond talk you into this," she muttered as she rummaged through the bag of provisions she'd packed for Olivia. "Livie likes the diapers with the fish on them," she noted, lifting one out of the bag so Sharon could see the trim, which featured a waist-band stripe of aqua populated by cartoonish drawings of sea life. "She refuses to wear the ones with the rocket ships. If you want to take them for Max, be my guest." She handed Sharon a few space-travel disposable diapers, then apparently remembered that she was supposed to be angry with Sharon. "So Raymond waltzes into your shop and gives you a sob story, and now you're on his side."

"I'm not on his side," Sharon insisted. She and Deborah had had this conversation twice before, but she was willing to go through it one more time. "All I said was, you owe it to yourself—not just him but yourself—to hear him out. You aren't going to resolve anything if you won't even talk to him."

"He had plenty of chances to talk," Deborah argued. "Unfortunately, he neglected to show up. He's missed sessions with the counselor, sessions with the lawyers, at least two dates with Olivia—"

"Because of work," Sharon reminded her.

"So, what does that tell you about his priorities?"

"He loves Olivia," Sharon pointed out. "He's got that much going for him—he loves his daughter." *Unlike some men who hate children.* She couldn't deny that the main reason she'd softened toward Raymond had been his devotion to his daughter. Even if he'd missed a couple of visits with Olivia, he did love her.

"All right. You've stuck me with him this morning, so if all hell breaks loose I'll know who to blame." Deborah poked through the bag one more time. "I've got her favorite cup in there, and a change of clothing, just in case."

"And Mr. Poochie?" Mr. Poochie was Olivia's beloved stuffed spaniel. Since Olivia was her future daughter-in-law, Sharon felt obliged to familiarize herself with the child's favorite dolls.

"Mr. Poochie's in there. Kids!" Deborah hollered down the stairs. "Time to go!" She handed the tote to Sharon. "And you're going to stop at the Children's Garden for me?"

"You're sure it'll be open?" The preschool Max and Olivia attended held classes from Monday through Friday; Sharon couldn't imagine why it would be open on a Saturday. But when Deborah had picked the children up on Friday she'd accidentally left Olivia's lunch box at the school. Olivia's pacifier was in the lunch box. She no longer used it—hadn't used it or a year now—but she fretted when it wasn't close at hand.

"I spoke to Molly Saunders-Russo a half hour ago. She assured me she'd be there until noon. She's running some kind of weekend program in the building. I didn't ask for details—all that mattered was picking up the lunch box.''

"I'll take care of it.''

"It's the least you owe me," Deborah grumbled before yelling once more for the children to come upstairs.

Five minutes later, Sharon had them both strapped into their car seats in the back seat of the Volvo. A drizzle misted the windshield, just enough dampness to prevent her from planning any outdoor activities for Olivia and Max. That was all right. She was going to detour to the preschool, pick up the forgotten lunch box, then take the kids with her to the studio. Angie would be there, and Sharon had stowed a carton of Duplo blocks, crayons and picture books in the trunk. She had a shoot scheduled at the studio— sisters aged three and five—so a couple of extra children probably wouldn't cause too much of a disturbance.

And if she was really lucky, and Max and Olivia were really good, she'd develop the film she'd shot around town for the Arlington commemorative book. She needed to get the pictures printed so she could figure out what her portfolio lacked and how much more work she ought to do on it. The deadline for submitting proposals was the first of September, less than a month away. Sharon had to get her submission in order, fast.

That impending deadline was the other reason— besides wanting Deborah and Raymond to work things out between them, one way or another—that Sharon was glad to have custody of Olivia for a few hours today. When Max was with Olivia, he didn't demand as much of Sharon's time. Ironically, two children could be easier to take care of than one, if those two children were best friends.

By the time she'd reached Hauser Boulevard, she had to switch on her windshield wipers. The rain rinsed some of the heat out of the morning and added a shine to the asphalt roads. Behind her, the kids giggled and argued about which one had a bigger *something*. Sharon didn't know what the subject of their competition was. All she heard was, "No, *mine's* bigger!"

"No, *mine!*"

"Mine is the biggest, biggest!"

"Mine is bigger than the biggest!"

Maybe they were bickering over the size of their egos, she thought with a smile.

If she'd been surprised to hear that the Children's Garden would be open on a Saturday morning, she was even more surprised to see ten or eleven cars parked in its lot. Did Molly offer regular weekend programs? If she did, Sharon had never heard about them. If she'd known about them, she might have taken advantage of them every now and then. She often had to schedule portrait sessions on Saturdays, like today's session with the Howland sisters. Clients couldn't always come to the studio on weekdays. Fortunately, Angie was flexible about putting in Saturday hours and keeping an eye on Max while Sharon took pictures, but on those Saturdays when neither Angie nor Deborah could help her out, she would appreciate the option of sending Max to the preschool for a couple of hours. He loved the Children's Garden. It contained more toys than Sharon would ever be able to provide for him at home.

"School!" Max and Olivia chorused from the

back seat as she pulled into a parking space outside the front door.

"We're just stopping here to pick up Olivia's lunch box," Sharon reminded them as she climbed out of the car. "We're not staying." It would have been easier for her to leave the children in the car for the two minutes it would take her to fetch the lunch box, but she'd read too many ghastly stories in the newspapers about children who were kidnapped from cars while the adult in charge had darted off to run a quick errand. Sharon wouldn't risk it.

She reached across Olivia's lap to unbuckle Max, then unbuckled Olivia. The children scrambled out of the car, commenting energetically about visiting their school on a day they normally wouldn't be here. Sharon clasped Olivia's hand, then turned and stretched to snag Max before he sped across the parking lot. That was when she noticed one of the cars parked in the lot: a silver Infiniti, the same model Brett drove.

Undoubtedly thousands of other people drove silver Infinitis of that model. Undoubtedly several of them lived right here in Arlington. Just because she was hung up on Brett Stockton...

No, she was *not* hung up on him, she resolutely assured herself. She was still thinking about him—rather obsessively—only because he was the first man to make a pass at her since Steve's death. A halfhearted pass at that, too, a kiss that insinuated more than it revealed. And she wasn't going to kiss him again, because he was a jerk. Only a jerk would be so bigoted against children.

Once she had a firm grasp on both Max and Olivia,

she marched across the damp parking lot to the building. The door was unlocked, and she pushed it open with her hip and drew the children inside. "Shh," she warned them as they tried to break free of her, to run past the front office and down the hall to the activity-filled room in back where they spent their weekdays. She heard voices drifting through the hall from the back room, Molly's and then a man's. Evidently, Molly's Saturday morning program included adults. The muffled thumps and high-pitched voices seeping through the ceiling told her children were present, too, in the upstairs play area. Sharon would have to hold very tightly on to Olivia and Max to keep them from charging up the stairs to join the youngsters.

The front office was empty, and Sharon led the children along the hall, searching for Olivia's cubby among the row of cubbies built into one wall. "Hello?" Molly suddenly called out from the back room. Sharon couldn't see her, but she halted. "Is somebody there?"

"It's just me, Molly," Sharon called back, then ventured a little farther down the hall. "Sharon Bartell. Deborah Jackson said she told you I'd be stopping by to pick up Olivia's lunch box."

"Oh—right!" Molly materialized at the opposite end of the hall. "I'm just running a class for fathers," she explained, approaching Sharon. "I've got the lunch box in the staff room. I rinsed the thermos out so it wouldn't smell bad. I'll be right back." She bestowed a bright smile upon Max and Olivia, who were clamoring for her attention.

"I need my lunch box!" Olivia informed her.

"It's got my 'fire.'" *Fire* was her abbreviation for "pacifier."

"I know you do, and I'm going to get it. Would you like to come with me?"

"Yeah!" Olivia tugged free of Sharon and slipped her hand into Molly's.

"Me, too!" Max demanded, grabbing Molly's other hand. Molly flashed Sharon a grin that said she didn't mind, and Sharon nodded.

Once they'd vanished into the office, she ambled down the hall to the large room in the rear of the building. It was partitioned into smaller spaces, each one designed as a miniclassroom for a different age group, but the partitions stood only waist high. Sharon could easily see the entire room, including the one partitioned area filled with men.

Brett Stockton sat among them, his tall body contorted as he perched on a tot-size table. He wore evenly faded blue jeans and a navy-blue T-shirt, and all that blue made his eyes look much too vivid.

What on earth was he doing here, at a child-care facility? He'd told her he had no kids. He'd told her he didn't like kids. And Molly had said she was running a class for fathers. If Brett was a part of that class... Was he a father?

The bastard had lied to her! Although she couldn't begin to guess why. If he was a father, why would he say he didn't like kids? Was it that he simply didn't like *her* kid? Or that he didn't like to date women who had children, even though he evidently had a child himself? Was he, in fact, married, too? Or divorced and uninterested in spending a Saturday with his own child when he could spend it with her, the way he had last week? What the hell was going on with him?

She spun away, endeavoring to muster a smile for Olivia and Max, who accompanied Molly back into the hall from the office. Olivia clutched her lunch box in her free hand, and she held it up proudly. "Look! My lunch box!"

"We got Livie's lunch box," Max reported, bristling with self-importance.

"That's wonderful," Sharon said, the words sounding as flat and faded as old parchment. "Now we can go to the studio, and Molly can go back to her class. Thanks, Molly," she added, lifting her gaze to the preschool director.

"No problem." She delivered Max and Olivia to Sharon, then bent down and beamed a smile at them. "See you later, guys!"

"Bye-bye!" They waved, then skipped toward the front door ahead of Sharon. She managed another quick thank-you before chasing after them.

They emerged into the cool, gray morning, two buoyant children and one deeply troubled woman. *Why the hell was Brett in that class for fathers?* The question drummed inside her skull as she crossed the lot with the kids, unlocked her car and got them strapped into their seats. Why hadn't he told her he was a father? Why had he claimed he didn't like children? Why had he lied?

I'm just sorry that things are the way they are, he'd said after kissing her. She'd thought she understood what he was trying to tell her when he'd spoken those words—but now she realized she had no idea what he'd meant, no idea about the way things were.

All she knew was that he'd kissed her and he'd deceived her, and she was outraged.

MOLLY SAUNDERS-RUSSO was a remarkable woman, he thought as he stuffed a dime in the parking meter and then strode down the sidewalk to the Bartell Studios. Not only had the petite, energetic woman allowed him to sit in on her Daddy School class, but he'd gotten her to tell him where Sharon had gone off to. He'd convinced Molly that he was a good friend of Sharon's, and that he wanted to stop by and talk to her about the class he'd just sat through.

The second half of that statement was true: he did want to tell her about the class. The first half, though... In light of the furious glare she'd sent him while she'd been lurking in the hallway, he didn't think "good friend" was the term she'd use to describe him.

He could understand her being vexed by him. He was vexed by himself—which was why he'd sacrificed a Saturday morning to sit through a seminar on how to view the world through a child's eyes. He'd actually found Molly's insights edifying. He had never given an instant's thought to children's perspectives before. To be sure, he couldn't remember ever viewing the world through a child's eyes, even when he'd been a child.

The comments of some of the fathers in the class had been useful, too, although for the most part Brett had felt little kinship with the men. They were all enthusiastic daddies, dedicated to and enchanted by their own children. They attended Molly's class to learn how to become better fathers. Brett remained determined never to become anybody's dad.

But he wouldn't mind becoming the friend—possibly even the good friend—of somebody's mom. Max Bartell's mom, to be precise. He wondered who the other child with her had been. A friend of Max's, obviously—and a fellow classmate at the Children's Garden. Molly Saunders-Russo had explained the interruption to the fathers once Sharon and her charges had left. According to her, young children became attached to certain objects—for instance, their pacifiers—and the little girl needed her pacifier back in order for her universe to return to its proper alignment.

Brett couldn't recall ever becoming attached to certain objects as a child. Anything he considered his own—his toys, his clothing, his bedroom, even his mother—had eventually wound up belonging to the younger kids, his half brothers and half sister. "You don't need this anymore," his mother would say, taking away some toy he'd long outgrown but still considered his own. "You're a big boy now. Let the children play with it." He'd been five when his brother Andrew was born and his bedroom had been converted into a nursery, six when his brother inherited all his stuffed animals, seven when his brother James was born and eight when the twins arrived. "Keep an eye on the children," his mother would say. "Mommy's got to run to the store. Take care of the children for me, Brett."

Eight years old—and he'd no longer been a child.

He wasn't going to let Molly's Daddy School class reopen wounds that had healed years ago. He'd made his peace with his mother and his siblings. He was a healthy adult, a productive citizen, a successful businessman. Was it a crime that he had vowed never to have to take care of any more children in his life?

He didn't want to think about it. If he was going to come away from Molly's class with anything worthwhile, it was the notion that kids approached the world in a more straightforward way than adults, with fewer preconceptions and defenses. Fair enough. He'd remember that when he had to deal with Max.

But the person he really had to deal with was Sharon. Why had she frowned at him with such anger? He'd hoped to surprise her with the news that he was attending this school for fathers at the recommendation of his poker buddies, that he was trying to overcome his antipathy toward her son because she meant something to him. He couldn't put her out of his mind, so he was going to take some classes that might enable him to make a little room in his mind for her kid.

Whatever had offended her about seeing him in the preschool that morning, he had to straighten it out with her. He sure as hell wasn't going to sit through any more Daddy School sessions if she was going to act as if the mere sight of him caused her indigestion.

He entered the studio, the door announcing his arrival with the tinkle of an attached bell. As soon as he was inside he heard the racket of several children—more than the two Sharon had had in tow that morning—performing a hearty and painfully out-of-tune rendition of "This Old Man."

A woman Brett recognized from the day he'd picked up his proofs emerged from the back room, smiling. "Can I help you?"

"I'm here to see Sharon Bartell," he told her. "Is she here?"

"Yes, but—" the woman glanced over her shoulder and through the open doorway "—she's kind of busy right now."

"Leading a children's choir?" he asked as the kids on the other side of the doorway bleated, "'Knick-knack, paddy-whack, give a dog a bone!'" Their diction left much to be desired.

"She's photographing some children. She should be done soon."

"Maybe I could help. I know the words to that song," he said, surprising himself. When was the last time he'd sung "This Old Man"? He was pretty sure the lyrics included a rhyme of "seven" with "heaven," but other than that, he'd have to fake it.

"I think it would be best if you waited out here," the young woman said. "It's a little hectic back there."

Her comment was punctuated by a rousing finale, with the children stretching out the concluding line of the song: "This o-man came rooo-diiing ho-o-o-ome!" *Roding* home? he wondered. That Daddy School teacher might give a special class in toddler grammar.

A peal of laughter preceded the appearance of Sharon's son and his friend. They scampered through the door, racing each other, elbowing for advantage as they careered around the counter. "I'm faster!" the little girl boasted.

"I'm faster!" Max argued.

Faster than a caterpillar, maybe, Brett thought as the two of them hustled into view. Their legs were too short to carry them with any speed—and thank

God, too, because they were veering toward the door. Reflexively, he bent over and snagged one in each arm. "Hey, calm down," he scolded.

They shrieked and giggled with apparent delight at being caught. Panting, they stared up at him and sobered. They'd probably received their share of lectures about not letting strange men touch them, and there he was, a strange man touching them.

Gradually, Max seemed to recognize Brett. "I know you," he said uncertainly.

"I'm a friend of your mother's."

The little girl stuck her thumb in her mouth and stared at him. She was a pretty pipsqueak, with latté-hued skin, curly black hair and round, dark eyes.

"He's Mommy's friend," Max informed her. She said nothing, just stared at Brett with those intense brown eyes. If he was in tune with kids, able to view the world from their perspective and all that, he might be able to interpret her state of mind from her gaze: afraid of him, or reassured, or resentful that he'd intercepted her before she could escape into the rain outside. But one Daddy School class wasn't enough to connect him to children on that intuitive level. A million classes wouldn't be enough.

"Mommy's taking pictures," Max announced.

"She's working today, huh?"

"She takes pictures."

Brett nodded. "Is she going to be done soon?" he asked. The sooner she was done, the sooner she might rescue him from this awkward conversation.

"She takes pictures," Max answered.

They seemed to have reached a dead end. Brett straightened up, releasing the kids but positioning himself in front of the door so they couldn't escape the building. They peered up at him, craning their necks, and he peered down. When he stood at his full height, they looked awfully small.

"She'll be done soon," the woman behind the counter promised. "If you can keep an eye on those two, I'll go back and see how she's doing."

Before he could object to that arrangement, she disappeared through the doorway.

He felt abandoned. Trapped. He preferred not to attempt another exchange with Max; the kid would probably just say that his mother was taking pictures. So he simply stood blocking the door, arms crossed and legs slightly apart, feeling like the Jolly Green Giant towering over a field of unripe peas.

After a minute, the girl removed her thumb from her mouth and glanced at Max. "Let's run," she said.

Max hooted and ran toward the wall. She trotted along beside him, and they both barreled into the wall and squealed with laughter. Brett eyed the framed photos on display. None seemed to have been knocked askew. Evidently, two toddlers hurling themselves full force at a wall couldn't do too much damage.

They about-faced and charged toward the opposite wall. As long as they didn't attempt to break past him and out the door, everything would be all right. Boring, annoying but not disastrous. He hoped Sharon's assistant was right about how much longer Sharon would be busy in the back.

The twerps hit the opposite wall, breathless with laughter, and then U-turned and zoomed back to the first wall. Brett entertained himself with thoughts of what he would have been doing that day if not for

Sharon. Certainly he wouldn't have spent two hours pretzeled into position on a puny table in a nursery school and followed that by stationing himself in front of a door, observing two pint-size maniacs as they literally bounced off the walls. He would have spent an extra hour enjoying his coffee that morning, browsing through each section of the newspaper. Then he probably would have met up with a friend at the tennis club—they had indoor courts, so the rain wouldn't have been a problem—and played a couple of sets. In the afternoon, he would have reviewed the week on Wall Street while simultaneously watching the Red Sox game on the wide-screen TV in his den; he could set up his laptop on the coffee table and check the online stock and bond indicators during the commercial breaks. In the evening, he would have gone out to dinner with one of his women friends. He had a few who could be available on short notice, who didn't need time to rustle up a baby-sitter first. Women like him, unattached and glad of it.

Ever since he'd met Sharon, though, he hadn't been quite so glad.

He wasn't looking to get attached, of course. When women started thinking about attachments, what they were really thinking was children. Especially in his age range, women in the market for commitment were really thinking about marriage and babies.

Brett had nothing against commitment and marriage. It was the notion of babies that always screwed things up. That was why most of the women he dated these days were older, single by choice or divorced and unwilling to make the same mistake twice.

So why was he contemplating it now? Marriage

was about moments like this—tedious stretches of time watching two noisy munchkins go giddy over stupid wall-to-wall races.

"Let's go in circles!" Max suggested, sticking his arms out as if they were airplane wings and spinning around.

"I'm dizzy!" the little girl screeched even before she started spinning. In short time they were both weaving and staggering and collapsing onto the floor, convulsed in laughter.

Brett's head throbbed. He had a bottle of aspirin in his car, but if he went outside to get it, they might tear the place apart in his absence, or climb up onto the counter, make themselves dizzy and then tumble off and crack their skulls open when they hit the floor. If the assistant came back, he could escape, but she was gone and he was stuck overseeing two little dingbats who seemed to take inordinate pleasure in reeling and staggering into each other like drunks on a bender.

Finally, he heard promising noises from the back room—not shrill, juvenile voices warbling "This Old Man" but adult voices, another woman's and then Sharon's. "In a week to ten days," she was saying. "As far as your Christmas cards, you're way ahead of schedule. I'm sure there'll be some really nice shots to choose from...."

She emerged through the open door, leading a woman and two girls in frilly matching dresses and glittery hair ribbons. Both girls were sucking on lollipops. Sharon immediately spotted Brett—he was hard to miss, being the tallest person on his side of the counter—and froze.

"Hi," he said.

She pressed her lips together as if to prevent any words from slipping out. Then she deliberately turned from him and smiled at the mother of the two party-dressed children. "We'll call as soon as the pictures come in," she said evenly.

"Okay. Girls, did you thank Ms. Bartell for the lollipops?"

"Thank you," they singsonged, then resumed sucking on their treats. Brett wondered whether Sharon had had to resort to belly-dancing dolls to get them to relax in front of her camera.

She watched as they walked around the counter and headed for the door. Since he was standing right in front of the door, she couldn't avoid looking at him. Damn, he thought, studying the hard glint in her eyes, the grim set of her lips. He might not be able to interpret the facial expressions of children, but he could sure interpret Sharon's. It said, *I hate you.*

What had he done to provoke such animosity? He'd been honest with her. He'd kissed her—but he hadn't forced her to kiss him back. He'd blown two hours that morning sitting in an uncomfortable room designed for toddlers so he could learn how to tolerate her kid. And she hated him.

The bell above the door tinkled as the woman and her two chic little darlings left the studio. He was scarcely aware of their departure, and of the continuing silliness of Max and his friend as they spun around and flung themselves to the floor. The photos decorating the walls blurred into meaninglessness; the counter that separated him from Sharon was irrelevant compared with the invisible wall of ice that stood between them.

"What's wrong?" he asked.

"Why are you here?" she asked simultaneously.

Before either of them could answer, Sharon's assistant bounded through the doorway, carrying a clipboard with a form attached to it. "Is it okay if I leave after I process this order? I wanted to get down to the mall this afternoon, and—"

"Sure, Angie. Go," Sharon said, her voice leaden, her chilly gaze never leaving Brett. The assistant busied herself for a moment at a desk behind the counter. The rumble of a metal drawer being open and shut offered a counterpoint to the high-pitched giggles of the kids. She filed her papers, then eyed Sharon, then eyed Brett, then eyed Sharon again. After plucking her purse from a shelf below the counter, she scurried around the counter and out the door, obviously eager to leave before the tension between Sharon and Brett erupted in some sort of catastrophic manner.

All the tension was coming from Sharon, he thought. Well, almost all. The only thing making him tense was her inexplicable wrath.

"Max, Olivia," she said briskly, "no more dizzy games. One of you is going to get hurt."

"It's fun," Max asserted, spreading his arms and launching into another spin.

"It won't be fun when you crash into the counter—or into each other. Come on. Livie? Both of you. I've got crayons in the back room."

"I wanna get dizzy," the little girl said.

"Not anymore. It's coloring time now."

Reluctantly, the children pulled themselves to their feet, regained their bearings, then staggered around the counter and out of Brett's view. He was impressed by Sharon's ability to get them to obey her. She hadn't had to threaten or punish them. She'd simply said it was coloring time, and after token resistance, they'd yielded.

What about him? Was he supposed to follow them around the counter? If he did, would he be rewarded with a crayon or a slap in the face?

This was America; he was supposed to be advised of the charges against him. If he walked around the counter, though, he couldn't help wondering whether his punishment would be meted out without his ever learning what he was guilty of.

One thing he was surely guilty of was lust. Despite Sharon's obvious displeasure, she looked wonderful to him. He loved being able to read her mood—even though it was a bad one—in her eyes, her lips, the tilt of her head. He loved the slender width of her shoulders and the sleek length of her arms extending from her simple white camp shirt. Her skin wore a golden undertone from months of summer exposure, and her hair shimmered with sun-lightened streaks. He recalled the kiss they'd shared at the Dairy Queen last week, a kiss haunting in its unfulfilled promise.

He wanted her.

Was that a crime?

"Are you going to talk to me?" he asked.

She shot him a quelling look, then turned and followed the children into the back room. "Over here," he heard her tell them. "Right here at this table— that's where we're going to set up."

"I'm hungry," one of the tykes whined.

"We'll have lunch very soon. Mommy has a few things to take care of first."

Was Brett one of the things Mommy had to take

care of? He'd be damned if he was going to stand around in the front room, waiting for her to deign to tell him what she was so pissed about. He strode around the counter and through the doorway.

To his left was an area surrounded by gray velvet curtains, with stuffed animals and cushions on the floor and photographic lamps on stands, all aimed at an upholstered bench positioned in front of a blank screen. A large camera on a wheeled tripod stood in one corner of the area. "This is where you do your studio shots?" he asked.

"Children's photos," she replied tersely. That she even bothered to answer was a positive sign.

"She takes pictures in the other room," Max offered. Brett interpreted that to mean the studio had a second area for taking photographs. Clearly, it was not the area where the children were kneeling on chairs and hunching over sheets of paper, a plastic tub of crayons open between them.

Brett glanced at Sharon, hoping for her to elaborate. Instead, she busied herself gathering the stuffed animals and storing them in a colorful toy chest.

His patience was like a rubber band, stretched to the point of snapping. He took a deep breath and followed her into the curtained area. "Okay, give me a hint," he murmured, keeping his voice down so the children wouldn't hear. "What's going on?"

She methodically gathered a Nerf ball and what appeared to be a stuffed raccoon from under the bench and tossed them into the toy chest. "You're a liar," she said.

He was many things, but a liar wasn't one of them. He'd been completely candid with Sharon, despite knowing his honesty would likely cost him his chance at a relationship with her. If he was a liar, he could have told her he adored children. If he had, she would have kissed him back. They would have been well beyond kissing by now.

"What did I lie about?" he asked, aware of the challenge in his tone.

"Being a father."

"What?"

She straightened up and met his gaze. "I saw you in that class this morning. You know I saw you, because you looked straight at me. That was a class for fathers."

"I was there as a guest."

Her eyebrows fluttered slightly upward. She appeared skeptical.

"I told you I don't like kids," he whispered, then peeked at the children to make sure they weren't listening. Engrossed in their drawings, they paid no attention to Sharon and Brett. "I'd make a hell of a lousy father, given that fact."

"Then what were you doing in a class designed specifically for fathers?"

"Trying to learn how to like kids. I heard about the class from some guys I know. Some of my best friends are fathers," he added, hoping to tease a smile out of her.

He failed. But she seemed to thaw a little, anger replaced by bemusement. "So your friends told you about this class, and you decided to go as a guest because…?"

Wasn't it obvious? "Because you've got a kid."

"You were taking the class because of *me?*" Her eyebrows fluttered more, widening her eyes, giving her a startled look.

"Because of Max." He peeked at the table again. Max was handing a fat yellow crayon to the girl. "Now I'm worrying that there's more than one kid in the picture. It's going to take me a truckload of classes to get me to the point where I can stand one kid. But two?"

"She's Max's best friend," Sharon explained. "Maybe his future wife. The details haven't been worked out yet."

"His future wife."

"She lives next door. Her mother needed the morning free, so I took both kids."

"Even though you had to work?"

"I'm a good juggler—and I happen to like kids." She surveyed the area and nodded, satisfied at its tidiness. "So you were taking that father class for my sake."

"Yeah. For what it's worth." As her gaze softened, he struggled to look indignant. He wanted her to feel guilty for having misjudged him.

Far from guilty, she looked amused. "I don't see how taking a class is going to get you to love Max."

"I don't have to love him," Brett argued. "I just have to—" He faltered.

"You just have to what?"

"Tolerate him? Learn how to spend a few hours in his company without having my nerves rubbed raw? I don't know, Sharon." He raked a hand through his hair. He didn't know how classes could teach him something that ought to be instinctive, how a Daddy School could replace what was missing from his heart. He didn't know if attending lessons at a preschool could make it possible for something to develop between him and Sharon—and if it did, where he hoped that development would lead them. He could wind up graduating from the Daddy School and discovering Sharon was all wrong for him. Or he could take class after class and never learn how to coexist with her child.

"I don't know," he repeated softly, regretfully.

To his surprise, she smiled. "You are the strangest man I've ever met."

"I'm not strange," he objected.

"You're certainly not typical." Sizing him up, she shook her head. "I'm not sure what to think."

"Think I'm wonderful," he suggested. "Think I'm noble and sexy and—"

She pressed her fingertips against his lips to silence him, then glanced toward the children. They were busy scribbling all over their sheets of paper. They hadn't heard him, but even if they had, he doubted they knew what "sexy" meant.

"I think you're amazing," she said, her voice hushed but warm. "Definitely strange, but amazing."

He could live with that. In fact, it didn't sound half bad. Maybe if he sat through another class or two of the Daddy School, he could get her to drop the "strange" from her evaluation.

Maybe he could get her to replace it with something better. Like "sexy."

CHAPTER EIGHT

SHARON FELT as dizzy as Max and Olivia must have felt when they'd done their whirling-dervish routine in the front room. In just one week, she'd gone from puzzlement over Brett's confession that he didn't like children to soul-deep disappointment that this man whom she found so alluring was utterly wrong for her, to rage that he'd apparently lied to her, to dazed affection that he had actually spent that very morning attending a class to learn how to get along with her son.

Now, as she dialed Deborah's number, she spied on him as he hovered near the kids, watching over them as they scrawled incomprehensible doodles on large sheets of scrap paper. He seemed to be exerting himself to pay attention as Max and Olivia took turns explaining their drawings to him. "This is a big frog," Olivia informed him. "This is a tree that's very, very big," Max noted in counterpoint. From Brett's expression, Sharon could tell that he saw neither a big frog nor a very, very big tree in the abstract slashes and squiggles of crayon, and that he was exercising enormous willpower to keep himself from telling the kids they were full of it.

His earnestness made her want to laugh.

His stance made her want to do other things. His head was cocked slightly and his hair was tousled, lending a rakishness to his usually polished looks. His eyes were blue enough to shame the overcast sky outside. He'd hooked his hands on the back pockets of his jeans, and the pose stretched the dark cotton of his shirt tight across his torso. His shoulders appeared boulder solid, his chest sleek and strong. If only the kids weren't present, she'd—

"Hello?" Deborah's voice came through the phone after three rings.

Sharon turned her back on Brett and the children. If she couldn't see them, she wouldn't be distracted by them. "Hi, Deb, it's me," she said. "I was wondering if you want me to bring Olivia home."

"Oh…um, no," Deborah said. Her voice sounded muffled, as if she had wads of cotton stuffed into her cheeks. "Not yet. We're not done yet."

"How's it going?" Sharon asked.

"It's going horribly—but at least it *is* going." Deborah didn't sound horrible, though. She didn't even sound upset. Just a little preoccupied. "I really can't talk right now, Sharon."

"Are you still angry with me? Because—"

"I'm not angry, but I can't talk. Can you keep Livie for a while longer?"

"Sure. How long? A couple of hours?"

"That'd be great. Gotta go." Deborah hung up before Sharon could question her further.

She stared at the phone in her hand, shook her head and then placed the receiver back in its cradle. If things were truly going horribly between Deborah and Raymond, Deborah would have demanded that Sharon return home at once—with a police escort, if necessary. Not that Sharon believed Deborah would ever be in danger with Raymond, no matter how horrible their meeting was going. Raymond was a calm, quiet man. His greatest sin, in Deborah's eyes, was not that he was controlling or meddling but quite the opposite, that he was too disengaged.

Well, maybe they were making headway. At least they were in the same room, which was progress— even if they were only progressing toward a divorce.

Sharon pivoted back to the children. "Mine is a biggest, biggest, big tree," Max was telling Brett. "These are the birds in it." He peppered the paper with shapeless brown blobs. "They live in the big tree."

"Uh-huh," Brett grunted, looking neither convinced nor particularly interested. Sharon supposed toddler art criticism had not been a part of that morning's Daddy School curriculum.

"Who's hungry?" she asked. "I think it's lunchtime. How does McDonald's sound?"

Her announcement was greeted with gleeful whoops from the children and a smile of soul-deep relief from Brett—a response she suspected had little to do with hunger. "Clean up the crayons first," she reminded the children, who in their jubilation had tossed their crayons onto the table and bolted from their chairs. They must have really wanted lunch badly, because they clambered back onto their chairs without complaint and dumped all the loose crayons back into the bucket, their small hands moving with surprising dexterity.

Sharon snapped the lid onto the bucket, stacked Max's and Olivia's masterpieces into a neat pile and shepherded the kids out the door. She felt Brett behind her, close enough to warm her back. When he brushed a hand against her shoulder, the warmth turned to heat. She remembered his casual way of touching her at the Leukemia Foundation dinner—to get her attention, to excuse himself when he had to take care of some hosting duty—and his less-than-casual way, when they'd danced and later, when she'd been sure he was going to kiss her.

And the way he'd touched her when he did kiss her.

As ravenous as the children were for lunch, she was even more ravenous for a man's touch. Not necessarily a sexual touch, though that would be lovely, but just what Brett was doing now, a moment of connection. A way of saying, "I'm here. You're not alone." She'd been alone too long. When Brett touched her, she didn't feel so alone anymore.

The rain had increased in the hour and a half since she and the children had arrived at the studio. The children pranced around the corner to the alley, where she had a reserved parking space. They tilted their heads up, stuck their tongues out and bragged to each other about how much rain they were drinking. Sharon didn't mind. The air was muggy—the temperature had to be above eighty-five degrees—and no one was going to catch a chill from remaining outdoors during a steady rain. In fact, a part of her wanted to stick her tongue out and sip a few raindrops, too.

Would Brett think she was unforgivably juvenile if she did that? Would he decide he couldn't like her because she was childish and he didn't like children?

He had moved beside her, and she noticed the rain glistening in his hair and dampening his shirt. "I should have brought an umbrella," he said apologetically.

"Why? It's just water." And then, to test him, she flicked out her tongue and captured a raindrop.

He halted, staring at her so intensely that for one brief, dangerous moment she lost all track of the children. She saw only him, the tension that tugged at his mouth, the stark desire that glinted in his eyes. Surely she didn't look her best—her hair was lank, her face streaked with moisture—but he gazed at her as if his life depended on that one inane gesture: her attempt to taste the rain. She saw the bone in his neck slide as he swallowed, and then he reached out and touched her cheek, wiping a stray raindrop from her skin. There was nothing casual about his touch this time. It communicated much more than simply that he was there and she wasn't alone.

"Open the car!" Max hollered. "It's locked, Mommy! Open it!"

Brett's eyes glinted again, desire replaced by irritation. He fell back a step and spun around to glare at the kids as they yanked futilely on the door handles. She wondered if everything he'd learned in his class that morning had been undone by Max's impatience.

Well, who could blame the child for being impatient? It was raining and he was famished. He wanted to get into the car and go to McDonald's.

Sighing, she shoved a damp lock of hair back from her face and hurried to the car to unlock it. Brett watched her buckle the children into their seats—she was just as glad that he didn't try to help her, since he probably wouldn't know how to hook all the straps correctly.

The children squirmed. Olivia fretted. "I'm wet! I got wet on my knees!" Sharon leaned across the front seat to the glove compartment and pulled out some napkins she kept stashed there. She dried off Olivia's legs, but the child continued to whimper. Hunger mixed with fatigue, Sharon diagnosed it.

"Let's go get something to eat," she said, tuning out Olivia's whiny litany. She wondered whether Brett would be able to tune it out, too.

He settled into the passenger seat, struggling to fit his long legs comfortably into the space. Sharon revved the engine, turned on the windshield wipers and pretended not to hear Olivia as she querulously listed every part of her that was wet—her hair, her fingers, her chin, her diaper.

"Not exactly dinner at Reynaud," she joked, shooting him a look.

He didn't smile. "Not exactly."

"Go with the flow," she urged him as she steered out of the alley and down the street. "Did Molly teach you that in Daddy School?"

He shook his head. "That must be the curriculum of the advanced class. I'm just at the intro level."

He still wasn't smiling, but his comment assured her that he had some humor about the situation, after all. "So, what did you learn in your intro-level class?"

"The class wasn't intro level. I was way out of my depth. All the other students were real fathers, and most of them actually *liked* their kids. Maybe they didn't understand their kids a hundred percent, or they might be struggling with them, but they *liked* them."

And maybe someday Brett would like kids, too, but Sharon didn't say that. "What was the class like?"

"Molly talked about children's perspectives, about how their intellectual development and immaturity alter their ability to interpret the world. She was trying to get us all to erase everything we'd learned since turning three, so we could figure out how a two-year-old would see things."

"And...?"

"I found that pretty nearly impossible."

"It is hard," she assured him, not wanting him to grow disheartened so soon. "Did Molly lecture the entire time?"

"No. There was lots of discussion, questions and answers. Kind of a support-group feel to the whole thing." He eyed her plaintively. "I'm not a support-group kind of guy."

"You were very brave to do this, Brett."

"Brave or stupid. Or maybe they're the same thing."

She pulled into the McDonald's parking lot, and Olivia stopped crabbing. "McDon-o's!" she crowed.

"Lunchtime!" Max bellowed.

Brett cringed. Sharon would bet he was feeling more stupid than brave right about now. That was a shame, because—as he was about to learn—taking two toddlers to lunch at McDonald's on a rainy Saturday was the sort of activity that required a great deal of courage.

"Buck up," she exhorted. "You're about to experience a whole new world."

"God save me," he muttered as he got out of the car.

THE NOISE LEVEL inside the McDonald's was excruciating, on a par with air-raid sirens, fingernails on a chalkboard and jackhammers chewing up concrete. Brett had been aware of the clamor upstairs in the play area above the room where the Daddy School class had been held, but that noise hadn't been painful. He'd been a level removed from it, of course, and the ceiling had muffled the children's strident voices.

Nothing muffled the cacophony in the fast-food restaurant. An indoor playground occupied a corner of the dining room, and the shrill, jubilant voices of some eight or nine children, hard at play, echoed off the walls and floor. Every hard surface—and the restaurant was full of hard surfaces—bounced the shrieks back at him.

When they'd entered the restaurant, Sharon had immediately hustled the children down the back hall to the bathroom. Brett could guess what she was doing with them in there, and he was grateful not to be a part of it. While they were gone, he snagged the only available table big enough for four. It was adjacent to the play area, close enough that he could feel the exuberant screams and laughter of the children vibrating in the soles of his feet. As soon as Sharon emerged from the ladies' room, Brett volunteered to join the line weaving toward the counter so he could place their orders. The counter was on the opposite end of the building, as far from the play area as he could get without evacuating the building.

The distance didn't do much to reduce the noise. He stared at the people sharing the line with him— a few teenagers, boys in baggy shorts and girls in skimpy tops—and one silver-haired man with a stoop to his shoulders, but mostly people of parent age, youngish mothers and fathers who'd brought their kids to McDonald's for a quick lunch. Afterward, perhaps, they'd be taking their charges to the mall or to the multiplex for a movie. It was too rainy for Little League and soccer games, for outdoor playgrounds or picnics or swimming at any of the lakes that dotted the hills and woodland surrounding Arlington.

Most of the people in line with him had probably chosen to be parents, he thought as he inched closer to the counter. They loved their kids. Maybe they even enjoyed eating lunch with their kids at restaurants where the stools were bolted to the floor and the food was served wrapped in waxy paper. Maybe this was their idea of the perfect Saturday outing.

He moved closer to the counter. In front of him, a woman in denim shorts and a Six-Flags T-shirt hunkered down to confer with her child. "I think you like the vanilla shakes better than the chocolate ones," she said in a cooing voice. "You sure you want me to buy you a chocolate one today?"

The kid nodded gravely.

God, what patience. What empathy. Brett reminded himself that she was the normal one, he the oddball. Most people liked kids—liked them enough to take the time to discuss with them which flavor milkshake to buy.

Brett had jotted down Sharon's and the kids' lunch selections on a napkin. He wanted to get their orders correct so they wouldn't start crying. He could still remember the horrible noises his brothers and sister used to emit whenever he didn't do exactly what they wanted—a ghastly keening sound that pierced his brain like bolts of electricity. In this cacophonous room, of course, a few wails from Max and Olivia would probably go unnoticed.

At the counter, he read his notes from the napkin. A perky young woman in a crisp uniform tossed wrapped burgers and lidded cups onto a tray. Once he'd paid, he pocketed his wallet, lifted the tray, and threaded a path through the tables to where Sharon waited for him. She sat by herself, the children gone. His dream come true, he thought with a wry smile—just Sharon and himself, without their two tiny, screechy chaperons. Alone, Sharon looked magnificent, an oasis of serenity in the bedlam that was McDonald's at lunchtime.

He set the tray on the table and lowered himself onto the stool across from her. "Where are the kids?" he asked, even though he didn't really want to know.

She motioned with her head toward the play area. Max and Olivia were jumping in a pile of colorful plastic balls inside a pen, flopping around and tossing balls at each other and several other children in the pen with them.

"I thought they were hungry."

"They're always hungry, unless something better comes along." She removed items from the tray and distributed them around the table, leaving the children's food at their empty places and then poking a straw through the lid of her diet cola.

Brett took a sip of his ginger ale and suppressed a sigh. He liked good food and soothing ambience. If he couldn't have that, he'd take fresh deli sandwiches and real ale, not a semisweet beverage the name of which was as close as it got to anything alcoholic. But gazing at Sharon—and remembering how she'd looked when she'd poked out her tongue and caught a raindrop on it—was more satisfying than feasting on the finest gourmet meal and the most exquisite vintage wine in the most elegant surroundings. With Sharon filling his vision, he could even put up with the rowdiness arising from the play area.

At least, he could in theory. That was the whole point of his experiment with the Daddy School—to figure out if he could put up with it in practice.

Because especially now, when his vision was filled with her and his knees bumped hers under the table, he was convinced that Sharon Bartell would be worth putting up with pretty much anything.

"Tell me more about yourself," she urged him as she delicately unfolded the wrapper of her chicken sandwich. "It's amazing how little I know about you. How did you wind up in Arlington?"

"I was born here," he told her.

"And you loved it so much, you couldn't leave?"

He smiled. Arlington was a great little city, with a dense, generally prosperous downtown area surrounded by residential neighborhoods, which were in turn surrounded by rolling countryside, orchards and farms and forestland. It had decent shopping, a well-stocked public library, an outstanding regional hospital and easy access to New York City. He couldn't imagine anyone falling passionately in love with it, however. "My father died when I was two, and my mother and I moved to Boston, which was where she was from. She remarried a few years later, and we moved to a suburb north of Boston. That was where I grew up."

"And you came back to Arlington as an adult because you remembered the city? Or because of your father?''

Her voice was so gentle he didn't mind her inquisitiveness. "I didn't remember either the city or my father, to tell you the truth. All I remembered was that I was happy here."

She reached across the table and gave his hand a squeeze. It seemed unpremeditated, an impulsive gesture of comfort. He wasn't looking for comfort or pity or anything remotely resembling sympathy. He wasn't racked with grief, a prime candidate for intensive therapy, a bereaved specimen unable to overcome his early loss. He honored his father's memory by raising money for leukemia research, and he and his mother got along fine these days. He didn't believe in clinging to past sorrow. You endured it, you recovered from it and you got on with the business of living.

That was one of the things that drew him to Sharon—besides her height and her long legs and those lovely cheekbones, the hollow at the base of her neck where her collarbones met and the glints of multicolored light in her eyes. She'd suffered a catastrophic loss, but she refused to let it flatten her. Like him, she was getting on with the business of living.

"So how did you wind up in Arlington?" he asked her.

"I met my husband in college. We were both photographers, and we went to New York City looking for work after we graduated. The cost of living was too high, though. We couldn't afford to start our own business. We couldn't even afford the rent we were paying for a dark, cramped apartment in a seedy part of Manhattan. Lots of New Yorkers had weekend homes here in Western Connecticut, so we came up and visited and decided Arlington was just the right size for us.''

Max and Olivia chose that moment to scamper over to the table. "We played with balls!" Max shouted. Brett would have heard him if he'd spoken in a normal tone, even with the surrounding din, but the kid was obviously pumped up from his grand adventures in the play area.

"I want to eat," Olivia declared.

The children ate. Not without some difficulty—the drinking straws in their cups inspired a lot of dribbling, squirting and sloppy slurping, and the hamburgers had to be broken into manageably small pieces, a task Sharon attended to. She was like the other people at the restaurant, the normal ones, the parents who didn't mind ignoring their own food while they mopped spills and dribbles and all but hand-fed their children because they loved those children and wanted them and couldn't think of anything they wouldn't do for them—including sacrificing their ability to eat their own meals.

He admired Sharon's sacrifice—but he also resented it because it stood as a barrier between them, a manifestation of what might keep them from ever getting beyond their current level of closeness. He thought again of the pink tip of her tongue sliding between her lips when she'd stood outside in the rain, and he felt a tug in his groin, wholly unexpected in this most unseductive of settings. He wanted to get beyond his current level with her, wanted it so much he was devouring a Big Mac while being serenaded by a chorus of overexcited children—including the two messy, giggly punks at his table who had discovered the tactile joy of tearing French fries into little pieces and smearing their soft insides all over the tabletop.

"What's on tap for this afternoon?" he asked, not sure what answer he expected—or wanted.

"Olivia's mom wants me to watch her for a while longer," Sharon told him. "I've got some film I need to develop. I was figuring I'd take the kids back to the studio and maybe, if I get lucky, they'll crash. I could develop the film while they nap."

"And if they don't nap?"

"I'm up the creek."

"You wouldn't get any work done if they were wired, would you?" He didn't ask so much as state it as a fact.

She shrugged. "It wouldn't be the first time they interfered with my ability to get work done. I might get some paperwork done, though. Not the darkroom stuff, because to do that I have to shut the door, and I can't open it for any crises without ruining the film."

"What film do you want to develop?" he asked.

She slid a French fry into her mouth. Unlike the children, whose mangling made the fries look decidedly unappetizing, the way Sharon bit off a piece of her fry, pursing her lips around the morsel, struck him as inexplicably erotic.

She chewed, swallowed and shrugged. "The pictures I've been taking for my submission for the Arlington commemorative book. Those shots I took last week, among others. But I can probably get them done tomorrow. Olivia's mother owes me some baby-sitting time."

He must have been crazy. Her eyes and the sweet curve of her mouth were messing with his brain, and he thought of her trying to hold everything together without complaint, to assemble a proposal that might open all sorts of doors for her if she won the commission—which she was too proud to ask him to help secure for her. He thought of her grit, her determination, her refusal to lean on others—her incredible heroism.

Yes, spending time with her, gazing into those magnificent eyes and witnessing her steadiness in the midst of chaos, must have made him lose his mind.

Or else he'd just decided it was time to set himself a new challenge. Because he said, "If you want to get your work done, I could watch the kids for you."

CHAPTER NINE

THE KIDS dropped off in the car on the drive back to
the studio. Brett carried Max inside, and Sharon carried Olivia, who was marginally lighter. She led Brett
to the curtained area where she'd photographed the
Howland sisters that morning. The floor was carpeted
and scattered with cushions; it would serve as the
dormitory area for the two sleeping beauties. She
knelt and lowered Olivia onto one of the cushions.
Brett eased Max down onto another cushion.

From Olivia's tote bag she retrieved Mr. Poochie
and tucked it into the curve of Olivia's arm. She
brought Max's stuffed teddy bear to him, then adjusted the dimmer switch so the space was relatively
dark. Satisfied that the kids were deeply asleep, she
tiptoed out, Brett right behind her.

"My darkroom is in the basement," she told him.
"You really don't have to stay if you don't—"

"Are you kidding?" He glanced over his shoulder
at the slumbering children. "This could be the easiest
time I've ever spent with kids."

If he was willing to keep an eye on them while
they dozed, she'd be a fool not to accept his offer.
"I've got some magazines, if you'd like something
to read." She hurried through the doorway to the
shelf behind the counter where she stored a variety
of magazines—news magazines, photographic jour-

nals, material she kept on hand to occupy waiting customers and to spark ideas when her vision went stale and inspiration eluded her. She returned to Brett, who seemed vaguely amused by the magazines.

"I'll be fine," he assured her.

He would be, she knew. As long as the kids were asleep, he wouldn't need any of his Daddy School training to keep an eye on them. She remembered long days—long weeks and months—during which she'd sworn that the times she loved Max best were the times he was fast asleep. Maybe Brett would learn to love Max over the next half hour.

She raced downstairs, aware that a half hour might be all the time she had before the kids woke up. Her landlord had let her build a tiny darkroom using the basement lavatory below her studio. It was too small for the quantity of photos she took during the course of her work, but a sink, a few basins, some clothesline, a worktable and a red lamp were all she needed to develop proofs of the photos she'd taken for her proposal for the Arlington birthday book.

She shut herself inside and began mixing chemicals. The familiar, tangy smells carried her back to the early years of her career, when she and Steve had moved to New York, hoping to become a part of that city's bustling art world. It had been a fun dream, the sort a childless couple in their twenties could afford to indulge in. Actually, she'd been the one to suggest, after a few years of starving-artist romance, that they move someplace where they'd be able to support themselves and start a family. If not for her urging, Steve might still be living in that ghastly walk-up on the Lower East Side with the bathtub in the kitchen and the mildew-stained tiles surrounding the toilet, and lugging his portfolio of black-and-white images from gallery to gallery. Steve had loved living on the edge.

He'd died on the edge, too. Once they'd settled into a more middle-class existence in Arlington, he'd found his thrills elsewhere—rock climbing, bike racing and hotdog skiing. Strapping on a pair of skis and gliding down a hill hadn't been enough for him. He'd had to try snowboarding, snow blading, navigating moguls and attempting ski jumps. He'd said he loved the thrill of it, but she suspected he also loved the immaturity of it. Growing up would mean accepting one's mortality and taking responsibility for others. Even after she got pregnant, Steve hadn't been able to do that.

And now he was dead.

Fresh out of college eight years ago, Sharon would not have imagined herself feeling such attraction to a man who spent his days sitting at a desk, wearing a tie—a staid, colorless one—and manipulating money for a living. Brett's world seemed so safe, so square. But now that she was a mother, with more responsibility than she'd ever had before, she respected Brett's square, safe existence. Someone like him would never test his own life expectancy just for a thrill. Perhaps he got his heart pounding by placing some of his fund money in high-risk investments, but she couldn't imagine him hurtling down an icy forty-degree slope on snow blades, jumping and attempting a three-sixty in the air. Just for the thrill of it.

Attending a class for fathers at the Children's Garden might well be the most perilous thing he'd ever done. And he'd done it for her.

She put the film through its baths, checking her watch frequently, wondering how Brett was holding up. As long as the kids remained unconscious he'd be fine. But if they woke up, she couldn't race upstairs and rescue him. Once the film entered this process, opening the darkroom door would destroy it. Brett was on his own.

He was putting forth such a noble effort for her— not just keeping an eye on the kids for now, not just his attendance at Molly's Daddy School class that morning, but lunch at McDonald's. She smiled as she recalled Max's dragging him over to the ball pit to show him the balls, and—when Brett fled back to the table—Max's screeching, "Look at me! Hey, Mr. Man, look at me!" while he climbed the jungle gym and scooted down the slide into the ball pit. Sharon had told him Brett's name, but apparently he didn't remember it.

Once the proof sheet was drying, she washed her hands, turned off the red lamp and emerged into the basement, which was scarcely brighter than her darkroom had been. Old file boxes lined the shelves along one wall—her landlord's records, not her own, which were kept upstairs in the studio, mostly on computer disks. She heard no terrifying sounds spilling down the stairs, but she hurried up the flight quickly just in case. She raced through the larger portrait studio, where she took photos using a screen on which she could project various backgrounds for customers who preferred to be photographed in front of a realistic-looking country bridge or a glen filled with flowers, or a slightly less realistic classic Corvette in glossy red. And on into the smaller studio, where she stumbled to a halt.

Brett lay on the carpeted floor, looking like Gulliver surrounded by Lilliputians. Two Lilliputians, to be precise. Max and Olivia were perched on their knees on either side of him, rolling the Nerf ball back and forth across his chest.

She couldn't see Brett's face from where she stood, but that didn't stop her from reaching for the camera. "Don't you dare," Brett growled before she could angle it to capture the scene.

She still couldn't see his face, but she hoped he could at least smile at his predicament. His two pint-size captors were obviously quite pleased with their conquest. "Throw the ball!" Olivia commanded, and Max nudged the squishy ball across Brett's torso. His leg twitched as Max's knee dug into his side.

"Look, Mommy!" he boasted. "We play ten-its!"

"Tennis," Brett corrected him, rising onto his elbows and peering at Sharon with an expression that seemed to shout, *Thank God you're here.* "I'm the net."

"And a fine net you are, too."

"Nothing else worked," he complained, shoving himself higher, until he was seated and the ball accelerated down his chest and rolled past Olivia. "It was either let them play tennis on my stomach or watch them tear the place apart. One of the magazines got sacrificed, I'm afraid."

"That's all right," she assured him. "They're pretty old."

"I noticed."

"I'm hungry," Olivia whined, ignoring the ball and rushing to Sharon. She flung herself at Sharon's leg and wrapped her arms tightly around her knee.

"Me, too." Max abandoned the "net" and staked

his claim on Sharon's other leg. "Let's go to McDon-o's!"

"We've already been to McDonald's," Sharon reminded him. "It's time to go home."

"I wanna go McDon-o's," Olivia wailed. Max decided to join her, manufacturing a mournful sob and a few impressive-looking tears.

"No McDonald's. We're going home. You can have a snack when we get home."

The children brayed in harmony. The noise seemed to pain Brett as he hoisted himself to his feet. "I don't know what your plans are," she told him, maintaining a conversational tone in spite of the keening duet, "but you're welcome to follow me back to my house."

"I'm not getting into a car with those two," he said, glowering at the children. "It was hard enough teaching them tennis when they were hell-bent on destroying your studio. I'm not going to put up with this screaming, too."

"I don't blame you." She patted his arm. "You did make an awfully cute net, though."

A smile almost escaped him, but he snuffed it before it could take hold.

Getting the children organized, the tote bags packed and the studio locked up was more difficult when the children were cranky than when they were in better spirits. But Sharon was used to their inconvenient moods. She was even, in an odd way, used to Brett's scowl. Each day she spent with him was a little more comfortable, a little more natural than the last. From a posh benefit dinner to a summery outing to this, a day when Brett felt confident enough with Max to simulate a tennis net, she saw a steady improvement. Maybe he didn't hate children as much as he thought he did. Maybe if he told her *why* he hated them, she could help him get past that hatred—she and Max and Olivia.

Max and Olivia were not in the mood to help anyone with anything right now. They continued to cling and howl and lament their undernourished state as she half led, half carried them outside to the car. The rain had let up, easing into a mist that washed every surface. The alley's asphalt glistened like patent leather. The brownstone walls of her studio's building and the adjacent beauty salon shone as if they were wearing a coat of fresh paint.

Once she'd gotten the kids strapped into their seats, she backed out into the road. Gazing into her rearview mirror, she saw Brett's silver Infiniti pull up behind her. She permitted herself a smile. He was definitely salvageable. He never would have allowed himself to be used as a tennis net if he hated children *that* much.

No cars were parked outside her town house or Deborah's next door as Sharon steered up the winding street where she lived. Raymond must have left, finally. Sharon wondered how Deborah was faring—and how much she resented Sharon for having made their private encounter possible. If Deborah was still recovering, Sharon would be happy to keep Olivia with her for a while longer. She had plenty of snacks for the famished children, and a decent supply of toys and animated videos they could watch.

She pulled into her driveway, and Brett braked to a stop at the curb in front of her house. Olivia and Max had sniveled and hiccupped most of the way home. Sharon had managed not to let them distract her, but she was glad to get out of the car.

"I have to drop off Olivia," she explained to Brett as he joined her in the driveway. He took the tote bags while she unbuckled the kids. Max didn't bolt, and Olivia was too distraught to run anywhere. "We're home now, Livie," Sharon murmured, lifting the melodramatic girl into her arms. "Do you want to see Mommy?"

"I want Mommy," Olivia whimpered, her cheeks tear-stained.

"Let's go see her, then." She trooped across the wet grass to Deborah's front walk. Her canvas sneakers soaked through, dampening her toes.

Deborah answered the door, looking rather damp herself. Her hair hung in glistening ringlets and her skin was dewy, as if she'd just taken a shower. "Livie, honey!" she said, extending her arms to take her daughter. Sharon gladly relinquished the load. "Any reason for all this fretting?" she asked Sharon.

"She wants to go to 'McDon-o's,'" Sharon explained, peeking past Deborah on the chance that Raymond might still be there, even if his car wasn't. The living room appeared empty, though—and Deborah looked far too refreshed and relaxed. If he was there, she'd be tense and testy.

"Come here, baby," Deborah crooned, stroking Olivia's head. "Are you a little sleepy? Do you need a nap?"

"The kids napped," Sharon reported, then glanced behind her at Brett, who stood warily on the front walk, two steps down from the porch where she and Max stood. His eyes were shadowed, his jaw rigid.

"How long did the kids sleep, Brett? Do you remember?"

"Not long enough," he muttered.

Sharon turned back to Deborah, whose eyebrows arched with curiosity. "Deborah, this is Brett Stockton. Brett, my neighbor Deborah Jackson."

Brett nodded. Any fantasies Sharon might have nurtured about his learning to love children dissolved. He looked surly and tired. The tennis net was sagging.

"Nice to meet you," Deborah called to him, then whispered to Sharon, "He hates children?"

Sharon shrugged, unwilling to concede the point.

"He sure is pretty. Maybe you can bring him around."

"So, how did things go with Raymond?" Sharon whispered back, not willing to dwell on Brett's shortcomings—or his beauty.

Deborah's cheeks darkened. "I can't really talk about it right now."

"Are you still pissed at me?"

"I haven't decided yet," Deborah told her, although she didn't sound angry. "We'll talk later. You've got Mr. Wrong to take care of."

"And you've got Miss Tragedy," Sharon observed, patting Olivia's back.

"Yeah, thanks. I send you off with a cheerful little girl and you return with this miserable creature. Any chance you brought home her evil twin by mistake?"

"None at all." Sharon smiled. She was eager to hear more specifics about Deborah's meeting with Raymond, but Deborah was right. Now wasn't the time.

She left the porch, and Max clamped a sticky wet

hand around her knee. Brett accompanied her back across the soaked grass to her own front door. Once inside, she let out a long breath.

"I'm hungry," Max grumbled.

"I know. Let's get your wet shoes off and then we'll get a snack."

Brett said nothing as Sharon pried off her own sneakers and left them, along with Max's, on the floor mat inside the door. She lifted Max and poked a discreet finger into the waistband of his shorts to check his diaper. Dry. She ought to perch him on his potty immediately, but that would mean abandoning Brett—probably for a good fifteen minutes. When Max tried to use the potty, it often turned into quite a time-consuming production.

Her heart just wasn't in it. Max could be toilet trained another day. Right now he was hungry and Brett seemed lost. She would rather devote her attention to him.

"Would you like a snack?" she asked as she carried Max into the kitchen.

"Have you got a beer?"

She smiled. A beer was the least he deserved. "In the refrigerator, on the lower shelf of the door. Help yourself." She settled Max into his booster seat.

Brett pulled out two bottles, twisted off both caps and left one on the counter for her. She might have considered this presumptuous, but the sight of that cold bottle and the happy hiss of released pressure as he'd opened it made her acknowledge that his presumption was correct. She wished she could sprawl out on the family room sofa with him, and they could enjoy their beers and talk about anything other than Max.

But that option wasn't available. Max was drumming his hands on the table, chanting, "Milk, milk, milk!"

She poured some milk into a lidded cup, peeled a banana and cut it into chunks on a plate, and arranged the snack in front of Max. Then she crossed to the counter, lifted her bottle and tapped it against Brett's in a toast.

"Have you ever actually calculated how much time you spend doing things for him?" Brett asked.

"God, no! If I did, I'd probably want to kill myself," she joked.

"Or maybe him."

"No, never him. It's not his fault. Children are time-consuming, that's all."

"I know."

Brett spoke casually, as if he were simply endorsing a universal truth. Yet Sharon sensed a gruffness in his voice, as if the words had been abraded by experience. She eyed him curiously. "How do you know?"

He gazed past her, through the small, square window above the kitchen table, where Max was mashing his banana with his fingers, more interested in playing with the fruit than eating it. The screen was mottled with raindrops, a dreary contrast to the cheerful blue curtains framing the window.

"I just know," he said quietly, then washed the words down with a drink of beer.

Nobody "just knew" how exhausting it was to raise a child. It was the sort of wisdom one acquired only through experience.

But what experience could Brett have had? He'd

told her he had no children. "Did you work as a teacher?" she asked.

He frowned. "No. Why do you ask?"

Studying him, she sipped her beer. She remembered the way she'd felt when he'd stared at her in the alley behind the studio earlier that day, and heat had flared between them. She was amazed, and even a little embarrassed, to admit how attracted she was to a man about whom she still knew so little.

He seemed to expect an answer. "You said you knew how time-consuming children were," she explained. "If you're not a father...I thought, maybe you'd been a teacher."

He shook his head. "I helped to raise my siblings," he told her.

All right. That made sense.

Max had reduced his banana to a mass of pulpy yellow goo. He clearly wasn't going to eat any of it. Sighing, Sharon lifted him out of his chair, carried him to the sink and turned on the water. She washed his gummy hands, dried them with a paper towel and lowered him to his feet. "I go potty," he announced.

She couldn't ignore his toilet training when he was specifically asking to use the potty. Sending Brett an apologetic smile, she let Max lead her out of the kitchen. Given Brett's practice with his siblings, he must be used to untimely interruptions, particularly those revolving around bodily functions.

But even as she hurried up the stairs after Max, her thoughts remained down in the kitchen, with Brett and his mysteries.

A MILLION TIMES that day, he'd wanted to leave. But there he was, at seven-thirty that night, still at Sharon's house.

After his potty adventure, Max had wanted to show Brett his waffle blocks. It had been bad enough offering his abdomen as a substitute tennis net, but sitting on the carpeted floor of the finished basement with Max while he wedged blocks together and took them apart, all the while yammering in an occasionally fractured English that he expected Brett to understand was worse. The hardest part was pretending he enjoyed such a tedious activity.

Sharon certainly seemed to enjoy it. She built structures with the blocks, chattered with Max and tried to engage Brett in their play. He watched her, amazed by her stores of energy, the ease with which she conversed with the kid, the apparent delight she took in erecting a colorful tower of blocks. Every now and then his gaze would settle on her long tan legs, her bare toes digging into the carpet pile, the graceful curve of her upper breast when she leaned forward and her blouse drooped at the neckline, and he'd wonder if the only reason he was still putting up with her noisy, obnoxious son was that he wanted to make love to Sharon.

He did want to. But that could never be enough of a reason for him to stay.

Other things were holding him here. Stubborn perseverance, perhaps. The desire to test himself. But mostly Sharon—his astonishment that she could do as much as she did for Max and still look fresh and buoyant and pleased with her life. It was a life that reflected his worst nightmare—not just parenting, but doing it without assistance. And not only did she seem to be enjoying it, but she clearly didn't feel any obligation to convince him it was the right life for him.

She accepted him. He was resistant to everything she'd devoted her life to, and she never made any attempt to show him the error of his ways. She didn't try to draw him into her nonsensical conversations with Max, or goad him into contributing to the waffle-block village she and Max were constructing. She just let him be himself.

She told him she planned to make macaroni and cheese for dinner, but he insisted on traveling into town for take-out Chinese. He savored the silence in his car during the drive through the rain, which had resumed in a steady shower, to the restaurant to pick up the food, and the warm spicy scent of Szechuan cuisine inside the restaurant. After paying for their order, he found himself walking unforgivably slowly back to his car. Not because he was reluctant to return to Sharon, but because this brief break hadn't been long enough for him to figure out how he felt about the day, about Sharon, about how he could possibly fit into her life.

Her life and Max's.

A drive to Boston and back wouldn't have been long enough for him to figure it out. And he wanted to return to Sharon's house while the tubs of shrimp in black bean sauce, chicken with straw mushrooms and fried rice were still hot. Even the thought of what Max could do with the dinner food, given his comprehensive mutilation of his banana earlier that afternoon, couldn't keep Brett from returning to Sharon's town house.

Max did manage to get at least as much food into his mouth as onto his clothing, his lap, his hair and the floor. Afterward, he needed a bath, and Brett politely declined Sharon's invitation for him to join them upstairs to observe this ritual. Left to himself while she brought Max upstairs to be dericed and desauced, Brett stacked the dishes into the dishwasher, packed the leftovers into the refrigerator and swept the floor. He remembered sweeping the floor in his mother's kitchen after the twins had eaten. "Why do I have to clean it up?" he used to ask her as she tucked one twin under each arm and hustled off to hose them down and slap fresh diapers onto their bottoms.

"Because you're my best helper," she'd say.

He hadn't wanted to be her best helper. He'd just wanted to be a carefree child. The memory jabbed him in his gut like a well-placed punch as he swept the stray bits of food into a dustpan in Sharon's kitchen. He was a big boy now, mature enough to be Sharon's best helper now, if that was truly what he wanted. At least this time it would be his choice, one way or the other.

He took another beer from her fridge and exited into the living room. Sharon's and Max's voices drifted down the stairs, his squeals of laughter in counterpoint to her soothing instructions. Brett moved slowly around the living room, studying the framed photographs decorating the walls. Some were of scenery: bucolic landscapes, an ocean wave erupting over a breakwater, a striking pattern of sloping roofs that, he realized after a moment, were a row of town houses in her complex. Others were portraits—of strangers; of two giggling toddlers he immediately recognized as Max and Olivia; of Olivia's attractive mother seated on a park bench, her legs drawn up and her chin resting on her knees. All the photos struck Brett as optimistic: sunny mornings or colorful sunsets and people with hope in their eyes.

How had Sharon, a young widow with so much responsibility and so much grief, managed to take so many upbeat photographs? Had she taken them all? Even if she hadn't, she'd obviously chosen them because she wanted to fill her home with cheering imagery.

Maybe this was why he'd had to come back to her house—because like the people in the portraits on the wall, Sharon had such abundant hope shining in her eyes.

"I still have to read to him," she said.

He turned to see her descending the stairs.

"I read to him every night before bed," she explained. "He won't go to sleep otherwise."

Brett gestured toward the photos. "Did you take all these pictures?"

She hesitated, as if thrown by his non sequitur. Maybe he should have commented on her bedtime reading ritual. But as far as Brett was concerned, how she got Max to bed wasn't as important as the photos on her wall.

"Yes," she finally answered.

"You're incredibly talented." He'd make sure Gail Murphy on the Arlington birthday committee knew just how talented Sharon was.

She laughed. "If I weren't, I'd be a fool to try to make a living at it."

"I'm sure taking these—" he again waved at the wall of pictures "—is different from taking pictures of little girls in party dresses at your studio."

"Not that different," she told him. "Photography

is about light and shape. Whether I'm photographing condominium roofs or little girls in party dresses, it's all a matter of getting the light to play over the shapes the right way and then capturing the moment. It's a little easier with rooftops, because they don't squirm.''

"How did you get that picture?" he asked, turning back to study it. The row of slanting black slate rectangles curved, the roofs equidistant and uniform in size and shape. They reminded him of a domino chain. "Did you rent a helicopter?"

She laughed again, low and melodic, and shook her head. "I climbed onto the roof of a town house across the street."

"You climbed onto the roof? You could have killed yourself!"

"I was careful. And it's a great photo, isn't it?"

He pictured her standing on a roof. Regardless of how dangerous it was, she looked fearless in his mind, focused on her camera and the roofs across the way, oblivious to everything but the shot she wanted to take. "You ought to include this in your submission to the town," he suggested.

"Do you think so? It's not really representative of Arlington, is it?"

"Of course it is. Village Green Condominiums is as much a part of town as the YMCA."

She drew to a halt next to him and scrutinized the photo. "Maybe you're right."

"No maybe about it." She was so close he was tempted to wrap an arm around her. She smelled of soap and baby powder from Max's bath, and her hair was pulled back in a barrette, exposing her slender throat. He ached to kiss that vulnerable skin.

"Mommy!" Max shouted. "Mommy, read me a book!"

She sighed and slipped away from Brett, moving back to the stairs. "You're welcome to come upstairs and listen to *Hop on Pop*," she said.

"I'll pass, thanks." He watched her climb the stairs and tried not to focus on the taut curves of her bottom. Her shorts weren't particularly tight, but...

Hell. She was going to spend the next half hour reading *Hop on Pop,* whatever that was, to her son. How could Brett possibly be fantasizing about her sexy rear end? There were plenty of other women in the world with equally sexy rear ends and no sons to read *Hop on Pop* to. Why was he in Sharon's home right now, instead of with one of them?

It didn't matter. He *was* in Sharon's home, and he didn't want to leave.

He finished his beer—and that day's edition of the *Arlington Gazette,* which had been lying untouched on her coffee table, no doubt since it had been delivered that morning. Mothers of toddlers must have little time to relax with the newspaper. He couldn't imagine not having time to read the newspaper as soon as he brought it in from his front porch. Yet he had to admit that none of the news it carried was so imperative that it had to be read first thing in the morning. Newspapers could wait if you chose to give priority to a child.

She appeared on the stairs as he was finishing a back-page article on a movement to turn golf into an Olympic sport. After such a long day, capped by a half hour of reading children's stories to a toddler, he would not have looked as refreshed as she did. Her hair was still pulled back from her face, but her skin was dewy, her eyes bright as she descended to the living room and smiled at him. "Did anything important happen today?" she asked, gesturing toward the newspaper.

Not according to the stories filling its pages—but yes, something important had happened. He'd spent nearly the entire day in Sharon's orbit, convinced that he could get past his lifelong aversion to children just because of her.

He stood and her eyebrows rose, two pale quizzical arcs above her eyes. "Are you leaving?" she asked.

"Do you want me to?"

Her gaze slid past him, then returned to his face, direct and honest. "I'd rather you didn't, but it's been a long day."

"Not that long," he countered. It had felt long to him when the kid had been awake, but he was asleep now, or close to it. "If anyone might be tired, it would have to be you."

"I do this all the time," she reminded him, grinning. "I've got stamina."

Stamina and a hell of a lot more. He moved around the coffee table and crossed the room to her. The line of her jaw beckoned, smooth and sharp and open to his view. He cupped his hand against it, then tilted her face and pressed a light kiss to her lips.

Her mouth softened against his and clung for a moment. He heard her breath catch.

It suddenly seemed to him as if he'd been waiting forever for the chance to kiss her, *really* kiss her. He'd tried to persuade himself he didn't want her, but he'd failed. Even knowing what her life was like, the diapers and whines and baths and storybooks, the dawn-until-dusk of it—he still wanted her.

He kissed her again, more deeply this time, and she sighed. One of her hands rose to his shoulder and he felt her strength in her fingers as they flexed against him. Her hands were strong enough to do all those things for her son: bathe him and diaper him and wipe his tears—but it wasn't just her physical strength he felt in her grip. It was her confidence, her resolve. Her willingness to do what had to be done, and to make the best of it. To go beyond just making the best of it—to celebrate everything her life had turned out to be.

He slid his hand to the back of her head, unclasped the barrette and felt her hair spill against his knuckles, soft and wavy from the rain that had washed it earlier that day. He wanted to kiss her hair, to feel its silken texture against his cheek. But his mouth was locked to hers, and he wasn't about to pull away. Instead, he slid his tongue between her lips.

A quiet moan escaped her. She touched her tongue to his, almost shyly, then broke the kiss, turning her head against his hand. "Brett," she whispered.

"What?"

"Please don't tell me you put up with Max all day because you wanted this."

For a moment he thought he'd have to lie to her—and he would hate to do that. But then he realized that telling her what she wanted to hear wouldn't be a lie. He'd put up with Max all day, and he'd wanted this—but he wasn't sure the two were connected.

Well, they were; Sharon was at the heart of both.

But even if he hadn't had the chance to kiss her like this, to twirl his fingertips through the tufts of hair at her nape and to have her standing so close to him he could feel the heat of her body through his clothing, he would not have regretted putting up with Max today.

He didn't know why that was. He just knew it was so.

"I want you," he told her. "Max has nothing to do with that."

"He should," she said. "He's a part of me."

"This is also a part of you," he pointed out, grazing her forehead with his lips, and the hollow below her cheekbone, and stroking his thumb along the edge of her jaw. "A different part. The part I want."

He covered her mouth with his once more. This time he sensed no hesitation in her. No questions. No reminder of the part of her—Max—who had dominated the day they'd spent together.

Max was asleep now. He wasn't a part of *this*. *This* was about Sharon and Brett and no one else, and he felt as if it were the culmination of not just one long trying day or a couple of thought-provoking weeks, but of his entire life.

This was the part he wanted.

CHAPTER TEN

THE NEAREST drugstore was less than ten minutes away—closer than Brett's house. Sharon felt awful sending him out into the rain, which was coming down harder again, a persistent muffled drumbeat against the roof, the windows, the lawn beyond her door. But he'd headed out the door, laughing and promising to return as soon as he could.

It had been nearly three years since she'd made love—and that had been with her husband. Condoms were not an item she'd thought to stock up on.

Ten minutes there, ten minutes back. She raced up the stairs, yanking off her clothes as she ran, and twisted the shower faucets to a warm spray. Just a quick rinse, to wash away the mingled scents of her day—soy sauce and ginger, baby soap and powder. She splashed a light fragrance behind her ears and between her breasts, then wrapped herself in her old terry cloth robe and wished she owned something silkier, sexier.

She wasn't used to being sexy. She was a mom. The only person she'd shared her bed with since Steve's death was Max, when he needed soothing after a nightmare or during the days last winter when he'd been afflicted with roseola. She and he would cuddle in bed together and watch cartoons on the small TV set in her bedroom, and he'd doze, his body steaming and his hair limp with perspiration.

She and Brett would not be watching cartoons tonight.

A faint tremor rippled through her, part anticipation but largely fear. Was she doing the right thing? Did this make sense? He was, as Deborah had dubbed him, Mr. Wrong. Until he changed his attitude toward children, their relationship had no future.

But it had a present. And she deserved to experience it, to revel in it. She deserved to be romanced by a man like Brett, if only for one night. She would deal with the future tomorrow.

The doorbell sounded. She peeked into Max's bedroom on her way down the hall to the stairs. He had graduated from a crib to a bed right after he'd recovered from roseola last January, and in the dim glow of his night-light she saw him in silhouette, a tiny island protruding above an ocean of mattress. She listened for the steady rhythm of his breathing that indicated he was asleep, then continued to the stairs and down.

Brett stood on the front porch, wet from the rain. His hair was pasted to his skull, his shirt to his chest. In his hand he clasped a small plastic bag.

Sharon drew him inside and closed the door. Ignoring the rainwater that rolled down his cheeks and arms, he pulled her into his embrace and kissed her, right there in the entry, a deep hungry kiss that settled any doubts in her mind, any hesitation, any concerns for the future.

"You smell good," he whispered.

"Thank you." He smelled good, too, even without having showered. He smelled of summer rain and mint. She slipped her hand into his and led him up the stairs, determined to focus only on now, on him. For tonight she would not be Max's mom, or even Steve's widow. She would just be Sharon, desiring this man who desired her.

They entered her bedroom and he shut the door. "Is it okay if we close it?" he asked, still keeping his voice low. "I mean, with your son and all—"

"He knows how to open a door if he has to," she said.

Brett eyed the door apprehensively. "I don't know if that's good or bad."

She smiled. "It's good. If there's an emergency, I'd want him to be able to reach me, no matter what."

"Right." Her answer clearly didn't thrill Brett, but he accepted it. He reached for her again, drew her into his arms and kissed her, kissed her like a man who couldn't care less about emergencies, who had no second thoughts about what might happen. All that mattered was what *was* happening in her quiet bedroom, where the only sounds were the whispers of his breath and hers, the crinkle of the bag as he tossed it onto the bed, the drumbeat of the rain against her window and the hush of his fingers sliding down her throat, down the front of her robe to the knotted sash.

And the thumping of her heart. She wondered if he could hear it—it was suddenly so hard, so fast. Three years since a man had touched her... Would making love be like riding a bike, one of those skills that, once learned, a woman never forgot? Or would she botch it?

He stopped kissing her so he could undo the knot.

Once it came loose, he lifted his gaze to her face again. He must have read the panic in her eyes, because he frowned. "Are you okay?"

"A little nervous," she admitted.

"Don't be." He kissed her brow. "We're friends."

"We are?"

"Do you think I would have volunteered to be a tennis net for your son if we weren't friends?"

She smiled. He was right. Only a friend would have put up with Max and Olivia the way Brett had. Only a friend would have kept Max occupied last week so Sharon could take some pictures—even though he didn't like children. Only a friend would race out in a downpour to buy contraceptives. A friend and a lover.

It was the lover part that made her nervous, but the warmth in his voice and his eyes, the gentle motions of his hands on her shoulders and arms, stroking her through the terry cloth instead of rushing to strip her naked, the solidity of him standing before her, patient and confident, when surely there were other women, women without children, whom he could pursue—all of that helped to put her at ease. If she tumbled off the bicycle, he'd be there. He would pick her up, kiss her boo-boos and help her back onto the seat. She could trust him.

She skimmed his chest with her hands, marveling at its hardness. Max was the only person she ever touched these days, and he was all baby, round and soft. Not Brett. She felt ribs layered with muscle, the thick bones of his shoulders, the tight flat stretch of his abdomen. He had the physique of an athlete, even though he spent his days seated behind a desk.

She wanted more than just to touch him through his shirt. She wanted to see him, to kiss him, to feel the heat of his skin against her palms. She wanted to find out just how much she remembered about the art of riding a bicycle.

She closed her hands around the dark-blue fabric and tugged it free of his jeans. His eyes narrowed slightly as he gazed down at her, and his smile faded. With a quick efficient twist, he wrenched the shirt over his head and off.

She had known he would have a gorgeous body, but actually viewing it, observing the flow of skin and lean muscle, the glints of raindrops trapped in the hairs on his forearms... She could have been a visitor to a museum, gaping at some magnificent sculpture, except for his warmth, the movement of his chest as he breathed and his hands as he reached for the lapels of her robe and spread them apart. His fingertips brushed against her and she felt a pang of longing so sudden and demanding it nearly staggered her.

She was going to embarrass herself. Just looking at him aroused her too much, and another brush of his fingers against her shoulders sent an ache deep into her womb. She considered explaining to him that she was out of practice, that she was starving and he was a banquet so rich, she was afraid that once she took a taste she would be unable to stop—but he kissed her before she could speak.

She tasted. She feasted. Her hands savored the texture of his skin. Her lips grazed his mouth, his cheek, the edge of his jaw. She arched to him and her body absorbed his maleness, his height and breadth and heat.

Her robe dropped to the floor, and his jeans and briefs joined it. Then he pulled her down onto the bed and she feasted some more. He seemed delighted by everything she did, smiling as she ran her toes along his shin, gasping as she trailed her fingers down his abdomen. It no longer mattered if she fell off the bike. She was beyond shyness, beyond embarrassment. Her senses filled with him, his scent, his bulk, the thickness of his wrists and fingers, the way his chest vibrated when he sighed. When he slid his thigh between hers she moaned, not caring if he heard her. When he bowed to kiss her breasts, she dug her fingers into his hair and held him to her, not caring if he thought she was too clingy, too needy.

When at last he rose above her and thrust deep into her, she lost all sense of tomorrow, the future, the impossibility of a true love existing between a woman whose entire life was her son and a man who had no interest in children. All that existed was this moment, this unspeakable pleasure, the satisfaction she felt as he filled her. No more hunger, no more need. She had everything she wanted right now, with Brett.

She came too soon, but he didn't seem to mind. He let go just after she did, pressing deep, pulsing inside her and releasing his breath in a barely audible groan. She wrapped her arms around him, wanting him to stay inside her as long as possible. He nuzzled her neck, exhaled a slow breath and lifted his head. He looked happy, dazed and a little sheepish.

"Was that quick enough for you?" he asked.

She smiled. "I'm not complaining."

He eased off her, and his absence chilled her. He looped an arm around her and pulled her against him, which warmed her again. She felt his mouth against her hair, dropping a kiss on the top of her head. "I'll go slower next time, I promise."

Next time. Her smile widened. "Brett, this was wonderful. Really. I was the one who went too fast. I—" She hesitated, unsure of how much to say.

His voice rumbled down to her. "You what?"

They were friends. And no matter what tomorrow brought, she trusted him. "I haven't made love in a long time."

He twined his fingers through her hair, gentle, thoughtful. "Since your husband died?"

She nodded. It wasn't that terrible an admission. Maybe other women wouldn't have waited three years to take a lover, but why should she be ashamed that she had? Sex was a wonderful thing—but only when it was right. And until tonight, she hadn't had the time, the energy or the craving to pursue it.

"You should have told me," he murmured. Had she made him uncomfortable? Would he have said good-night and gone home if he'd known? He reassured her by adding, "I would have done a better job of it."

She laughed and traced a line across his chest with her index finger. Hair grew sparse and wiry across the upper portion. His nipple stiffened as her hand wandered near it. "I'm not complaining," she repeated.

"Because it's been so long for you. You have no basis for comparison." He rose onto his side, forcing her onto her back next to him. She was relieved to see his grin as he gazed down at her.

"I know the difference between good and bad.

This was good, Brett.'' She sighed, reliving for a moment just how good it was.

''I usually have a little more lasting power. I just—'' He faltered.

''You just what?''

''I wanted this. A lot.''

''Well, good.'' She grinned.

He remained solemn. ''I haven't been able to stop thinking about you.'' He ran his fingers through her hair in a soothing rhythm. ''Pretty much from day one, I've been— Well, wanting you.''

''Really?''

''That first night, when you were wearing that sexy black dress—I was so turned on by you I thought I'd go crazy.''

The night she'd expected him to kiss her. ''Why didn't you do something about it?''

''The first night? Are you kidding?'' He brushed a misplaced lock of hair back from her cheek. ''I figured you'd shoot me down.''

''Why? Did you think I would have been shocked?''

''I didn't know. First date and all…'' He continued to toy with her hair, tucking it behind her ear. ''You weren't some sort of fast-lane lady. You were a mother.''

''Most mothers, by definition, aren't virgins,'' she pointed out.

He smiled briefly. ''The truth was, I didn't want to see you again. I didn't want to get involved with you. Knowing where you're coming from, and where I'm coming from…I'm not into casual sex, Sharon. I don't make love to a woman unless there's something real going on, you know?''

His willingness to talk about this moved her even more than the sex had. "So you think there's something real going on between us?"

"Yeah." He didn't look happy about it.

She knew her son was the reason for Brett's misgivings. She'd really hoped she wouldn't have had to think about her son for a few hours. But of course she couldn't really bar him from her thoughts, not even when she was lying naked with Brett. Max was so deeply embedded in her brain that to remove him, even temporarily, would probably kill her. "Max is not just an obstacle," she said, her voice quiet but steady. "He isn't going to disappear."

"I know." His fingers continued to weave through her hair, slowly, soothingly. His gaze never strayed from her face.

"How bad was it?" she asked. "With your siblings. Is that why you don't like children?"

He nodded. "It was bad. I was five when Andrew was born, seven when James came along, eight with the twins. They took over my life. I had nothing of my own after they were born. I'd come home from school and be stuck baby-sitting all of them, every day. I changed diapers. I fed them. I cleaned up after them." His thumb stroked the edge of her earlobe. "I don't have to tell you what it's like to take care of kids—only I had four of them and they weren't mine, and I was just a kid myself."

"Where were your parents?"

"My stepfather worked. He was an accountant—an okay guy, but very traditional. He didn't want my mother to get a job. She probably didn't want a job, anyway. I think she was overwhelmed, and depressed. As soon as I got home from school, she'd go off and leave me in charge."

"Maybe you should hate your mother instead of children."

"I don't know if I *hate* them," he assured her. "I just don't want them taking over my life again. And you know that's what children do. They take over your life."

True enough. But she'd chosen to hand her life over to Max. She and Steve both had wanted him, and when Steve had died she'd wanted Max even more. Not just because he was a surviving piece of Steve but because he reminded her, every day, with every breath, every smile, every dirty diaper and sticky kiss, that life went on.

"I suppose," she conceded, "people who don't want children shouldn't have them."

"And people who *do* want children *should* have them. Like you. You're a good mother."

She snorted. "I'm not so sure about that. I'm just winging it. Sometimes I'm convinced I'm doing everything wrong. I've got no one here to point out my mistakes or show me the right way to do it."

"But look at your kid. He's healthy. He's smart. He doesn't look deprived to me."

"He's messy."

"I raised four kids, Sharon. They're all messy at that age."

It amazed her to think Brett might know more about child rearing than she did. Not only did he have more experience, but he'd attended a Daddy School class. Except for one lecture she'd attended in her eighth month on bathing and burping techniques, safety standards for cribs and breast-feeding strategies, she'd never taken any classes at all. She wondered if Molly at the Children's Garden ran a Mommy School for women like her.

"Do you get along with your siblings now?"

"More or less. They all live in the Boston area and I'm here, so it's not like we see one another very often."

Sharon didn't point out that Boston was barely two and a half hours away, and that if he was close to his siblings he could see them as often as he liked.

"I think they know I resented them. But they all had one another. I was this older person, removed from them, yelling at them when they spilled something—and then mopping up the spill while they ran off to wreak havoc somewhere else. We get along now, sure, but I don't think we could ever be close."

Her heart squeezed tight for the little boy he must have been. He'd lost his father, and then he'd lost his home when his mother moved to Boston, and then he'd lost his mother to depression. He'd lost his childhood. She used to worry about how much Max had lost with Steve's death—but whether or not she was a great mother, she loved her son fiercely. She would never exploit him and ignore his needs the way Brett's mother had ignored his. She would never place so much responsibility on such tiny shoulders. She would never deprive her son of the chance to be young and silly and carefree.

She could think of no words that wouldn't come out sounding like pity or a condemnation of his mother and stepfather. So she said nothing. She only cupped her hand around his head and pulled him down to her so she could kiss him, kiss away some of the little-boy pain that still ached within him, kiss away the unfairness of his youth and the scars it had left behind.

He returned her kiss, using his lips, his tongue, playing his teeth against her lower lip. His kisses earlier had been hard and greedy, but this one was leisurely and thorough. He was taking his time now, and if everything he did to her felt as good as this one deep, consuming kiss...

It did. Everything. The unhurried forays of his hands across her skin, cupping her breasts, circling her waist, his warm breath against her nape as he rolled her onto her stomach and massaged the length of her spine and then turned her onto her back again. His mouth taking one breast and then the other, his palms on her hips, his legs between hers, knees pressing her inner thighs...it all felt better than good.

She touched him, too, because she couldn't lie passive while he made love to every part of her body. She raked her hands through his hair as he kissed her belly, clutched at his shoulders as he licked between her legs, pulled him up when she couldn't bear another moment without having him inside her. And then when he was inside her she couldn't bear that, either, because it felt so good, too good.

When she climaxed, he paused, then started again, deep slow thrusts that seemed to fill her soul as much as her body. Her eyes brimmed with tears and she closed them, and when she opened them again she saw only Brett, his beautiful blue eyes, his lips parted as he tried to keep his breathing even. She circled her arms around him, and her legs, wanting him to experience the pleasure she'd already known, but he held back, his muscles taut as he braced himself higher above her. The new angle created more sensations inside her, friction and pressure and love coiling together and pulling tight, tighter.

It hit her like an ocean wave, fluid yet hard enough to knock the world out from under her. He caught her cry with his mouth, kissing her, pumping hard until the wave crashed over him, as well. He shuddered, sinking heavily into her arms and gasping for air.

For a long time she remained incapable of lucid thought. When her brain finally cleared, her first realization was that he'd been right. Slower was better. She had a basis for comparison now.

He seemed in no rush to slide off her, and she was glad. He was heavy, his skin damp with sweat, and she loved the weight of him. She loved the harsh whisper of his breath through her hair, and the vague motions of his fingers against her upper arm.

Love, she thought. She had fallen in love with this complicated, stubborn, honest man. The wrong man, yes, but there was no denying it. She loved Brett.

SHE SLEPT SOUNDLY. Brett was egotistical enough to believe he deserved some credit for that. Three years without sex would have turned him into a perpetual insomniac. Now she was probably enjoying the first satisfied sleep since her husband's accident.

Unlike her, he was unable to fall asleep—and she deserved no blame for that at all. Her body felt surprisingly natural against his, slim yet soft, her bottom nuzzling his hip and her hair splayed across his shoulder.

After all that lovemaking, he should be out cold. But his eyes refused to close, his mind refused to shut down.

He was in trouble.

This hadn't been intended. Of course, if he analyzed it, he would be forced to acknowledge that he'd been heading straight down this path from the moment he'd decided to pick up the company photos instead of sending someone else to get them. That had been the crucial instant, the telling step. He'd decided, in spite of her son, that he wanted Sharon.

Nothing had detoured him from this moment, this night. Not his common sense, not the boy's brattiness, not the truth when he'd laid it out for her. Not a two-hour stretch in the Daddy School followed by a long afternoon immersed in child activities.

A small voice inside him had pleaded, *Save yourself! Get out while you can!* But he hadn't been able to save himself. Attempting escape would have been pointless. He'd wanted Sharon too much.

And now that he'd had her, he wanted her even more.

She knew him, at least. He didn't make a habit of bearing his soul, especially to women, but she deserved to know what she was dealing with. Certain things about him were never going to change, and she'd heard his explanation. She knew why he was the way he was.

If she could be foolish enough to let him remain in her bed after everything he'd told her, he could be foolish enough to stay.

CHAPTER ELEVEN

HE FELT HER SHIFT against his shoulder, sigh and lift her head. Groaning, he forced his eyes open and squinted at the glowing red digits of the clock radio on the night table beside him—6:34.

No one should ever be awake at 6:34 on a Sunday morning. But she was pulling away from him, shoving herself into a sitting position. Not only was she awake, but she seemed on the verge of getting out of bed, which struck him as criminal.

He pulled her back down onto his chest. "Ten minutes," he mumbled, a major compromise. If he was truly demanding, he'd suggest a couple more hours of sleep, followed by more lovemaking.

"I've got to get up," she told him, even though she snuggled against him.

"Why?"

"Max."

Brett listened, but he heard no noise beyond the door, no indication that the kid was at large and on a tear. Stillness filled Sharon's bedroom, and Brett thought it reasonable to assume it filled the rest of the house, as well. "He isn't up yet," he murmured. "You and I shouldn't be up yet, either."

She laughed gently. "Trust me, he's up."

"So, what terrible thing could happen if we stay in bed a little longer? What can he do? Go downstairs, get himself some Cheerios and watch cartoons on TV?''

"Sure. Except that for him to reach the Cheerios, he'd have to climb onto the counter. And then he could fall off and break his neck.''

Sharon evidently thought this would be a bad thing. Hell, Brett did, too. He didn't want Max to kill himself. He just wanted Max not to exist.

If Sharon ever found out he could entertain such an idea—even if only in jest—she'd kick him out of her bed and her life so fast the world would melt into a blur as he flew past. But this was merely one more reason he didn't like children: not just that they were pains in the ass but that they denied adults the right to linger in bed, groggy and affectionate; to cuddle up and mold themselves to each other, and maybe make love one more time and drift off to sleep for a little while longer.

For God's sake, 6:34. To get up now would go against the laws of nature.

"You can stay in bed," she said cheerfully, pushing herself back into a sitting position, the heel of her hand digging into his ribs. "Sleep as late as you want.''

He didn't want to sleep. Well, he did, but he'd slept so little overnight that he doubted a few extra minutes of shut-eye now would make much difference. What he wanted was her in his arms, soft and pliant and naked. What he wanted was the freedom to remain where he was with her, for as long as they both wanted to be there. What he wanted was for Max to disappear.

Damn. He was really going to have to develop a

new attitude if he hoped to make this thing—whatever it was—work.

What was it? A night of lovemaking and slumber. And talk. Too much talk. A night of revealing a lot more of himself than he was used to.

That was what had his sleep cycle so screwed up—all that talking about things he never talked about. To his amazement and regret, he'd loved opening up to Sharon. He didn't talk to people the way he talked to her.

He was apprehensive, but also exhilarated by the opportunity to give voice to thoughts he'd always been ashamed of. To confess his frustrations with his mother, his resentment of his siblings, the bitterness his childhood had left festering inside him, an old wound that had never completely healed. To be able to share it with Sharon was like winning a race barefoot. There was some pain involved, but mostly a sense of liberation and triumph.

He didn't want to give up the chance to be with a woman who could open him up that way and help him to heal. Not even her kid was going to scare him off.

She was already out of bed. He watched her glide around the room, a pale shadow in the darkness. Her movements turned him on as much as her body did. She was so sure of herself when she walked. Each step had purpose. She wasted nothing—her legs carried her where she had to go and then she stopped completely. No jiggling, no swaying, just a sublime motionlessness as she stood before her dresser, gathering herself. Once she had her intentions clear, she opened a drawer and pulled out fresh underwear. Then she shut it, spun around and vanished into her bathroom. Disappointment seized him like a cold fist at the fact that he could no longer see her.

He smiled at his mild dementia. She was a woman and she was getting dressed. That she had to use the bathroom was not the end of the world.

Yet it felt like the end of a small, contained world, at least, the exclusive child-free world of him and Sharon alone together in bed.

Cursing, he threw back the covers and shoved away from the pillow. Her bed held no appeal to him if she wasn't in it. He found his jeans in a pile on the floor. Last night's rain had dried out of them, leaving them wrinkled and stiff. He yanked them on and wished he'd thought to pick up a toothbrush when he'd raced out to buy condoms.

Sharon emerged from the bathroom, clad in a bra and panties more utilitarian than sexy. On her, though, the simple cotton underthings looked alluring. He saw the soft curve of her belly, the roundness of her breasts, the elegance of her throat and her long slender legs, legs that had wrapped tight around him, legs that had pulled him deeper inside her. His groin tensed at the memory.

If he asked her to come back to bed with him she'd say no, so he didn't bother. He simply snagged her as she headed past him, drew her into a hug and covered her mouth with his. She tasted like spearmint and smelled like plain soap, and his groin grew tighter still.

She returned his kiss without any reticence. Oh, this was so good. Even if she was a mother, with her kid allegedly running loose and wreaking havoc throughout the house, she could lose herself in a kiss for a minute, give herself completely over to it, take back as much as she gave. She leaned into him, nestling against his fly, and he cupped his hands around her bottom and arched into her.

A long steamy minute later, she eased back. "Don't tempt me," she whispered, smiling in a way that made him want to do nothing but tempt her until her resistance was gone.

But that wouldn't be fair. If anyone knew what kind of destruction an unsupervised toddler was capable of, he did. With a sigh, he released her and ducked into the bathroom, where it took another full minute for his muscles to relax enough for him to empty his bladder.

No sense asking himself why Sharon Bartell was the one. She just was. "Things happen that we can't explain," his mother had told him when he was young and grief-stricken over his father's death. "It can be something we don't want, but it happens anyway, and we have no choice but to accept it. There's really nothing else we can do."

Sharon had conquered him, and he had no choice but to accept that. Another woman might have been easier, better suited, more comfortable. But this had happened. He couldn't explain it, but Sharon was the one.

OF COURSE Max was up. Sharon didn't have to hear him to know that. A mother's connection to her child was intuitive; her cells started to vibrate whenever her child was on the move. The fact that Sharon had spent a long luscious night making love with Brett didn't change that fact.

He could have gone back to sleep if he'd wanted to. She probably would have preferred if he had. At this early hour, half-asleep and grumpy—and more than a little horny, she'd noticed—he was not going to be at his most tolerant. And Max was likely to be at his most intolerable. He was well rested and recharged, after all, ready to take on the day at full strength and top volume.

Well, Brett was just going to have to deal with it. He'd known when he decided to spend the night with her that the morning would mean Max. He could have left at any time, but he hadn't.

Still, Max could be a handful.

She paused in the doorway to her son's empty bedroom. His blanket shaped a rumpled heap at the foot of his bed, and his teddy bear lay abandoned on the carpet at the center of the room. The night-light was still on. She switched it off, then headed down the stairs.

"Hey, Max," she called from the top of the stairway to the finished basement. "Mommy's up."

"Mommy!" Max chirped. She heard his footsteps scrambling toward the stairs.

"I'm in the kitchen. Are you hungry?" she shouted over her shoulder as she entered the kitchen. She worked quickly to prepare a pot of coffee, hoping that a freshly brewed cup might make the transition from lover to child-resistant guest easier for Brett.

"Hungry!" Max announced as he stomped into the kitchen. His pajamas were designed with snaps to hold the top to the bottom, but he'd opened all but one snap and his tummy stuck out. He was growing, she realized. He'd need new pajamas—and probably new everything else, too. He seemed to grow so fast she sometimes imagined she could see him adding inches right before her eyes.

"Hungry, hungry, hungry," he sang, marching in a circle around the small room. "Pancakes!"

"No pancakes this morning."

"I want pancakes!"

Sharon wasn't in the mood to make pancakes. She was even less in the mood to clean the griddle, the blender and all the other utensils she'd have to use if she made them. And it was too hot. The sun had barely topped the horizon, but she could already feel its heat against the window.

"Would you like a bagel?" she offered.

"Pancakes!" Max halted at the center of the room, planted his little fists on his hips and glowered up at her, his lower lip protruding ominously. "I want pancakes!"

"I'm not making pancakes, Max. I've got bagels, cereal, toast, eggs—"

"No eggs! I hate eggs! Eggs is yucky. Pancakes."

Yesterday he'd eaten scrambled eggs without complaint. The only reason he suddenly hated eggs was that they weren't pancakes. "I'm not making pancakes," she repeated. Behind her the coffeemaker on the counter let out a promising gurgle, and the room filled with the aroma of coffee. "I could cut up some banana for you and mix it with some yogurt if you'd like."

"I hate yoga! I want pancakes!" He screamed it louder, as if increasing the decibel level would convince her to change her mind.

"No pancakes. I'll make you a bagel."

"No! No! No!" He flung himself onto the floor

and wailed like a police siren. "Pancakes! No! I want pancakes!"

Sharon let out a weary breath and started toward the refrigerator to get a bagel for him. She paused when she saw Brett filling the doorway, his brow dented in a frown. He glared at Max, then lifted his gaze to her. She read dismay and disgust in his face.

What could she do? Apologize for what was, unfortunately, rather typical behavior for a boy in his final weeks of the Terrible Twos? Max wanted pancakes. He wasn't going to get them. He was going to throw a tantrum, and he still wasn't going to get them. Such was Sunday morning life with a toddler.

"Would you like a bagel?" she asked Brett, the question barely audible above her son's caterwauling.

Brett's frown intensified.

"Or some earplugs, perhaps?" she joked.

He didn't smile.

Get used to it, she wanted to say. *This is my life.* Except that she wanted him in her life, too—and this was the difficult part of her life, the part that might scare him away.

"The coffee's almost ready," she told him, pulling a plastic bag of bagels out of the fridge and carrying it to the counter. "Let me get Max settled, and then I'll get you something to eat."

Still frowning, he shook his head—whether to indicate that he didn't want food or he couldn't hear her she didn't know.

She sliced a bagel for Max, slid it into the toaster oven, filled a lidded cup with milk and hoisted her son off the floor, holding him carefully so he wouldn't kick her. She settled him into his booster seat at the table, and he tried to squirm out of it. "No! No! I don't want yoga!"

"I'm not giving you yogurt. I'm making you a bagel."

"I want pancakes!"

"So you've said."

Max howled. Oh, it was terrible, disastrous, worse than death, worse than eternal damnation: a bagel instead of pancakes. His face was flushed, his breath wheezy, his nose dripping. She grabbed a napkin from the dispenser and wiped off the mucus. "No!" Max shrieked, twisting his face away. "No! No! No!"

Sharon wished she could find his Mute button. She wished Brett had stayed in bed for an extra hour. By the time Max took a bite of his bagel, he'd be fine. But until then, he was going to share his torment with everyone. Sharon had become inured to it, but Brett...

She glanced toward the doorway. He was no longer there.

Her impulse was to race after him, to apologize, to explain how Max could get sometimes. But she couldn't leave the frenzied little boy. Right now, he was her top priority. In fact, ninety-nine percent of the time, he was her top priority. Last night had been a reprieve, an oasis of nonmotherhood in the desert of her life. But this was the future she hadn't wanted to think about last night. This was her reality.

So instead of going off in search of Brett, massaging his temples and assuring him that Max wasn't his siblings and Sharon would never burden him the way his mother had, she pulled Max's bagel out of the toaster oven, smeared some cream cheese on it, gave

Max a chewable vitamin—which he threw across the room—found it, wiped it off and gave it to him again, and then delivered his bagel, which had cooled off enough for him to handle it. He took a begrudging bite, sniffled dramatically and stopped sobbing.

She poured herself a cup of coffee and again resisted the urge to find Brett. If he wanted to be with her, he would have to come back to the kitchen on his own. She couldn't beg him to put up with Max. Nor could she promise that Max would never again throw a fit like the one he was winding down from.

Brett knew the terms, and she could not coerce him into agreeing to them. She could only hope. Because if he decided he couldn't abide by those terms, if he left her... It wouldn't matter how many times she told herself he was wrong for her. Her heart would still break.

She sipped her coffee black, then leaned against the counter and stared at the sunlight casting a white glare across the window. The steam from her mug floated up into her face; the fragrance filled her nostrils. She sighed, feeling her pulse slow and her stress recede as Max quietly munched on his bagel.

"Where do you keep the mugs?" Brett asked.

She turned to find him entering the kitchen. He still looked grim, but he'd come back. He had voluntarily walked into this room. Warmth washed her like the morning sun against the windowpanes.

He'd come back.

"Here," she said, opening a cabinet and pulling down a mug for him.

"LEVI HOLT," the voice at the other end of the phone said.

Brett leaned back in his chair, gazed about his tidy, austere office and tucked his phone more securely between his ear and his shoulder. "Levi? It's Brett Stockton. You got a minute?"

"Oh, God," Levi said. "Should I sit down?"

"Why?"

"If you're calling me on a Monday morning, I assume it's to tell me my investments tanked over the weekend and I'm flat broke."

Brett laughed. His poker pal Levi had invested a large chunk of change in Arlington Financial funds. Under Brett's management, those funds were doing just fine. "You can stay standing if you want. Thanks to me, you're actually a bit richer than you were last week."

"In that case, sure I've got a minute. What can I do for you? You want me to build you a house?"

Brett had called Levi for his expertise not as an architect but as a father. He felt his smile slip away as he surveyed his office again. The walls were a muted shade somewhere between gray and brown, the name of which only the decorator and possibly Janet knew. The carpeted floor was uncluttered, the furnishings elegantly simple, and the lamp shed an oval pool of light on his desk. He liked neat surroundings. He liked the absence of chaos. He liked the silence surrounding him; the hum of his computer and his own voice were the only sounds in the room. It was all so peaceful, so relaxing.

"I wanted to talk to you about that Daddy School thing," he said.

Levi paused before asking, "What about it?"

"Well, I went to a class on Saturday. I don't know if one class is going to be enough for me."

"You can go again next Saturday. The class meets every week."

"What I meant was, I don't think one class *a week* is going to be enough. Do you know if they've got an intensive program? One of those total-immersion classes, maybe, like the language schools offer."

"You want to become fluent in childese?" Levi chuckled.

Brett didn't. "That's exactly what I want."

Again Levi hesitated for a moment. "This woman is special, huh."

"Yeah." Brett sighed. He wished he could explain just what it was about Sharon that made him want to go the extra mile—although learning how to get along with her son seemed more like trekking a thousand extra miles. Simply remembering the ghastly Sunday they'd spent together—a Sunday Sharon seemed to think was on the whole rather pleasant—caused his head to throb. There had been the pancake outburst; the pooping-in-the-potty episode; the hysteria when a certain stuffed animal turned up missing, the giddy relief when the animal was found; the rambunctious snack time, the walk to the playground, which was wet from the previous day's rain; the snit when Sharon said he wouldn't be safe climbing on wet apparatus; the furor over whether to go back home; the decision to go to the mall, which had an indoor play area that would be dry; the pleas for lunch at "McDon-o's;" the lunch at a real restaurant, where Max couldn't sit still for more than five minutes at a time, and since there was no ball pit like the one at "McDon-o's," Sharon had occupied him by taking frequent strolls with him around the dining room....

Brett would find it easier hiking to Patagonia than going the extra mile for her. Yet here he was, searching for additional training in order to deal with Max.

"Well, there's a Daddy School class that meets Wednesday evenings at the YMCA," Levi told him, "if you want to go twice a week. That one's for fathers of babies. It's taught by a nurse from Arlington Memorial."

"I don't care who teaches it, or who it's for. I'm not a father, anyway."

"But you want to take the course."

"Not really." He'd rather spend his free time playing tennis or reading a good book. But what choice did he have? One night with Sharon convinced him his heart had already made the choice for him. "I don't want to be this kid's daddy. I just want to be his mommy's friend. If there was a Friend-of-Mommy School, I'd sign up."

"These things aren't always so clear-cut," Levi remarked. "There are a lot of different ways to be a father. The Daddy School was helpful to me."

Brett didn't want to be Max's father in any possible way. But if he studied hard in Daddy School, he might eventually reach a point where he could get through a Sunday morning with the kid. And given that he hoped to spend lots of Saturday nights in Sharon's bed, learning some strategies for surviving Max's Sunday-morning pancake histrionics would be worth the effort.

"I'm pretty sure Allison still teaches the class at the Y on Wednesday," Levi was saying. "For a while it was meeting Mondays, but—"

"I'll call the Y and find out," Brett cut him off.

If Levi went on too long about it, Brett might find an excuse to avoid the class.

He really, really didn't want to have to do this. For Sharon, though… For her, he'd bite the bullet.

"Just as long as it doesn't meet Tuesday nights," Levi said. "Poker takes precedence."

"Absolutely." Brett thanked Levi, promised to pick his pockets clean at the card table the following evening and hung up.

Silence wrapped around him like fog, cushioning him. Outside his window the world was rolling along, hectic and cacophonous. Car engines roared and purred, faulty mufflers rumbled, people shouted. Children acted up and parents scolded. But the window was insulated to contain the air-conditioning, and he could pretend that noise, those acting-up children and their remonstrative parents—didn't exist.

No. He couldn't pretend. Sharon's existence in his soul was like a crack spreading through the window's glass, allowing the world entry. As long as he held on to her, he couldn't escape the noise, the anger, the frenzy.

His phone chirped, making him nostalgic for the days when phones just rang instead of producing polite flutelike signals. He lifted the receiver and heard Janet's piercing voice: "Evelyn and Bill are waiting for you in the conference room. Do you want me to get Leo on the line?" Leo was a trader affiliated with the firm, who worked on Wall Street, and Evelyn and Bill were Brett's senior fund managers. Every Monday morning, they had a conference call with Leo.

"Yeah, get Leo," Brett said, annoyed that he'd needed Janet to remind him of this week's meeting. He ought to know his own schedule—and if he didn't have every last appointment memorized, his daybook lay open on one corner of his desk, listing his obligations, minute by minute. But as soon as he'd let Sharon's kid hijack a piece of his brain, his memory about everything else crumbled. Meetings and talks with Wall Street traders took a back seat to panic about tykes and relationships and age-old wounds.

Once again he wondered how fathers did it. Maybe they were more emotionally stable than Brett. Or so deranged nothing bothered them. Maybe attending Daddy School classes would drive him so insane nothing would bother him, either.

What the hell—his decision to stick around and see what developed with Sharon proved that his mental health was already compromised. Maybe if he let go of his sanity, he'd be a lot happier.

He couldn't be more miserable, he thought as he shoved away from his desk and trudged to the door. Why did poets and romantics claim that love was such a great thing? He wasn't even prepared to consider himself in love, and already he was suffering from a sense of impending doom in the form of a small boy with golden hair, dimples and a teeth-rattling voice capable of shrieking, ''No!''

CHAPTER TWELVE

"IT'S BEDTIME," Sharon told Max.

"No bedtime," he said. If he was less engrossed in finding the piece that would complete the brontosaurus's head in his jigsaw puzzle, he might have argued more vehemently, but he was too deeply involved in the puzzle.

She glanced at her watch. Nearly eight. She still had to get his teeth cleaned, tuck him into bed and read to him—and she wanted him asleep before Brett arrived.

He was planning to come over after his Daddy School class, a midweek class he'd enrolled in to augment his Saturday-morning class. Sharon was so touched by his effort to learn fathering techniques she was willing to do anything to make things easier for him—including getting Max into bed before Brett arrived at her home. After two hours of Daddy School, she imagined that the last person he'd want to see was Max.

Max picked up a piece and walked around his half-done puzzle on the floor, an illustration of dinosaurs with large, squiggle-shaped gaps in it where pieces were missing. There was a pterodactyl's wing, a partial triceratops's horn with a patch of carpet peeking through, and, in the lower left corner, the trunk of a palm that as yet had no fronds.

"It's definitely bedtime," she said, wishing she had as much energy as her son did. She was exhausted. Her schedule at the studio was intense. As the summer wound down, more and more high school seniors had been setting up appointments to have their yearbook photos taken. Every day since Monday, she'd been inundated by teenagers anxious about their hair and their pimples—"Don't worry, they can be airbrushed out," she assured them over and over—and arrogant about their alleged sophistication—"This is my good side," they'd boast, or, "Make sure my eyebrow stud shows." She liked photographing them, and the money was great. But they drained her.

Given how much Max already drained her when he wasn't yet three years old, she dreaded what he'd be like as an adolescent. By then, who knew what sort of body piercing would be in style?

She tried to picture her cherub with a nose ring and laughed. He didn't even have a real nose yet, just a bridgeless little bump of flesh above his lips.

"You can leave the puzzle out and finish it tomorrow," she offered, reaching down and lifting Max off the floor.

He gave a shriek and clung to the puzzle piece in his fist. "No! No bedtime!" he screeched.

"Yes bedtime."

"I'm not done!"

"You can finish tomorrow."

"No, no! I have to put this piece!" He wriggled out of her grip and hovered above the half-finished puzzle, searching for where the piece in his hand belonged. Hunkering down and breathing heavily, he studied the picture.

The doorbell rang.

Sharon breathed a bit heavily herself—partly from frustration that Max was still up and about and partly from anticipation. She hadn't seen Brett since he'd left her town house Sunday afternoon. He'd phoned her Monday and Tuesday evenings and then asked if he could come over after his Daddy School class today, but she hadn't seen him.

Two days, and she'd missed him as if he were already a part of her life.

He was.

"Brett is here," she told Max, who ignored her. He was much too young to be probed for his opinion concerning his mother's boyfriend, but so far he'd accepted Brett without any noticeable balking. Brett concealed his opinions of Max well, thank goodness. Max seemed unaware of Brett's antipathy toward children.

Maybe today's Daddy School class had eroded that antipathy. Maybe after a few more classes Brett would be swearing he adored children.

She could dream, couldn't she?

She climbed the stairs, hurried to the front door and swung it open. The sight of Brett standing on her porch was enough to banish her weariness for a moment. Seeing him made her forget all the potential problems they faced, all the warning signs that flashed through her mind whenever she tried to envision herself in a long-term relationship with him. He had a wonderful way of making her live only in the present. It was irresponsible, reckless, probably idiotic—but when she was with him she couldn't think about what might go sour tomorrow. She could think only about what was so sweet right now.

He stepped inside and closed the door behind him. And then they were kissing—as if Max didn't exist, as if it wasn't bedtime, as if pieces of the dinosaur puzzle didn't lay scattered across the playroom floor. She sank as deeply into the present as she could for one lovely instant.

"Found it!" Max bellowed.

Sharon drew back, but Brett didn't release her. "What did he find?"

"The place where the piece was supposed to go. He's doing a jigsaw puzzle."

"Found it, Mommy!" Max summoned her. Evidently, he wanted her to witness his triumph.

"I'll be right back," she said, but Brett still didn't release her. He only gazed into her face, his eyes a wildflower blue, his smile unbearably seductive. She needed all her willpower to pull out of his embrace, turn her back on him and trudge down the stairs to Max.

Were Brett's sentiments contagious? Was hanging around with him going to make her resent her son, too?

No, she vowed. Absolutely not. Max was still Numero Uno in her life. He was her reality. Brett was...her magic.

"Good job," she praised Max, who had indeed inserted his puzzle piece into the right place, completing the T-rex's leg. "Now it's bedtime."

"Bedtime," Max confirmed, lifting his arms to her and giving her such an angelic smile she felt guilty for having allowed Brett, however briefly, to take precedence over him.

Guilt. Just one more complication she had to contend with as this new phase of her life took shape.

She hugged Max tightly and carried him up the stairs, savoring the wholesome scent of his baby shampoo, the soft cotton knit of his pajamas. "I wanna go potty," he announced just as she reached the top step.

"Good boy! I'm glad you told me. Let's try the potty right now," she said, then caught Brett's eye. He lounged in the doorway between the living room and the kitchen, and his smile was utterly unreadable. Was he grossed out by Max's potty training? Or perhaps by her gushing encouragement of him? Or had he learned in Daddy School that praising a child who took an active interest in toilet training was a good thing?

Or did he simply not care? Was he just going to humor her and pretend Max's well-being mattered to him, because he knew that was the quickest way to Sharon's heart?

He didn't have to pretend. He was already in her heart. "I'll be back soon," she called over her shoulder as she continued up the stairs to the second floor, where Max's bedroom and the potty were located.

She unsnapped his pjs, pulled down his bottoms, removed his diaper and planted him on the colorful plastic seat. He reached for the toilet paper and tore off a square, which he seemed content just to hold. She smiled optimistically. He fluttered the thin sheet of toilet paper through the air and ignored her.

Her phone rang. "I'll be right back," she said, scowling when she realized that was the same promise she'd made to Brett. She wondered if her caller was going to be someone else she loved, someone else who was waiting for her, yearning for her full attention.

It was. "Hi," Deborah said. "How are you?"

She hadn't spoken to Deborah since she'd returned Olivia to her on Saturday afternoon. And though it hadn't been at the forefront of her mind—not with everything else that had occurred over the weekend—she'd been wondering how Deborah's meeting with Raymond had gone. "Hi, Deb! I'm fine. I've got Max on the potty, so I can't talk long."

"Are you on your cordless?"

"No." Sharon had answered the phone in her bedroom. The cordless was downstairs. "It's all right. Max can sit by himself for a few minutes."

"Or else Mr. Wrong can keep him company. That's his car outside your house, isn't it?"

Sharon smiled, not minding her friend's nosiness. If she'd had a spare moment to call Deborah before now, she would have told her how things had been going with Brett. "Yes, that's his car."

"On a weeknight? What's going on?"

"He's visiting. We need to talk, Deb, but now probably isn't the best time."

"Indeed. I tried you on Sunday, but your line was busy and then Livie and I went out. And I haven't had ten minutes to myself since then."

"I know the feeling." Sharon sat on her bed, swung up her legs and leaned back against the headboard. Would Brett be sharing this bed with her tonight? Could they do that on a weeknight? Would it be as wonderful as Saturday night had been? "How did things go with Raymond last Saturday? You never told me."

"Oh, Sharon." Deborah sighed brokenly. "My life's a mess. But you can't talk with Max on the potty."

"Of course I can talk." Sharon straightened up and pressed the phone to her ear, as if that could bring her closer to Deborah. "What happened?"

"Well, we just…we made love."

"Ah." Was that really so terrible? They *were* married, after all. But estranged. On the way to a divorce. "How was it?"

"Honey, don't ask."

"That good, huh."

Deborah sighed again. "What am I going to do? I can't believe we did such a stupid thing. We were both so—I mean, first we were angry, and then we both started crying. And we've got this history of comforting each other when we're sad, you know? It's not like hugging each other was the most unnatural thing in the world. It was practically a reflex."

"So you hugged."

"And one thing led to another. I don't know what to do, Sharon. I miss him. He's a son of a bitch, and we've got lawyers, and I can't count on him to be around when I need him…and I miss him. Like I said, my life's a mess."

"Do you want to come over?"

"I just got Livie into bed. And you've got Max on the toilet. And what's-his-name cooling his heels."

"His name is Brett."

"That's right, Brett. You introduced us on Saturday, but I was a little distracted at the time."

"I noticed." And now Sharon knew why.

"So, what should I do?" Deborah asked. "Should I call off the lawyers or dig in my heels? For all I know, he was just using the oldest trick in the book to soften me up."

"I think he really loves you," Sharon said. "And I know he loves Olivia. The rest is just details." She wasn't sure she believed that. If love could solve every problem and iron out every detail, Brett wouldn't be taking father classes and she wouldn't be worrying about whether she had a future with him.

"I shouldn't take your time up with my problems now." Deborah issued one final sigh. "I'm sorry, laying a number on you like this. We've got to get together and talk, though. Sounds as if you've got more news than I do. You think you'll have a free minute at work tomorrow?"

"Not a chance. It's yearbook time."

"Right. Well, we'll have to connect soon. I need you to talk me out of getting together with Raymond again—at least not until I've got my head on straight. Raymond and I are supposed to see the marriage counselor tomorrow. God knows what I'm going to say to her."

"Tell her your life's a mess," Sharon suggested, then laughed. "Just kidding. Tell her what you told me—that you aren't sure whether Raymond really loves you or he's just manipulating you. See what he has to say for himself."

"But you think he loves me."

"As if I'm any kind of an expert. I'd better go, Deb. I haven't heard a sound from the bathroom in the past few minutes. That's generally a bad sign." When Max got quiet, it was usually because he was doing something naughty, destructive or dangerous.

"We'll talk later." Deborah said a quick goodbye and hung up the phone.

Sharon swung off the bed and strode down the hall to the bathroom. At the open door she froze. Brett was kneeling on the tile floor in front of Max, fastening the tapes of a clean diaper around the child's waist. His back was to her, his head bowed, his hands moving with a speed and intensity that amazed her.

He'd diapered babies before—a long time ago, but apparently he hadn't lost his touch. Max watched him, his eyes round with curiosity. He held his pajama top up, out of Brett's way.

"There," Brett said, smoothing the tapes. "Pull up your bottoms."

"You pull them up," Max demanded, although his voice was soft and awed.

"If you're big enough to use the potty, you're big enough to pull up your own bottoms."

Max looked uncertain, but he bent over and tugged at the elastic waistband. The front of his pajama bottoms rose higher than the back, which got caught on the bulk of his diaper. He struggled to get the pants all the way up.

Brett didn't help him. He simply moved to the sink and scrubbed his hands. When he glanced up, his eyes met Sharon's in the mirrored door of the medicine cabinet. His shrug warded off any comments from her. "You can clean out the potty," he said.

"Of course." She inched into the room, which was barely big enough to accommodate all three of them. Max scampered to her and wrapped his arm around her leg. "I use the potty," he boasted, but he still sounded subdued, as if the entire experience was skewed because Brett had been involved.

"Brett, you didn't have to—"

"He was done. He needed a diaper." He shook the excess water from his hands and dried them on a towel, then turned to her. His face was a handsome blank, offering no indication of how he felt about the whole thing.

Sharon knew how she felt about it—but she couldn't tell him without embarrassing him. To be sure, she didn't want to *tell* him. She wanted to show him, starting with a kiss and moving on to other things. And afterward, lying in his arms, she wanted to thank him for trying so hard to overcome his past, for silencing his demons. For changing a diaper, and changing all his plans and all his dreams, just for her little boy.

Just for her.

SEVERAL HOURS LATER, their bodies cooling side by side atop the wrinkled sheets, she felt she'd done a pretty good job of communicating how she felt. He had his arm around her and her head rested on his shoulder, which was really too bony to be comfortable. She didn't mind, though. She liked the cragginess of it, the way he trailed his fingers through her hair and along the edge of her cheek, the way his rock-hard hip pressed into hers. The way his body took up so much of her bed.

"Can you stay the night?" she asked.

"I didn't bring any fresh clothes with me." He traced the curve of her ear. "Not that that matters. Max'll wake us up so early. I'll have plenty of time to go home, shower and suit up for work."

"Is it hard, what you do?" she asked. He never talked about his work.

He chuckled. "So far, the hardest part of the job has been posing for photos for the annual report." His thumb made a foray behind her ear, definitely an erogenous zone. Her legs twitched and she stifled a tiny moan. "It doesn't seem hard to me, but that's because I've got a talent for it. To me, taking photographs would be hard."

"But you're investing all that money. People trust you with their life's savings."

"They trust me because they know I'll take good care of their funds. And I do. I can't control the market, but my funds almost always come out ahead of the game."

"Why don't you work in New York? That's where Wall Street is."

"I don't have to be on Wall Street. I've got computers, I've got phone lines and I've got an office down in Manhattan, with a small staff who take care of the hands-on stuff and pick up any gossip I might need to know. Investment fund managers are located all over the place, Sharon. You don't have to have a seat on the exchange to do what I do."

"Well, it's nice that you can live here in Arlington, where you want to be." She shifted onto her side, adjusting her head to rest on a less bumpy part of his shoulder, and let her hand come to rest on his chest. She could feel his heart beat, slow and comforting. Ten minutes ago, it had probably been racing as hers had been. But she liked the part of lovemaking that came afterward—the unwinding, the lassitude—almost as much as the sex part. "Where exactly do you live?"

"Would you like to see my house?"

"Not this minute."

"Of course not this minute. How about this weekend?"

Oh, God. This weekend was going to be jammed. When Deborah had phoned earlier that evening,

Sharon had been so startled by her news that she'd forgotten to ask if she could take Max for the day. What if she couldn't? What if she and Raymond were planning another little reconciliation? What if she was expecting Sharon to take Olivia?

"Sharon?" Brett prodded her.

"I'm sorry. I'm just so snowed under. I've got three yearbook shoots scheduled for Saturday morning. And in the afternoon, I was hoping I could finish getting my portfolio ready so I can submit it to the town birthday committee. I've still got to make some prints and get everything organized. The deadline is September 1st."

"How about Friday night?" he asked.

"You mean, to come to your house?" She frowned. Friday night she'd be dealing with Max. If Brett wanted her to bring Max with her to his house, he'd better first childproof the place.

"Why don't you get a baby-sitter for Friday night, and I'll fix us a nice dinner at my house."

What a lovely invitation! A man fixing dinner for her. She couldn't recall any man ever making dinner for her before. Not even Steve, not even after they were married. "I wouldn't be able to stay over, though," she pointed out. "Tracy's only sixteen. I couldn't have her spend the night here with Max. Assuming she even wanted to—"

"Get Tracy for the evening. We'll have a nice, peaceful dinner and then come back here for the night."

"Yes." She kissed the warm skin of his upper chest. "I'd love that. I wish…" She faltered. She'd learned long ago not to play that game, to wish things were different.

"You wish what?" he asked.

"That I didn't have such a wretched schedule lined up for Saturday."

"I'll take Max."

"What?" She jerked out of his arm and sat up so she could see his face. "You'll take him where?"

"You can go to your studio and get your work done. And the portfolio, too. I can bring Max with me to Daddy School—all the guys in the class did that last Saturday. The kids went upstairs and played while the dads had their class downstairs."

"Yes, but that would be just for the morning. Maybe Deborah could take him in the afternoon," she added, planning out loud.

"No." He sat up, too, and gazed squarely at her. "I'm saying I'll take Max for the day, so you can prepare your photos for the Arlington book."

"Why? Why would you do that?"

His grin was crooked, not quite heartfelt. "Because I'm a masochist?" he guessed, then shook his head. He gathered her hand in his, held it up, ran a finger along the lines that creased the curve of her palm. "Because," he said solemnly, "if this thing between us—whatever it is—if it's ever going to have a chance to work, I've got to get used to dealing with Max. There's no way around it."

Then he wanted "this thing" between them to go forward. He wanted to look ahead, to consider a future for him and Sharon. Her heart pounded harder than it had when they'd been locked together, cresting together. He was talking about love.

"It doesn't seem fair," she murmured, unable to look away from him. "You're making all the sacrifices, all the adjustments. You're going to the Daddy

School, you're willing to take care of Max for the day, you're—I don't know, hinting that you're rethinking your entire view of children. And what am I doing for you? What am I giving up?''

"Do you have to give something up? Do you think I'm giving something up?" He sighed. "I guess I'm prepared to find out if the rewards are greater than the sacrifices. Or maybe…maybe I just think it's time to get over it. I'm not eight years old anymore. And you're not my mother. You're not dumping your responsibilities on me." He lifted her hand and kissed the tips of her fingers. "I don't know if this is going to work out, Sharon. I'm pretty good at predicting stock trends, but I don't have a crystal ball when it comes to this kind of thing. All I know is, you're the first woman I've ever met who made me believe it was worth trying. So—I'm going to try."

Her eyes welled up with tears. A few spilled over and trickled down her cheeks. Brett's words were more romantic than his dinner invitation, more romantic even than a confession of love.

"What's with the crying?" he asked, his smile genuine this time.

She sniffled and brushed a stray tear away with her free hand. "I'm crying because I'm happy," she told him. "I'm so glad you came into my life, Brett."

"As I recall, you came into mine. With that belly dancer doll. That's what really turned me on, Sharon—that doll of yours."

She laughed. And cried. And climbed into his lap, wrapped her arms around him and held on to him as if he were a miraculous gift. For nearly three long years, she had struggled, gotten by, loved her son and made the best of her fate. But now she didn't have to use gels and angles to make her life look better than it was. The lighting was ideal, the focus perfect. Brett had made it so.

ONCE AGAIN, he couldn't sleep. She was practically comatose beside him. No doubt raising a toddler and running a business by herself sucked all the energy out of her.

Well, not all. She'd had enough energy to make him crazy with lust. If he chose to analyze it, he'd probably come up with a valid explanation for why sex was so damned good between them. Maybe because she'd gone so long without, and he was the lucky beneficiary of her voraciousness. Except she wasn't exactly voracious. She was eager, welcoming—but completely tuned in to him. It wasn't just sex she responded to. It was Brett.

He'd never been the sort of guy for whom any woman would do. He was responding to her just as specifically as she responded to him. The way her body felt around him, the way her eyes glazed and her breath caught and her hands slid across his skin... She was strong. He liked that. Strong and wholehearted. During those moments when they were loving each other, nothing else existed in her consciousness or his. It was all about Sharon and Brett, two people who needed and wanted and trusted each other.

But he didn't choose to analyze it. Some things were better left unexamined, simply accepted with gratitude.

He eased out of bed, then turned to check on her. She hadn't moved. Her eyes were closed, her lips parted, her hand dangling over the edge of the mattress. He grabbed his jeans, pulled them on and glanced at her again. The only sign of life was the rise and fall of her bosom as she breathed.

She had beautiful breasts, full and round. He lifted the top sheet over them so he wouldn't spend the next half hour staring at them and reliving their love-making.

Barefoot, he made no sound as he tiptoed across the carpet to the door. He eased it open and stepped out. Max's bedroom door stood wide, and the glow of his night-light laid a slash of amber across the floor of the hallway. He nudged the door wider and peered inside.

Max was a lump at the center of his bed. His butt was hunched upward, his knees tucked under him, his head half hidden by a stuffed animal. He snored faintly.

Once Brett's eyes had adjusted to the dim light, he surveyed the room. A mobile hung from the ceiling above the bed, airplanes floating on arched wires. A bookshelf by the bed held a collection of picture books, plastic blocks, a sturdy-looking boom box and a stack of cassette tapes. A chest of drawers stood against one wall, a toy chest against another, with a child-size chair and desk beside it. A convoy of yellow toy trucks was parked under the desk, along with a tiny sock and striped ball.

Brett recalled the miniature desk he'd sat on at the Daddy School class last Saturday. At least the class he'd attended at the YMCA that evening had featured adult-size furniture.

The class itself hadn't offered him much. The teacher was intelligent and knowledgeable, but the subject—injuries and illnesses in children—wasn't relevant to him. He needed to learn how to feel comfortable around children, not how to remove splinters or deal with chronic ear infections or how to know when to race to the emergency room.

But he'd gained something from the class anyway: an awareness that he wasn't all that different from other men. They loved their children but felt overwhelmed by them, many of them harboring a secret fear that they'd lost an essential part of themselves to their offspring. "When I'm with him, I feel as if I'm not really human," one new father had confessed. "I'm just this machine that supplies things. Strained carrots, clean diapers, a shoulder to burp on. I'm like a slave."

Brett could sure as hell relate to that sentiment. So, apparently, could most of the other fathers. Allison Winslow, the neonatal nurse who taught the class, let them talk about that for a while, kind of like a support group. The discussion didn't solve anything, but it made Brett realize that he wasn't a freak, missing the vital gene for nurturing. These were fathers, men who had voluntarily decided to bring a new life into the world, and yet they resented their children, the precious babies they loved. They suffered from doubt and rage, just like him.

But they were managing. They were serving as the supply machines to their children, and doing it willingly, doing it without letting themselves get knocked out of alignment. Why? Maybe because they loved the children. Maybe because they loved the children's mothers.

Brett was no slouch. He was smart, he was successful, he was wealthy, and he was one of the top ten tennis players at his club. If these other men could cope, he could, too.

He didn't love Max. But Sharon?

He could do this for her.

CHAPTER THIRTEEN

"DID I TELL YOU I'm not much of a cook?" Brett asked, his smile tinged with guilt. Across the polished-granite counter in his kitchen stood the evidence: a disposable foil pan filled with lasagna, a plastic-wrapped loaf of garlic bread, plastic bags filled with ready-to-serve salad fixings and several empty shopping bags featuring the logo of a major supermarket.

"After working all day," Sharon said, "I didn't expect you to come home and cook a complete meal."

"I can cook a few things," he admitted as he set the oven temperature and turned the oven on. "Fried eggs. Hamburgers. Steak, as long as you don't mind if it's a little underdone or overdone. Oh, and I can pour a mean bowl of cereal."

Sharon laughed. "Cereal, huh? And fried eggs. Breakfast must be your specialty."

"Someday you'll have to let me show you." His smile faded just a bit.

Sharon felt hers wane, too. To have Brett demonstrate his breakfast talents for her would require an overnight stay at his house. And she would love to spend the night with him here.

Thanks to Max, that was hardly likely to happen. If only...

No, she wouldn't let her mind wander down the if-only path. Brett was doing his damnedest to overcome his resentment of Max. Sharon couldn't let herself move in the opposite direction, chafing at the obstacles Max imposed on her love life.

In fact, having Brett fix her steak and eggs and cereal after spending the night in his bed might not be a complete impossibility. Deborah had offered more than once to let Max sleep over at her place; one of these days, Sharon ought to accept. Then she and Brett could dream together, limbs entwined, breathing synchronized. They could wake up slowly, drifting together in that netherworld between sleep and consciousness. They could make love in the morning, without having to cringe at the clock or strain for the sound of Max prowling around the house. And then they could sip coffee and indulge in a leisurely breakfast feast, one that included no spills, no drumming on the table with tiny fists, no discussion of potties and diapers—and not a single mention of the word *no*.

It could happen. Maybe someday it would.

She wasn't sure what she'd expected Brett's house to be like, but she was surprised by the reality. He lived not on the ritzy west side of town but on the east side, in a cozy neighborhood of well-maintained residences and ancient trees. From the outside, his house looked like a modest ranch, sided in weathered gray shingles and trimmed with simple white shutters. But interior walls must have been removed to open the space, creating airy, light-filled rooms. The wall paint was clean and devoid of smudgy little fingerprints. The floors were hardwood, warmed by beige rugs. Such pale rugs were utterly impractical, she thought—a mother's reflexive appraisal.

She'd arrived at his place at seven, after having fed and bathed Max, showered, donned a summer-weight slacks outfit and gotten Max and Tracy organized with one of his favorite videos. Brett had obviously showered and changed from his work clothes, too; he wore jeans and a polo shirt the same blue as his eyes. His hair was still damp and scored with tracks left by his comb.

She was also surprised by how comfortable she felt in his house. Probably because he himself was so comfortable. Without Max underfoot, he seemed relaxed. His mouth settled easily into a smile.

He filled a goblet with red wine and handed it to her. "I've got some stuff still to do here," he said, waving grandly at the bags of prewashed vegetables conveniently cut into chunks. "You're welcome to keep me company, or you can go explore."

Much as she'd love keeping him company, she couldn't resist his generous invitation. "I think I'll explore," she said. "It would break my heart to have to watch you slaving over a hot stove."

He shot her a sharp look, then laughed and got busy searching his cabinets, probably for some utensil he never used because he rarely cooked.

She carried her wine out of the kitchen, through a dining area and into what appeared to be a den extending off the back of the house. It overlooked a slightly overgrown yard, one she could envision a bit neater, with a vegetable garden cut out of one corner and Max's colorful plastic tricycle parked on the patio.

No, she mustn't think that way.

Turning from the sliding glass doors that opened onto the yard, she surveyed the room. It looked like a typical male lair: big-screen TV, oversize leather couch and chairs, state-of-the-art stereo equipment, VCR and DVD. Just like Max, Brett filled his playroom with his toys.

She scanned the teak bookcases lining one wall. Judging by the books on his shelves, she concluded that he had a taste for popular history and biography and novels about financial skullduggery. Some classics were mixed in among the thrillers—holdovers from his college days, perhaps. At the bottom of one shelf, half-hidden by the bulky swivel recliner, a thick leather-bound book lay on its side.

A photo album.

She glanced behind her, as if afraid to get caught snooping. But he'd invited her to explore. If certain parts of his house were off-limits, he should have warned her.

She was a photographer. Of course she'd be curious about his photographs. Maybe the album contained pictures of old girlfriends, or of exotic places he'd visited. Or his family.

She lifted the heavy book, sank into the recliner and spread the cover open across her knees. The first several pages were filled with pictures of a dark-haired, blue-eyed man who looked uncannily like Brett.

His father. Sharon's heart squeezed painfully as she studied the pictures. Like her own son, Brett had lost the most important man in his life. All he had left of his father were his memories and these photos.

In a couple of the pictures, Brett's father was alone. In a few, including a somewhat stiffly posed wedding picture, he was with Brett's mother, a pretty woman with a round face and fluffy brown hair, both her and her new husband youthful and hopeful and unnaturally prim in their formal attire. And then, on the next page, a precious collection of photos of Brett with his father—as an infant in his father's arms, a baby perched uncertainly on his father's knee, and a few months older, gleefully straddling his father's shoulders, his hands poked triumphantly into the air. She could see traces of the man she knew in that adorable little boy's smile, his radiant eyes.

Brett didn't appear the least bit troubled in that picture, or in the one where he stood with his tiny feet balanced atop his father's big ones, his hands safely within his father's and another powerful smile on his chubby young face. Or in the one where he sat in the bend of his father's arm, his head higher than his father's as he reached into the branches of an apple tree.

She turned the page. Brett was no longer a toddler in the next array of photos. He was already a school-age child, and his smile was gone.

She studied the pictures more closely. Other, younger children populated them—his half siblings, no doubt. They occupied the foreground, an infant propped up in front of Brett, or filling his lap and obliterating most of his face. On the next page, more infants and toddlers, hamming it up for the camera while Brett retreated into the background, an anxious expression darkening his face. A picture of an eight-year-old Brett struggling to hold up a two-year-old. A picture of all four siblings standing in a row on a porch, dressed up for some fancy occasion, and Brett lurking behind them, barely visible. A photo of the younger children in party hats while Brett carried plates of birthday cake to a table.

A well of rage erupted inside Sharon. She wanted to flip back to the first pages, to scream at the blandly pretty face of his mother, the woman who had made an eight-year-old boy serve birthday cake to his raucous siblings. Why were there no photos of *him* at a table in a party hat? Didn't he ever get to celebrate?

She forced her anger down. His mother had suffered a tragic loss—if anyone knew how painful such a situation could be, it was Sharon—and then had battled depression. But still, why was the album filled with page after page of photos featuring happy youngsters and an older brother being nudged out of the way, upstaged, forced into the shadows? Why weren't there any pictures of Brett front and center, with his siblings gazing up at him, admiring him, allowing him his moment?

No wonder he didn't like children. And no wonder he didn't like having his photo taken. If these pictures represented the sum of his experience facing a camera...

"What are you looking at?" his voice broke into her thoughts.

"Oh, Brett, I—" She had no reason to feel guilty, but she did. Not for peeking at his photo album but for seeing so much in it, for understanding so much. "I didn't think you'd mind."

He crossed the den and lifted the heavy book off her lap. His expression was noncommittal as he scanned the page she'd had it open to. "That's my family," he said.

"I figured."

He gazed at the pictures for a minute longer, then

closed the book and slid it onto the shelf. ''Dinner's ready.''

She wasn't sure what to say. She doubted he would want to hear her instant psychoanalysis of him based on what she'd seen in the pictures, or her critique of the photographs themselves, their composition and subtext. He extended his hand to help her out of the chair's deep cushions, and when she peered into his face she knew he didn't want her to say anything at all.

But he was Brett, a man trying so hard to overcome so much—for her.

She took his hand, let him hoist her to her feet, and then wrapped her arms around him. ''I love you,'' she murmured into the hollow of his neck.

He remained silent, unmoving. She'd probably startled him, maybe alarmed him. If there was anything some men feared more than being psychoanalyzed, it was hearing the words *I love you* spoken to them by a woman.

She hadn't said them to pressure him, or to extract promises or commitments from him. She'd said them only because her heart ached for the child he'd been and soared at the man he was, the man he was trying to become. She'd said them because they were true.

Slowly, his arms closed around her. She felt acceptance in his embrace, in the light kiss he planted on her forehead. He might not be able to say he loved her, but at least she hadn't scared him away. He was still here, holding her.

HE DREAMED she was slipping away from him. He reached for her and felt only air, and his arms dropped back to the bed, useless. Then he opened his eyes and discovered he hadn't been dreaming.

"Shh," she whispered from across the room. "Go back to sleep. I'll wake you up later."

He glanced at her clock radio, winced at the red digits—6:42—and closed his eyes. Sleeping without Sharon, he'd discovered, was nowhere near as satisfying as sleeping with her—but sleeping with her often meant not getting much sleep at all.

He rolled over, drew the covers up and shut his eyes. Let her handle the first shift with the kid, get him cleaned, dressed and fed. Brett would have to take over soon enough.

Why had he agreed to this plan? He knew the logical reasons: he wanted Sharon to finish her proposal so she could submit it to the city's birthday committee. He wanted to be helpful. He wanted to get over his old hang-ups about children. He'd be attending his third Daddy School class later that morning, and three classes ought to be enough to make him an expert.

But there was another reason. There had to be. He'd long ago jettisoned the need to prove anything, to himself or Sharon or anyone else. He had a successful business, a nice home, an active social life. He didn't have to pad his résumé.

If he wasn't so damned tired, he might be able to figure out the real reason he'd volunteered to take care of Max for the day. To slay his demons? To make peace with his past? To show Sharon...*something*. Something about how he intended to fit himself into her world.

Someone patted his shoulder, then gave it a gentle

shake. He flinched. She'd told him to go back to sleep. Why was she bothering him now?

"Brett? It's eight-thirty. I've got to leave."

Eight-thirty? He opened his eyes and his vision filled with her. She looked fresh and neat, ready to depart for her studio. Her skin glowed; her hair was pinned back from her face, and she seemed almost girlish, her cheeks and jawline somehow softened. Freedom made her youthful, he thought. Shedding her maternal responsibilities and knowing she could work undisturbed for an entire day, not just on paid assignments but on a project she was doing on spec, probably stripped ten years off her age. He could only wonder at the burden being a mother placed on her.

That was it, the reason he'd been groping for earlier: he had offered to take care of Max so Sharon could be carefree. He had agreed to be a substitute daddy for a day so she could take a break from being a mommy. It was his gift to her.

He sat up and threw off the covers. Her gaze drifted down his naked body, and he responded the way any healthy man would respond when a woman looked at him like that, her eyes smoky and her cheeks growing pink. He found himself contemplating other gifts he could give her, gifts that would bring him as much pleasure as they brought her.

With a wistful smile, he rose and reached for his jeans. They'd had yesterday evening at his house. And last night, after they'd come to her place and sent the baby-sitter home. And they would have tonight. Whatever thoughts were floating through her head—and he felt safe in assuming they resembled the thoughts floating through his—would just have to wait until that evening, when Max was asleep and they could put down the parent burden for a few precious hours.

Meanwhile, it was time for him to shoulder that burden for the day.

He headed into the bathroom, and when he returned to the bedroom she was gone, no doubt making sure Max wasn't climbing through a window or scribbling with crayons on the walls. That was how Brett was going to have to spend his day, he thought grimly—preventing Max from destroying the house and/or himself. The Daddy School class would eat up most of the morning, and then maybe he'd take the kid to "McDon-o's" for lunch and frolicking in that sea of plastic balls. And then Max would nap. So it would really be only a couple of hours in the afternoon when Brett would actually have to play a father-son duet with Max.

Once he was dressed, he descended the stairs. Sharon waited near the door, her patience a thin veneer. "I wish I could stay while you had your breakfast," she said, the words rushing out as she checked her watch, "but I've got to run. Help yourself to whatever you want in the kitchen. You know where the diapers are, and all Max's toys. I got his car seat out of my car—" she pointed to it, resting on the floor near the front door "—so you can put it in your car. Make sure you strap it firmly to the seat. And I wrote down the phone number at the studio and left it on the kitchen table. And Max's favorite milk cup—"

"Go," Brett said, sounding more confident than he felt. "Max and I will be fine. Where is he, anyway?"

"Downstairs. I already said goodbye to him. He was too busy playing to care. I guess he won't miss me." She smiled and reached for the doorknob.

"I'll miss you," Brett assured her, meaning it more than just romantically. He'd miss her whenever it was time to change Max's diaper, whenever Max demanded food, whenever he started to whine.

"If I have a free minute, I'll give you a call to see how things are going," she promised. "If you're really desperate, bring him to the studio. I'll be there."

"Go," Brett ordered her again, covering her hand with his and twisting the knob. The door swung open, and he kissed her. He'd shaved yesterday evening, but he could feel the roughness of his own cheek against her smooth one.

She didn't seem to mind. She kissed him back, then sighed, stepped out onto the porch and said, "Have fun!"

He smiled, waved, closed the door and cursed. *Have fun.* Yeah, right.

Okay. He'd agreed to do this for her, and he was going to do it. Fun wasn't the point of the exercise.

He strode toward the kitchen, then paused at the top of the stairs. "How're you doing down there?" he called.

"Busy," Max called back.

Good. He might be busy applying a snub-nosed scissor to the carpet or gluing scraps of construction paper to the TV screen, but he wasn't asking for Brett's supervision, so Brett chose not to provide it. He continued into the kitchen, filled a bowl with cornflakes and milk and smiled when he spotted the fresh pot of coffee and the mug Sharon had left for him. He filled the mug, then turned around and leaned against the counter, propping the bowl in his hand and scooping a spoonful of cornflakes into his mouth.

Max suddenly appeared in the doorway, clad in a pair of shorts and a T-shirt with Look Out, World! printed across the front. He dragged his stuffed teddy bear behind him. "Where's Mommy?"

"She went to work," Brett told him, then shoveled another spoonful of cereal into his mouth. He had the feeling Max wasn't going to allow him to enjoy a leisurely breakfast.

"I want Mommy," Max said, his lower lip quivering.

"She's not here right now."

"I want her!" Max's voice grew louder and more tremulous. "I want Mommy."

Ten minutes into the day, and already the shit was hitting the fan. "She's working today," Brett said, setting the bowl in the sink and taking a bracing sip of coffee. He needed caffeine more than he needed cornflakes. "She's working," he repeated to the little boy, who stared up at him dubiously. "You and I are going to hang out together till she gets home. Didn't she explain this to you?"

"I want my mommy," Max said, his eyes welling with tears, but his volume decreasing. "I want her."

"Why don't we go downstairs and you can show me what you've been up to?"

Max considered his options for a long moment, then turned and stomped down the stairs. A small victory for Brett.

The playroom at the bottom of the stairway was a scene of bedlam. Toys covered the floor—brightly colored plastic blocks, brightly colored plastic ani-

mals, brightly colored plastic cars, a toy telephone
and a space shuttle. Although the finished basement
room had no windows, Brett wished he had his sunglasses to shield his eyes from the glare of gaudy
plastic.

Max plopped himself onto the floor amid all that
color and wept.

Oh, hell.

Brett placed his mug on a shelf and lowered himself to the floor next to Max, careful not to sit on
any toys. He felt a surge of the kind of panic he used
to feel when his brothers and sister cried and he was
the only one around to comfort them. He'd been so
miserable, how could he possibly have cheered them
up? Who was going to cheer *him* up?

He wasn't a pathetic child anymore, though. He
was an adult with his own life. He could handle
Max's sadness without feeling put upon. No one had
put anything upon him, anyway. He'd chosen this.

Awkwardly, he arched his arm around Max. The
child bawled, first resisting him and then crumpling
against him. "Mommy! Mommy!" he lamented, as
if grieving over a death.

Was he afraid he was going to lose his mother?
He'd never even known his father, but maybe he understood the idea of loss. Maybe in his subconscious
he recognized the permanence of death. Brett could
relate to that.

"She'll be back later," he promised. "Your
mother will be home later."

"Want her now!"

The side of Brett's shirt was damp from Max's
tears. The kid was small but sturdy, with broad
shoulders and a head as hard as a bowling ball. He'd

make a hell of a football player someday, Brett thought. Possibly a tennis player. He hoped to God the boy didn't decide to take up skiing, the sport that had killed his father.

"How about if I read you a book?" he suggested.

"No."

"Do you want to build something with your blocks?"

"No."

"How about pushing the cars around for a while?" Brett asked, nudging a vibrant orange vehicle across the carpet. He knew better than to present Max with an open-ended question: *What do you want to do?* When he used to ask his siblings that question, they'd always provide dreadful, if honest, answers: "I want to fly!" "I want to have ice cream!" "I want to hit my sister!" He'd learned his lesson; he wasn't going to ask Max.

Max showed no interest in toy cars, so Brett gathered up an assortment of books, some from a shelf and others from the floor. He grabbed his now tepid coffee and resumed his seat next to Max on the carpet. He read *Curious George; The Cat in the Hat;* a yawner about a butterfly that couldn't decide which flower to land on; *Curious George* again; a bowdlerized version of *Alice In Wonderland,* and, at Max's insistence, *Curious George* yet again. As he read, he thought longingly of how hot and fragrant the coffee had been when he'd entered the kitchen. He thought of that morning's edition of the *Arlington Gazette* sitting on the table. If not for Max, he could have relaxed with his breakfast, read the paper and savored every sip of his coffee.

Instead, there he was, his butt sore from sitting on

the floor and Max beside him, jabbing a pudgy finger at the *Curious George* book and saying, "Read it again."

Finally, the hour rescued him. "No more *Curious George*," he said. "We've got to leave."

"Where?" Max demanded. "Where we going?"

"To your preschool. You'll get to play there."

"My school?"

"Right."

"I have to go potty."

So they did the potty thing. Brett discovered that Sharon had bought Max disposable training pants. He suggested that Max try wearing one of those, but Max balked and insisted on not just any diaper but a diaper with rockets printed across the waistband. The kid seemed so fragile, like a bubble about to burst. Brett wasn't going to push him on something as trivial as underwear.

It took him a while to get Max's car seat set up in his car. While he worked the straps, Max raced around the lawn that spread in front of the row of town houses. "Livie is here!" he shouted, pointing to the town house next door to his own. "I play with her!" His spirits seemed to improve in the warm morning sun. Maybe he'd just needed some fresh air and a little running room.

At last Brett had the seat secured. Max decided to flee from Brett, but he didn't get far; Brett snagged him, hauled him back to the car and buckled him into his seat. Then he deposited the tote bag Sharon had packed with diapers, juice, crackers and assorted toys on the floor behind the driver's seat and got in.

He arrived at the preschool a few minutes late. He hadn't realized how much extra time it took to get places when you were transporting a toddler. But the class had barely begun, and after Max spent a minute shrieking Molly's name, he joined the other children upstairs, leaving Brett to soak up wisdom with the fathers downstairs.

For a woman with two children of her own, Molly Saunders-Russo struck Brett as unnervingly serene. "When my stepson was two, he was terribly moody," she told the fathers, who, like last week, were grouped within a partitioned area of the first-floor room, some seated on the floor and others, like Brett, perched on tables and counters. "He had valid reasons for his moodiness," she continued. "Children can't always articulate the things that set them off, but just because they can't tell us what's bothering them doesn't mean nothing's bothering them. We might ask, 'Are you upset about not having a birthday party this year?' and they'll say no, or they'll start talking about something else, and we'll assume they're okay. But their mood will emerge in some other way. Let's discuss how we can help our children cope with their moods, even when they don't know or can't tell us what's bugging them."

The conversation became spirited. As with last week's class, and the class he'd attended at the YMCA on Wednesday evening, Brett kept his mouth shut and his ears open. He wasn't a father. But he could learn something. Max struck him as a moody little boy—and why shouldn't he be moody? He had no father, his mother worked and he didn't always get his way.

"Sometimes when my daughter is really in a state over something," one of the fathers ventured, "I can calm her down by giving her something—like a cookie, or a special toy. I have the feeling that's not a smart move, but it works.''

A lot of the other fathers nodded.

''Just because something works doesn't mean you should do it,'' Molly gently chided. With her petite build and her cute round face, she looked like a pixie, someone magically connected to the world of children. Yet she sounded more mature than any of the fathers in the class. ''When you give your daughter a cookie to calm her down, she learns that if she throws a fit she'll get a cookie. That isn't a good lesson for her.''

They analyzed other strategies, most of which fell into two categories: leaving the kid alone and smothering the kid with attention. Brett wasn't sure how helpful that advice was.

But he continued to listen, to absorb the debate. The most important thing Molly said, as far as he was concerned, was that children felt losses in ways adults weren't always aware of or sensitive to. Again Brett's mind wandered to Max, heroically trying to live his life without a father. Brett hadn't had a father, either, and he'd soldiered on just as heroically— because he hadn't had a choice. By the time his mother had remarried, he'd realized he was never going to get his father back. His stepfather was the best he could hope for, and while the guy hadn't been evil or obnoxious, he hadn't been Brett's father, either. Nothing could ever alter the loss he'd suffered.

Had he been moody? Definitely. He'd been stoical in public, doing what was demanded of him, never complaining...but the resentments had piled up inside him, the pain layering into a laminated wall that separated him from his family, from his sister and brothers, from all children. He liked to think he wasn't moody anymore, but the wall was still there.

With a few cracks in it, thanks to Sharon.

He was still mulling over thoughts about children and loss and temperament when noon arrived and children stormed down the stairs, hollering for their fathers and swearing that they were dying of hunger. Max was no exception. He seemed delighted when Brett suggested McDonald's.

"We go McDon-o's!" Max crowed, so excited he had to jump and clap his hands. "We go McDon-o's!"

Definitely moody, Brett acknowledged. Max had traveled from inconsolable despair to rowdy exuberance in one morning. Just thinking about such a journey exhausted Brett.

McDonald's was as noisy as it had been last week. Even though the weather was nicer, the place was packed with children and their parents. Brett let Max flop around in the ball pit while he stood in line and purchased their food. When Max made milk squirt out of his straw, Brett didn't scold. When Max smeared ketchup on his nose, Brett only sighed. The symphony of shrill children's voices from the play area throbbed inside his head, but he simply ate his burger, sipped his soda and resolved to ask Molly at next week's class how she managed to stay so calm. After all, as the director of a preschool, she thrived within this sort of pandemonium every day.

"Are you done?" Brett asked Max, who seemed to be playing with his fries more than eating them.

"Go on the slide," Max said, wriggling down from his seat and heading back toward the play area.

Brett drank the last of his soda and watched as

Max climbed the ladder to the slide and rode it down, landing with a plop in the balls and giggling. If a kid was going to have a mood, Brett supposed a manic mood was better than a depressive one. Max climbed the ladder and slid down again, and again. Brett fantasized about popping a couple of aspirin as soon as they got back to Sharon's place.

Please, Max, he prayed silently, *get sleepy. If you take a nap, I'll be a happy man.* As Max rode down the slide yet again, Brett smiled. The more energetically he played here, the more pooped he'd be when they got back to the Village Green Condominiums.

Watching Max career down the slide, he caught glimpses of Sharon in the boy's face—his fair coloring, his sharp chin, his concentration as he scaled the ladder. His determination, his refusal to let sorrow crush him.

She'd made a miracle out of her son, he realized. Even a man who didn't like children could admire what a widowed woman had accomplished without any help: she'd raised a healthy, headstrong boy who, despite everything, refused to quit.

Brett gathered the trash from their table and deposited it in the nearest trash can. Max might still seem full of energy, but the drive home would probably tucker him out. Then he'd nap and Brett would call the day a success.

Max raised only a token protest when Brett summoned him from the ball pit. "I want to play," he asserted.

"It's time to go home." The sudden shriek of a little girl who'd spilled her soda convinced him of that. The building practically shook from the intensity of her screams. What a perfect time to leave.

Max reluctantly let Brett take his hand and lead
him from the restaurant. He climbed into his seat and
remained still while Brett strapped him in. He must
be tired, Brett thought hopefully.

Neither of them spoke during the drive home. Beyond the windows the world shimmered with heat,
but inside the car the air-conditioning whispered
gently, cooling the edges of Brett's headache. He
glanced in the rearview mirror and saw Max clinging
to his stuffed bear and staring out the window.

Once he got Max into bed, he thought, he'd fix
himself some coffee and read the paper. He'd have
the leisurely breakfast—minus the cereal—he'd been
denied that morning. He'd unwind. He'd think about
Sharon getting her portfolio together, preparing her
submission. He'd have to give Murphy's wife, Gail,
a call this week to let her know Sharon's proposal
was on its way. Ultimately, the committee would decide whom to award the commission to, but Brett
would make a case for Sharon. She was talented; she
worked so hard—she performed miracles. She deserved the job.

He pulled up to the curb in front of her town
house, glanced in the mirror again and saw that Max
was still awake, although he seemed on the far side
of mellow. Smiling, Brett climbed out of the car,
opened the back door and unbuckled Max's seat belt.

As if he'd emitted an electrical charge to the kid,
Max scrambled out of his seat, completely reener-
gized. "I want to play!" he yelled.

Brett cursed. He didn't want to play. He wanted
the kid to go to bed so he could have a little time to
himself.

But Max had shifted into high gear. He shoved

past Brett and out onto the grass, knocking over the tote bag in his eagerness. Brett tossed the spilled items back into the bag, hauled it out of the car and slammed the door. "Let's go, Max," he said, stalking across the lawn.

Max gave a little leap and darted away. "I play now!"

"Get back here," Brett scolded, dropping the tote bag so he could chase after Max. A juice box and a few diapers spilled from the tote, and he paused to cram them back in.

Max giggled and ran some more.

"Max! Get back here!"

The brat halted, laughed and then ran on, his legs pumping hard. "I play!" he cheered. "You can't catch me!"

That was a lie. Brett easily caught him, clamped his hand hard around Max's upper arm and yanked him to a halt.

Max let out a howl. "Ow! Let go! It hurts!"

"No." He was annoyed, he was tired and he wasn't going to let Max make a fool out of him.

"Let go! Let go! Ow!" The kid started crying real tears.

Brett took a deep breath. He was letting his anger and frustration rule him. His hand was big and strong—maybe he was bruising Max's arm. He immediately relented, loosening his grip.

Max slid his arm free, then burst into laughter. "I play!" he taunted, spinning and running away from Max again.

"Get back here!" Brett shouted, rage and impatience bubbling over inside him. He'd devoted his entire damned day to the kid, and now the kid was mocking him, laughing and running and ignoring the fact that Brett was also a human being, deserving of a little respect.

"I play!" Max hooted, charging across the lawn.

"Play, then," Brett snarled, glaring at him.

Max grinned. "Catch me!"

Brett shuddered. He might as well have been eight or nine or ten again, with his brothers and sister squealing, "Brett! Brett! Do this for me! Do that for me! Watch me, Brett! Help me, Brett!"

"Catch me!" Max challenged him.

"No." Brett stormed over to the tote, stuffed its contents securely back into it and started toward the front door.

"Catch me! Catch me!"

In his peripheral vision he saw Max race toward the curb that separated the front lawn from the street. *The street.* "No!" he shouted, dropping the tote and charging after Max.

Max was moving fast now, fueled by his lunch. The only cars Brett saw were parked—but a teenager suddenly zoomed down the asphalt on a skateboard, barreling down the road, traveling way too fast.

"Max!" he shouted. "Stop!"

Max spun around and gave Brett a brash grin. Behind him, the teenager leaped off his skateboard, unable to control it. The skateboard veered up the curb, its speed launching it off the ground, and slammed into Max's back.

Brett had heard a lot of children's screams in his life—but none of them sounded as horrible as Max's utter silence as he fell.

CHAPTER FOURTEEN

DON'T FALL APART, Sharon ordered herself, skidding the old Volvo to a stop between the painted lines of a parking space outside the emergency room entrance to Arlington Memorial. *You can't fall apart. You mustn't.*

Her heart felt as if it had risen to the base of her throat and was choking her with every pulse. Her baby. Her baby was hurt. On the phone, Brett had told her it wasn't bad, but if it wasn't bad why were they at the hospital?

It was bad. Oh, God. It was bad.

Don't fall apart.

He was standing right inside the sliding glass door, watching for her. Ordinarily, she would have flown into his arms, seeking comfort. But she was too distraught. Her baby was hurt. She had to see her baby. She couldn't think about anything else.

"He's fine," Brett told her before she could ask.

"Where is he?" She wouldn't believe anything anyone told her until she saw Max.

"He's right over here." Brett took her arm, but she could only see his hand cupping her elbow. She couldn't feel him. This man could usually arouse her with a single touch, but right now she was numb, removed from her surroundings. Until she was with her baby, nothing else existed, not even Brett, not even her love for him.

He was leading her somewhere, but before they got far a woman in civilian apparel intercepted them. "Is this the mother?" the woman asked.

"Yes," Brett said.

"I'm going to need some information, insurance and authorizations—"

"Let me see my baby," Sharon whispered.

"We'll take care of the paperwork later." Brett nudged the clerk aside and ushered Sharon around a bend in the hall to a curtained alcove. On the other side of the curtain, she saw Max seated at the center of a hospital bed. A nurse in crisp blue scrubs sat behind him on the mattress, her hands on his shoulders and her legs hanging over the edge. A doctor stood to one side, jotting notes on a clipboard.

"Mommy!" Max smiled.

He looked okay. Really. A scrape on his chin, covered with a small surgical bandage, and splatters of blood on the front of his shirt. Both knees scabby with blood and taped with gauze. But he was okay. He recognized her. He was reaching for her.

She flew across the enclosed space and wrapped her arms around him. "Not too tight," the nurse cautioned when Sharon would have smothered him in a hug. "He's got a pretty nasty bruise on his back."

"Oh, my baby, my sweetie!" Now that she knew he was okay, she could fall apart, and she did, releasing great, heaving sobs of relief. "Oh, Max! My love. Are you all right? I love you!"

"Mommy," he sighed into her neck.

"He's fine," the nurse told her. "He had the wind knocked out of him, but he's going to be fine."

"Are you sure?" Still clinging to him, she twisted to view the doctor, searching for confirmation.

He peered up from his clipboard and nodded. "Some bruises and abrasions, but nothing serious. No fractures, no concussion, no internal injuries. That's one tough little boy."

"What happened?" Now that her heart was beginning to settle back down into her rib cage and her arms were filled with her precious son, she could start thinking again. Her gaze sought Brett. He stood at the edge of the curtain, as far from the bed as he could be without leaving the area. "All you told me was that there was an accident and you'd brought Max here. What happened?"

"He got hit by a flying skateboard," Brett told her.

"I got hit," Max said proudly.

"The skateboarder lost control of it...." Brett sighed and looked away for a minute. "Anyway, he got hit hard, and I—I didn't know how bad it was. I brought him straight here."

"I got hit," Max repeated.

"Oh, my poor baby! It must have hurt."

"It hurt," Max declared. "A lot."

"I think your friend made the right call, bringing him here," the doctor said with a nod toward Brett. "An accident like that, you don't want to take a chance. There could have been organ damage."

Organ damage. God, that sounded so scary. But there wasn't organ damage. Max was okay. He was okay.

She sniffled back her tears and kissed Max's silky blond hair. He felt so warm and solid on her lap, so familiar. Only his smell was different—a sharp, antiseptic scent instead of his usual baby-powder sweetness.

"Can I have a cookie?" Max asked.

A weepy laugh escaped her. If he was asking for a cookie, he was definitely okay. "When we get home," she promised.

"I'm going to need you to sign some papers," the clerk who'd tried to corral her earlier announced. She had materialized beside Brett at the edge of the curtain. "I'm sorry, Ms. Bartell, but it has to be done."

"Of course." Sharon could handle signing papers now. She could handle anything. Her baby was okay. She turned back to the doctor. "What should I do? Does he need to have any special treatments?"

"Those are just superficial scrapes on his knees and chin," the doctor told her. "Keep them clean, use an antibiotic ointment on them and they should heal up fine. He'll probably be a bit achy, but Children's Tylenol or a similar product should help. If he can tolerate it, you should ice the bruise on his back today. It'll keep the area from swelling."

"You can put compresses on it while he watches TV," the nurse suggested. "Or while you read to him. I have the feeling this isn't a little boy who sits still very often."

Sharon nodded. Compresses. Antibiotic ointment. Children's pain reliever. What did she have on hand in her medicine cabinet? Should she stop at the drugstore on her way home?

Brett would pick up what she needed.

She turned back to him. He had saved her son's life. He'd rushed her little boy to the hospital. A mixture of gratitude and love swelled within her, prompting a fresh spate of tears as she gazed at him.

He looked solemn, tense—and no wonder, after what he'd been through. As terrified as she'd been, he must have been even more frightened. He'd witnessed the accident. Yet he'd remained calm and done what was necessary. He'd brought her baby to the hospital. He was her hero.

She would make sure he knew how much she appreciated his levelheadedness and control. She'd give pain reliever to Max and a nice cold beer to Brett. They'd spend a quiet evening at home—she'd order out, and they'd eat, and they'd watch whatever Max wanted on TV and put cold compresses on his back. They were on the safe side of this crisis, and they would celebrate.

She smiled through her tears, but Brett didn't smile back. His eyes were chilly, glinting with fear. "It's all right," she said to him, realizing as soon as she spoke that he might have no idea what she was referring to: not just that Max was all right, but that *everything* was all right. The world was all right. Life was all right. Even being afraid of what might have happened was all right.

She refused to let go of Max when the doctor sent them out of the treatment area with the clerk. She carried her son back out into the reception room and held him on her lap as the nurse reviewed form after form with her. Insurance policy number. Primary-care pediatrician. Releases for the radiology department, where Max had been taken for X rays. Her poor baby, having to lie still while a big scary X-ray machine roamed over his back, searching for fractured ribs, bruised kidneys and God knew what other injuries he might have incurred. She should have been with him through his ordeal.

But Brett had been with him, thank heavens. Brett had taken care of Max as if he were the boy's father. He must have advocated for him, comforted him, reassured him. Maybe he didn't like "children" in the abstract. But when Max had needed a daddy, Brett had been there.

At last, she'd signed the final form the clerk had for her. Still gripping Max, who was noticeably less squirmy than usual, she stood and searched the reception room for Brett. He hovered near the door, his hands plunged deep into his pockets and his expression unreadable. At her approach, he took a few steps toward her. "Do you want me to put his car seat in your car?" he asked.

She'd expected him to say something a bit more personal—like, "Let's go home," or "I'm glad that's over with," or "Time for this little guy to have a cookie." But he still appeared shaken and grim. Perhaps viewing the accident had been more traumatic than she'd realized. Perhaps spending all that time at the hospital, not knowing whether Max would be all right, had wrung him out.

"Yes," she remembered to answer. "I'd like his seat in my car." She wouldn't have been able to bear being separated from her son for the fifteen minutes it would take to drive home.

The automatic door slid open and Brett preceded her and Max out of the building. Max rested his head against her shoulder—he must be drained, she realized. Once they got home, she would probably feel drained, too. But right now, she was still running on adrenaline, her senses too acute, her heart in its proper location but thumping much more fiercely than normal.

She spotted Brett at his car, leaning into the back seat. When he straightened up, he was holding Max's car seat. Sharon crossed the lot to her car, which she hadn't even bothered to lock, and continued to hold Max while Brett strapped the car seat into place. She wished she could have Max in the front seat next to her, so she could see him at a glance. But he would be safer in back.

"I'll meet you back at my house," she told Brett once Max was buckled into his seat.

Brett hesitated for a moment. "Sure," he finally said, then pivoted and strode back to his own car.

She had never seen him so tense before, so unreachable. Even at his touchiest—that first day, when she'd taken pictures of him for his company's annual report—she'd broken through to him. She'd made him smile, made him laugh—and she'd gotten quite a few good photos of him. And one stunning photo, the one she'd kept, when he'd dropped his guard and she'd seen him as he could be, at home in his skin. But now, it was as if he'd donned an armor of frost.

Once they were back at her place, she'd pull out her belly dancer doll and see if she could tweak a smile out of him. She had let go of all her stress with her tears. It was time for Brett to let go, too.

She monitored his car in her rearview mirror as she drove home. The sun glared against his windshield, so she couldn't see his face. She could see Max's in her mirror, though. The bandage on his chin was a darker tan than his complexion. If he'd fallen harder, he could have broken his jaw. Or his nose. He could have bitten through his lip. He could have injured himself badly enough to require plastic surgery. He could have—

No. She wasn't going to fret over what could have been. Her baby was fine.

At her house, she carried Max to the door. He was probably able to walk, but she wanted to hold him. She was vaguely aware of the tote bag she'd packed for Max lying on the lawn. Brett must have dropped it when the accident occurred. It had lain there, spilling clean diapers and a lidded cup out onto the grass. No one had bothered to pick it up.

"Can I have a cookie?" Max asked as she unlocked the front door.

"Of course you can. What kind would you like?"

"Chocolate chip."

"Okay." She stepped inside and headed straight to the kitchen. Behind her, she heard Brett enter and close the door. "Does your back hurt?" she asked Max as she lowered him onto his booster seat at the table. "Would you like Mommy to give you some of that red medicine that makes the pain go away?"

"I want a cookie."

Sharon smiled. A cookie might ease his pain just as effectively as an analgesic could. She pulled a couple from a package of chocolate chip cookies and put them on a plate, then filled a lidded cup with milk for Max. She couldn't resist the urge to kiss him as she set the plate and cup before him on the table.

Once Max was happily munching on a cookie, she glanced toward the door, expecting to see Brett. She had assumed he would join her and Max in the kitchen. But he hadn't. She didn't know why, or why he'd seemed so remote at the hospital, so tightly strung. If she was able to recover from her shock and fear, why wasn't he?

She told Max she'd be right back—not that he cared; he was greedily devouring his treat—and left the kitchen. Brett was in the living room, his back to her as he stared at the photos she'd hung on the far wall.

"Brett?"

He turned, and she saw in his face that he was a long way from recovering. His brow was creased, his eyes pained, his lips pressed together in an austere line.

"Are you all right?" she asked.

"I've got to go."

Go? Why? They were home. Max was safe. Everything was all right.

Everything but Brett. He remained at the far end of the room—a small room, but she felt as if he were miles away. She took a few steps toward him, yet she couldn't seem to close the emotional distance between them.

"Go where?" she asked.

"I shouldn't be here now."

"Of course you should be here. You saved my baby's life! You got him medical care, and—"

He laughed, a brief bitter sound. "I didn't save your baby's life, Sharon. It was my fault."

"What?"

"The accident. It was my fault."

She shook her head, refusing to believe him.

"I wasn't paying attention. He wanted to play, and I didn't. He was running, and I didn't chase him. That's how he wound up in the path of that skateboarder."

"Oh, Brett..." She wanted to hug him the way she'd hugged Max, to reassure him. He mustn't blame himself for what had obviously been an accident. Max could be wild—if anyone knew that, she did. He could tease, he could scamper, and sometimes she couldn't keep up.

But Brett's forbidding expression warned her off. "I didn't *want* to chase him," he explained. "I was tired of him. I'd dealt with him all morning, and all through lunch, and I just...I didn't want to deal with him any more."

She took a slow deep breath. All right, then. That was a little different from just being too fatigued to chase Max when he was on a tear.

"Taking care of a toddler is hard," she conceded. "Sometimes I burn out, too."

"You don't let him run away, though. It wouldn't matter how burned out you were. You wouldn't have let him escape. I did. I'm sorry, Sharon. I didn't want Max to get hurt. But at that moment—at the moment he got away from me, I—" he closed his eyes, as if he couldn't bear to look at her "—I let him go. Because I wanted to." He opened his eyes again, and the remorse, the self-condemnation in them sent her reeling as much as his words had. "I can't do this, Sharon. I'm sorry, but I can't."

He broke from her, walked to the front door, stepped outside and closed the door behind him.

"Mommy!" Max hollered. "I want another cookie!"

But she couldn't move. She could only stare at the door, at the emptiness of her living room.

She refused to believe the accident had been Brett's fault. He might believe it, but she couldn't. She loved him.

And maybe her love was blinding her to the man

he really was: one who had let her child place himself in harm's way. One who perhaps could have prevented this calamity, but hadn't—because he hadn't wanted to.

Maybe she *could* believe it. But believing it would mean believing she'd been wrong about Brett, he'd been wrong about himself... It would mean acknowledging that he was not the man she needed him to be.

Max was all right. But Brett wasn't. And she wasn't. What had just occurred in her cozy living room could not be treated with ointment and painkillers and ice. She wasn't sure it would ever heal.

BY DINNERTIME, he was on his third beer but still had no appetite. He sat in his den, watching the shadows grow as the sun slid down to the horizon. Just last night, he'd had Sharon here with him. They'd eaten lasagna and garlic bread, sipped wine, talked about his cranky assistant, Janet, and Sharon's timid assistant, Angie. They'd debated the governor's most recent highway initiative and argued over whether *Gladiator* had really deserved an Oscar. Then they'd cleaned up and returned to this room, to the plush area rug in front of the fireplace—which lacked a fire, because it was August—and made love. "This feels so wicked," she'd murmured, lying naked in his arms. "So—public."

"There's nobody here but us," he'd pointed out.

"I know. If we were at my house..."

She hadn't had to finish the sentence. He knew what she was thinking: her den belonged to Max. Her whole house did, with the exception of her bedroom.

She didn't have the freedom to make love wherever she wanted in her own home, because she had a son.

A son who could have died, thanks to Brett's incompetence, his selfishness.

The voices had echoed inside his head all evening: the ghost voices of his siblings demanding that he help them, that he play with them, that he pick them up or put them down or get them a snack or walk them across the street. And his mother's voice, chiding him for having not done enough: "While you were sitting here reading a book, the children were tearing pages from the road atlas! Why weren't you keeping a closer watch? What's wrong with you?"

He'd wanted to answer, "I'm one of the children, too." But in spite of his age, he hadn't been a child. He'd been the one in charge, and he'd resented it. So he'd buried his nose in a book.

That was what had happened today. He'd tried to keep a close watch on Max. He'd done his best all morning and through lunch. But then…he just hadn't been able to do it any longer. What was wrong with him was that he lacked what it took to be a daddy, even a substitute daddy for a few hours on a Saturday.

He had thought that if he loved Sharon enough, he could handle anything: Daddy School classes, full-time caretaking, Max. He'd thought loving her would make him more patient, more imperturbable. He'd thought it would help him break free of his past. He'd thought: *I can do this for her.*

But he couldn't. He had failed her and her son— and himself.

He contemplated phoning her, just to see how Max was feeling. The welt on his back where the skateboard had struck him wasn't as bad as it looked, the Emergency Room pediatrician had assured him, but it had looked pretty damned bad. And his barked knees. How many knees had Brett cleaned and bandaged as a kid? It seemed as if one or another of his siblings was always falling down and scraping a layer of skin off a knee. And then they'd come running to him, screaming, and he'd have to drop whatever he was doing so he could scrub the knee and cover the wound with an adhesive strip. His sister had always insisted on the bandages with pictures on them, stars or cars or Mickey Mouse.

And Max's chin… He could have really hurt his face. Nobody cared about a scar on the knee, but what if he'd knocked out teeth? What if he'd needed stitches? What if he'd injured an eye?

All because Brett had shut down. All because he couldn't be a daddy.

He wouldn't phone Sharon. If he heard her voice, he would want to be with her. And if he went back to her house, he'd have to stand by while she took care of her son, gave him compresses and cookies and whatever else he required. Max's needs *did* take precedence; Brett couldn't dispute that. The kid came first for her. He had to.

Brett didn't mind that Max was Sharon's top priority. But he couldn't bring himself to accept Max as his own top priority. He was a selfish bastard, but he couldn't sacrifice himself to the needs of a child again.

"OH, MY GOD!" Deborah exclaimed when she saw Max. "Oh, look at his chin!"

Sharon actually thought his chin looked better today than it had last night, when she'd eased off the bandage before his bath. She'd kept the wound covered overnight, but it was scabbed today, clean and dry, and since he said the bandage itched, she decided to leave it off for a while. The rain was going to keep him and Olivia indoors, so the likelihood of dirt getting into the sore was slim.

"He's all right," Sharon assured Deborah.

"And he's not even achy?"

"Not that I've noticed." She watched Max traipse down the stairs after Olivia, the two of them yammering about building a choo-choo train. "He was a little fragile last night," she admitted, turning toward the kitchen, where Deborah was fixing a pitcher of lemonade. "I think the whole thing—the accident, the hospital—I think it shook him up. He got weepy. I let him sleep with me."

"Of course." Deborah filled two tumblers with lemonade and handed one to Sharon, who carried it to the table and slumped into a chair. "Did Brett mind that arrangement? Or is it none of my business?"

"It's none of your business," Sharon said with a sad smile. "Not that that matters. You and I have no secrets, Deb."

Deborah smiled as well, sat across the table from her and gave her hand a squeeze. "So where did Brett sleep while you shared your bed with Max?"

"In his own house. He left."

"He left?" Deborah reared up indignantly. "With all you were going through, he didn't stay?"

"He stayed until he was sure Max was all right. Seriously, Deborah, he was wonderful through the worst of it. He got Max to the hospital, got him treated, called me, saw us home, hung around long enough to be sure Max was okay—and I was okay, too—and then he left.''

Deborah clicked her tongue. ''Some men are like that. They're so tough and macho, but show 'em one drop of blood and they're ready to swoon.''

''That wasn't why he left.'' Sharon took a sip of the tart, cool drink and sighed. ''He thought it was his fault.''

''The accident?'' Deborah shook her head. ''I've seen those teenagers fly through the neighborhood on their skateboards. It's amazing more people don't get knocked over. They're crazy on those things.''

''I know. But Brett... It wasn't the accident he felt responsible for. It was that he'd let his attention falter. He was—'' the words stuck in her throat, and she had to swallow to loosen them ''—tired of Max.''

''Max can tire anyone out. Even Livie.''

''Not that way. He was tired of dealing with Max, I think. Tired of having to be responsible for him.''

Deborah mulled that over. ''Well, what's so strange about that? I bet you feel that way sometimes.''

Sharon nodded.

''Of course, you've got more justification. I mean, he'd had Max only, what, three or four hours?''

''It's not a responsibility he's used to. But none of that should matter. I think...'' She traced a line in the condensation on the surface of her glass, then swallowed again. ''I think he feels guilty because— well, you know how kids can get. Sometimes, you just look at them and think, *Oh, go away!* And Brett had reached that point. So then, when something terrible happened—it was as if he'd wished it.''

"But he didn't *really* wish it,'' Deborah argued.

"I know that. He'd know it, too, if he was thinking logically. But when something like that happens, a scary accident...you don't think logically.''

"So he feels as if he somehow brought this down upon Max.''

"I'm only guessing, but yeah, I think that's what's going on.''

"Mr. Wrong.'' Deborah shook her head. "He was good-looking.''

"Better than good-looking. He was smart and thoughtful and stable.'' And loving. Tender. Sexy. Caring. "He was trying so hard, trying to get it right with Max.''

"Men,'' Deborah muttered.

"How are things with you and Raymond?'' It hurt Sharon too much to think about Brett. She'd rather dump on Deborah's husband than dwell on her own pain over Brett's abrupt departure from her home, from her life.

"Raymond,'' Deborah said, then sighed. "Well, they're going better.''

"Meaning...?''

"We're talking.''

"Anything besides talking?''

"Well...'' Deborah blushed. "That, too. He dropped by Friday night, took me and Livie out to dinner, and wound up spending the night. He had tickets to a Red Sox game yesterday, so we all drove up to Boston for the day. Olivia ate cotton candy for the first time. She freaked out.'' Deborah grinned, obviously remembering her daughter's reaction.

"She just couldn't figure the stuff out. It was so soft and airy and sweet. Anyway, I sent Raymond home last night. I thought, I'm not about to get into a habit with him. Not until we've reached some understandings."

"Do you think that's possible?"

Deborah reached for Sharon's hand again, this time seeking approval rather than offering comfort. "I'm afraid to hope, Sharon, but I think it's possible. You wouldn't believe what the man said to me."

Sharon leaned forward, delighted to share her friend's excitement. At least something was going right, someone's love life showing promise. "What did he say?"

"Are you ready for this? He said, 'I'm sorry.'"

"You're kidding."

"I swear."

"I didn't know men knew how to say that." They both laughed.

"Well, he said it," Deborah insisted. "He said he was sorry about focusing on his job at the expense of our marriage, sorry he was missing milestones with Olivia—he said he didn't realize how much he was missing until we were really gone and he was missing us all the time. He said he's been working with his supervisor, trying to figure out a better way to schedule his trips so they don't keep him out of town so often and on weekends." She smiled sheepishly. "He just apologized and apologized. I don't know if men realize what an aphrodisiac those two words can be."

"So, are you going to get back together with him?"

"Not so fast," Deborah said, holding up a hand

like a traffic cop slowing down a speeding car. "But we're talking. He's been coming to the sessions with the marriage counselor, and calling me every evening after work—and he's getting home from work by six instead of seven-thirty or eight, like he used to when we were together." Her smile grew poignant. "I still love him, Sharon. I never stopped loving him. I'm afraid to be too optimistic, but I think we might work things out."

"That's wonderful." Sharon sprang out of her chair, circled the table and gave Deborah a hug.

"I shouldn't be telling you all this," Deborah said once Sharon had returned to her chair. "Here things have gone south for you and Mr. Wrong—"

"You're the one who coined the name," Sharon reminded her. "And it's accurate. He's all wrong for me. I knew that going in."

"But you had hope."

Her eyes met Deborah's. Deborah looked as if a shroud had lifted from her face. She now had hope of putting her family back together again. Was having hope such a bad thing?

In the years since Steve's death, Sharon hadn't even considered it. Hope was a luxury, and she'd had no time for luxuries. Sure, she'd hoped Max would stay safe and healthy, and that he'd grow up to be a strong, kind, moral man. But to hope for love? She hadn't been able to afford that kind of hope.

Then love had crept into her life and caught her unaware. Hope had infected her like a joyful virus. She'd suddenly found herself believing love could exist between her and a man like Brett Stockton.

Apparently, it couldn't. But she'd experienced

hope, and she didn't want to be cured. Let the virus slip into remission if it had to, but she wanted it to remain in her blood.

Maybe someday she'd have reason to hope again.

CHAPTER FIFTEEN

"DID YOU BRING Max with you today?" Molly Saunders-Russo asked.

Brett shook his head. He wasn't even sure why he'd brought himself to the Children's Garden Preschool for another session of the Daddy School. Perhaps it was just to confirm in his own mind that he truly lacked the daddy spirit.

He'd just slogged through the longest week of his life. He'd skipped Wednesday's Daddy School class at the YMCA, choosing instead to spend that evening whipping his friend Murphy's butt on the tennis court. But all that sweating and running and whamming a ball with his racket hadn't made him feel any better. Nor had Murphy's comment that his wife had received a submission of photographs of Arlington and its environs from Sharon Bartell for the city's birthday committee to consider. "If you want to put in a good word for your girlfriend, now's your chance," Murphy had said, swabbing his face with a towel. "You've just humiliated me in two straight sets. You may as well collect your spoils."

"She's good," Brett had claimed, trying not to choke on the words. "Her work speaks for itself." He hadn't seen the photographs she'd submitted, but he knew the pictures she had hanging in her living room. He'd practically memorized them, certain he would never have a chance to view them again. His mind conjured her photo of the staggered town-house roofs; the shot of the curling ocean wave breaking over the stone jetty; and the portrait of the children, her son and his friend Olivia, looking deceptively cute and peaceful.

God. He couldn't think of Max without remembering that day, the deathly silence that lingered long enough to stop his heart followed by a scream loud enough to knock Mars out of its orbit. Max, flushed and bleeding and moaning with each labored breath, and screaming in shock and fear, screaming the way Brett would have liked to scream.

All because he'd had his fill of children. Because he'd grown tired of Max's neediness, his leechiness, his oppressive presence. The accident had been his fault.

"So, any hints you want me to pass along to Gail?" Murphy had asked.

"Tell her to give Sharon a fair shake, that's all. She wants the commission and she deserves it. I'm sure she's got more talent than any of the other photographers in the running." He'd busied himself zipping his racquet into its case, not eager to think about everything he'd given up when he'd walked out of her house last Saturday.

He loved her.

That was the cruelest irony, of course. If he didn't love her, he could have continued to see her. Building a rapport with her son would not have been necessary. He and Sharon could have enjoyed each other's company and moved on when they were done. But loving her meant signing on for the whole package, and the whole package included Max.

Even if Brett had been willing to accept Max, he couldn't remain in their lives. Max wasn't safe with him.

So what was he doing at the Daddy School?

Obviously, Molly was wondering the same thing. "I didn't bring Max with me, no," he answered her.

"He's recuperating really well," Molly remarked. "His chin is nearly all healed, and that bruise on his back has gotten a lot smaller. He was so lucky."

Not lucky enough, Brett thought with a surge of self-recrimination. If Max had been truly lucky, he would have spent Saturday with someone capable of taking proper care of him, someone who wouldn't have grown sick of him and tuned him out just when harm was careering toward him in the form of an out-of-control skateboard.

But Brett held his face impassive and nodded at Molly's comments. "It could have been worse," he agreed.

The other fathers were already assembling in the enclosed area where the class met. The morning was milder than usual, September sucking a little of the oppressive heat out of the air. Someone—a teacher from the preschool, Brett assumed—had escorted the children who'd accompanied their fathers through a back door and outside to a fenced-in playground. The back door remained open, and through it drifted the sounds of laughter and chatter.

Molly gestured for Brett to join the group. He took his usual place on one of the low tables. Several smeary paintings lay across the surface to his right, apparently left there to dry. More paintings were tacked to the corkboard lining one wall, brightly col- ored abstracts, slashes of random color. Ugly paintings, he thought—but they were displayed with as much pride as the photographs on Sharon's living room wall. The kids who painted them must consider themselves brilliant artists.

And why shouldn't they? They were two and three years old. They should be allowed to believe whatever they wanted about themselves: that they were artists or doctors or kangaroos or kings and queens. Why not hang their paintings and let them think what they'd created was important?

He tried to remember if his mother had ever displayed any of his childhood artwork in his house. He couldn't recall ever owning a set of paints, but he would have created pictures with crayons or colored pencils. He had no doubt produced his share of meaningless masterpieces. But he couldn't recall ever seeing one of his drawings on display.

His brothers' drawings, yes. And his sister's strange collages, composed of construction paper and sparkles and scraps of cloth glued onto cardboard. They'd been displayed because *he'd* displayed them. He distinctly remembered using magnets to fasten his sister's collages to the refrigerator, thinking they were grotesque but figuring that if he didn't hang them up, his mother would never bother to do it. His sister used to beam when he hung her designs in the kitchen. She used to puff up and grin. She'd probably felt like a queen.

"I want to talk about identity," Molly said, sitting on one of the child-size seats. Given her petite build, she fit into the chair much better than any of her Daddy School students would. "Specifically, I want to talk about your children's identity, and your identity, and where the line forms between the two."

He had no idea how such a discussion might help him—but then, he had no idea how the Daddy School could help him at all, now that he was no longer a part of Sharon's world. Identity was an interesting issue, however, so he leaned forward, stretching his long legs so they wouldn't cramp from his improvised seating.

"How many of you have ever spent such a long stretch with your children that after a while you forget who you are?" she asked. Most of the men chuckled and nodded. Brett couldn't relate at all. "It's almost like—what do they call it in science fiction movies? A mind meld," she went on. "You suddenly realize you haven't had a lucid adult thought for the past ten minutes. Your mind is completely wrapped around whether your son is going to spill his milk, or whether your daughter is going to keep up that awful whining. Nothing else exists in the world—or in your head. Your child has taken over your thought processes." More nods and laughter.

"Sometimes that lack of a boundary between you and your children is a good thing. It means you're on your child's wavelength. You can almost read his or her mind. But other times it's almost scary. You think you've completely lost your mind, that your brain has been replaced by your child's brain. You're not a teacher anymore, or an engineer, or an investment manager—" she glanced toward Brett "—but instead, all you are is this child-care machine. I know. I'm a mother. I feel that way, probably more often than most of you."

More nods. Without thinking, Brett bobbed his head, too. That was how he'd felt with his siblings, years ago—and how he'd started to feel with Max last Saturday afternoon: as if he'd lost his sense of himself and his ability to think the kinds of thoughts that mattered to him. Max had been begging him, "Catch me! Catch me!" until the chant had overpowered Brett. If someone had asked him his name right then, he wouldn't have known what to answer.

"There's another way a mind meld can happen, which might not be so bad for fathers but is much worse for kids. This is when fathers are convinced they can make their children think like them, or act like them. The classic overbearing Little League dad would fall into this category—the kind of father who thinks, 'I loved Little League as a boy. I was one of my team's stars. I know my son is going to be a star, too.' The father is imposing his thoughts on the child, just as in the earlier version the child seems to be imposing his thoughts on the father."

Brett settled back on the table. This aspect of the topic had nothing to do with him. He'd never played Little League. He hadn't taken up tennis until he was eleven, and his stepfather hadn't been particularly interested in his athletic ability. He couldn't imagine trying to influence Max to think as he did when it came to sports. Max or any other kid, he silently amended.

"Let's talk about these boundary issues. When do you feel you're losing your identity? What sorts of situations make you feel as if your kids have taken complete possession of your minds?"

The fathers contributed examples from their own lives. Several of them alluded to periods of intense frenzy—when their kids were running wild, when they were late for an appointment, when the house was a mess. One fellow said reading children's books over and over altered his vocabulary after a while. "I'll suddenly start rhyming words, like I'm Dr. Seuss or something," he said, prompting a round of laughter. Yet another father insisted his mind had vanished the day his daughter was born, and it had never really come back.

Brett was glad Molly didn't call on him. She knew he was just an auditor, not an official student. What would he have said if she'd forced him to contribute to the discussion?

He'd lost his mind not from Max but from Sharon, when he'd lost his heart to her. He wasn't sure exactly when it had happened but it had, and his mind had gone into a swoon right along with his heart. He'd been drawn by her unshakable balance, her rootedness, her knowledge of what mattered in life. Her determination. Her morality. Her ability to look at a row of condominium roofs and discover something beautiful in them, and to capture that beautiful image on film.

He'd lost his mind enough to pursue her, despite her son. And then Max had devoured another chunk of his brain. He'd pulled up his mental drawbridge on Saturday afternoon because he'd had to defend against invasion. Max had been storming Brett's skull like a hostile army, threatening to declare Brett's mind his own.

Catch me! Catch me! Catch me!

Max had been the one to catch Brett—and Brett's response had been to try to escape.

"It's normal," Molly was saying. "It's perfectly normal to resent when this happens. But it's going to happen anyway, so rather than give in to resentment, you can accept it, go with it, trust that your mind will return to you eventually.''

Brett could confirm that. His mind had already come back to him, more or less. He'd read the newspaper uninterrupted every morning for the past week, perusing articles about food shortages in central Africa, feminism in Japan and bickering in the U.S. Senate. He'd savored his coffee while he'd skimmed the stock market listings to see how the stocks he'd been monitoring had performed the previous day, and how his mutual funds were doing compared with the funds of his competitors. He'd parried Janet and sat in his quiet office and worked with his managers, and then gone home and eaten something he'd have thrown together or brought home with him, a meal without food spilling off the plate or ketchup smeared on anyone's nose. When he'd played tennis with Murphy, and the following night with a fellow member of his tennis club, his mind had been his own.

No one else was rattling around in his head, imposing, demanding, forcing him to redraw those boundaries Molly was talking about. It had just been Brett.

Yet he was so lonely it hurt physically, like a hunger pang.

That pain could go away if he let them in—not just Sharon but Max. He could cure himself of the pain if only he was willing to sacrifice his identity.

As always, the class seemed to fly by. It ought to have dragged; it was utterly irrelevant to his life— except that it actually wasn't. He wasn't learning about how to survive Max here. He was learning about how to survive himself.

Noon arrived, along with the boisterous intrusion of the children from outside. Brett signaled his thanks to Molly above the heads of the tykes who swarmed around her, and he made a quick exit, reminding himself how fortunate it was that none of those noisy tykes was attached to him. But he suffered another pang, deep and sharp in his soul.

He got into his car—his spacious, quiet, clean car with its lack of a child's car seat in back—and steered out of the lot. A few cottony clouds drifted through the sky, and the electric hand-shaped sign in the window of the palm reader's parlor next door seemed to wave at him. He pointed his car in the direction of the Village Green Condominiums and pressed harder on the gas.

He was going to have to face reality—the reality that he needed the Bartells, not the reality that he had to avoid them. If Sharon could possibly forgive him for his lapse with her son last week, he'd try harder. If Max could forgive him… Did Max know how much blame Brett deserved for his injuries? Did he know Brett's resistance to him had put him in harm's way?

They probably both did. They probably didn't want to see him again. But he'd try to get through to them, somehow. He'd plead his case. He'd beg.

It hadn't occurred to him that they might not be home. He rang the bell three times but heard no sound inside. Great. He'd finally built up his courage to the point where he could bare his hopes and fears to Sharon and implore her to give him a chance to be as good a man as she needed him to be—and she wasn't home.

A car cruised to a halt by the curb as he turned

from her door. His hope that it might contain her and Max faded as soon as he saw the late-model sedan instead of Sharon's clunky old Volvo. The car pulled up in front of his and the doors opened.

He recognized Sharon's neighbor and her young daughter as they emerged from the car, but not the man with them, a tall dapper fellow with a neatly trimmed mustache. The woman—Deborah, Brett recalled—spotted him descending from Sharon's front porch and strode across the grass toward him, her little girl skipping alongside her.

"She's not home," Deborah said, her expression far from welcoming. He could blame her squint on the sun, but he interpreted it as a frown of disapproval.

"I noticed."

Her little girl giggled and clasped her mother's hand. Brett wondered if she remembered how he'd lain on the floor of Sharon's studio and let her and Max toss a ball back and forth across his chest. "She won't be back for a while," Deborah added, as if afraid he was planning to camp out on the porch until Sharon returned.

That wasn't a bad idea, actually—unless she was *really* gone. How long was a while? Had she left town with Max?

He shrugged away his panic. "Where did she go?" he asked in an impressively level voice.

"The mall."

Thank God. She was still in the Arlington vicinity.

"It's a party," the little girl chirped. "Max's party."

Deborah glanced at her daughter and sighed. "Yes, that's right."

"Max is having a party," the girl repeated happily.

Deborah turned back to Brett. "They went shopping to get what they needed for Max's birthday party," she said, her voice as acidic as lemon juice. Maybe she wanted him to feel even guiltier for having brought on Max's injury so close to his birthday.

"When is his party?" Brett asked, trying not to wince at the thought of a three-year-old's birthday party. A houseful of kids, cake and ice cream, games and toys and noise. A universe of noise.

"Next Saturday."

"He's turning three?"

"I'm two," the girl boasted, extending two of her fingers to illustrate her statement.

"You'll be three in a couple of months, sweetie," her mother told her.

"I go to Max's party."

"Yes, you'll be there."

Abruptly, she turned and let out a whoop. "Daddy!"

The man had remained apart from them, but at his daughter's acknowledgment he hunkered down and spread his arms wide. "You got some sugar for your daddy?" he asked.

She scampered off, evidently bored with her mother's conversation. Deborah seemed relieved, and Brett realized why as soon as she started to speak. "I don't know what your game is," she said, "but Sharon doesn't need your kind of trouble in her life, okay?"

"Trouble?"

"You're there, then you disappear. She's already lost the man she loved once, and she shouldn't have to go through that again. And neither should her son.''

''I know. I—''

''Her son gets hurt, it's one of the worst moments in a mother's life, and what did you do? You abandoned her. You walked away just when she was depending on you.''

Brett didn't feel like defending himself to Sharon's friend, but he couldn't let her accusations go unchallenged—especially since they contained more than a few drops of truth. ''I walked away because I was the last person she needed,'' he said.

Deborah sniffed cynically. ''Things get tough, and some men disappear. Sharon deserves a man who isn't going to disappear on her. We all do,'' she added under her breath, then glanced behind her at her daughter, now shrieking in ecstasy as her father gave her a piggyback ride. Sniffing again, Deborah returned her gaze to Brett.

''Do you know when Sharon will be back?'' he asked.

''Did she know when you'd be back?'' Deborah retorted.

He sighed. As much as the woman exasperated him, he admired her. She was a loyal friend to Sharon, stalwart and protective. He wanted Sharon to have someone like Deborah in her corner.

And maybe she was right. Maybe he didn't deserve another chance with Sharon. He'd blown it not once but twice, first by letting Max get hurt and then by abandoning her, as Deborah said. Whether or not he was the reason things had gotten tough for Sharon, he'd disappeared when she'd needed someone to remain with her, to provide support and reassurance and love.

He couldn't refute Deborah. Whatever defense he might have had crumbled beneath her condemnation.

He nodded, muttered, "Thanks," and stalked down to his car. He wished he wasn't the kind of man who disappeared. But he was honest enough to acknowledge the possibility that he was.

ABOUT MIDWAY through the birthday party, Sharon ducked into the bathroom and downed four aspirin. She'd had a pretty good idea how much hullabaloo six two- and three-year-olds could produce, even when their mothers were present to keep them calm. London Bridge had disintegrated after five minutes. A sing-along had lasted maybe eight. The children were too excited to sit still for cake; they'd plundered the sheet cake Sharon had baked last night, and then romped off, leaving the kitchen table and floor littered in golden crumbs and smears of chocolate frosting.

The mothers were not as much help as Sharon had hoped. To them, Max's birthday party was an opportunity to schmooze with other mothers. They sipped the coffee Sharon had brewed for them, issued occasional reprimands to their children and then resumed their conversations about potty training and flash cards and the rumor that one of their children's classmates at the Children's Garden Preschool was still being breastfed at three and a half years of age.

Of all the mothers, only Deborah was actually making an effort to help Sharon maintain order. She marshaled the children in and out of activities and scolded a youngster she saw pushing another guest in a tussle over a balloon. She made sure the mothers got unmangled pieces of cake once the children had departed from the kitchen. While Sharon organized the kids in an overly giggly game that had them pretending to be different animals, Deborah quietly gathered up some of the toys the children had strewn across the playroom floor.

Sharon was more grateful for Deborah's assistance than she could measure. To have to host Max's birthday party after the worst two weeks of her life was bad timing, to say the least.

The worst two weeks of her life? No, that wasn't true. Even as she arranged the children into a line for a simple game of Simon Says, her mind wandered back through the long days after Max's accident and Brett's desertion. Surely she'd been through worse, hadn't she? What about when Steve had died?

Max hadn't been born yet when she'd lost Steve. And she'd been too inexperienced to realize how difficult the job of raising a newborn alone would be. And Steve...of course she'd loved him. But she'd also been furious with him for being so stupid, so reckless on the ski slope. That anger had gotten her through the dark days.

Brett's departure from her life didn't anger her. It left her sad, regretful, wishing there was some way he could escape the ties that tethered him to his past.

"Simon Says, touch your nose," she said slowly. Olivia was the first to find her nose. One little boy had to think a minute, but eventually he remembered where his nose was. "Great! Simon Says, touch your ear." Amid bubbly laughter, the children all touched an ear. "Okay. Touch your other ear." All of them obeyed. "Oops—you're all out," she said, then laughed to assure them no one was going to lose this game.

Except, perhaps, "Simon" herself. The aspirin hadn't diminished her headache. Her watch told her the party still had fifteen minutes to go. And once the children were gone, she would have to hose down the kitchen, steam-shovel the playroom and remove Max from the ceiling, where he might just wind up, given how bouncy he was.

"Simon Says, jump up and down," she said, foolishly hoping she might coax the kids into burning off some of their excess energy. They jumped—and shrieked, just for the hell of it. "Simon Says stop jumping up and down!" she shouted above the din. They stopped, out of breath and giggling. "Start jumping again." Three children jumped, and all the children dissolved in wild laughter. They flopped onto the floor, guffawed so hard they burped, screeched one another's names and gasped at the hilarity of it all.

She checked her watch again. Twelve minutes before this would be over.

"Sharon?" one of the mothers called from the living room. "There's a man at the door."

"You want me to get it?" Deborah offered. "It's probably Raymond."

"Sure." The one bright spot in her otherwise worst two weeks had been the first tender buds of reconciliation sprouting between Deborah and Raymond. He'd been so diligent and devoted, phoning every night, stopping by to see if she needed anything, bringing her car to the shop for its tune-up. "I've talked to him more in the past week than I did in the six months before we separated," she'd confided to Sharon just that morning. "He's part of our lives again. All those months when he was always traveling with work, putting in the hours and not even bothering to phone home—he wasn't in our lives then. He is now."

Sharon was thrilled for Deborah, and for Olivia, too. Children needed fathers.

Her gaze followed Deborah up the stairs, then came to rest on her own son surrounded by his playmates on the carpeted floor, all of them convulsed with hysterical laughter. He needed a father, and she'd hoped... Damn it, *she* needed a partner as much as Max needed a father. Not because she couldn't cope on her own, not because she couldn't support herself and her son. She could. She'd been doing it for three long years.

But she wanted someone by her side. Someone to lean on, to talk to, to share with. Someone she trusted. Someone honest and smart, someone who knew himself and didn't have to prove anything to anyone.

"Hi." A male voice she recognized too well reached her through the hubbub.

She spun around to see Brett descending the stairs, a gift-wrapped box in one hand.

What was he doing here? She hadn't invited him to Max's party!

Silly thought. She would never have invited him. She understood that a children's birthday party would likely be his definition of hell. All the ruckus, the clutter, the high-decibel revelry. All those little bodies darting around the room, throwing soft foam balls and balloons and broken pretzels at one another.

It was *her* concept of hell—or it would be if Max didn't appear to be having the time of his life.

He was in the thick of the pretzel battle, flinging crumbs in all directions. Shuddering, Sharon backed toward the stairs and figured she would attack the room with her vacuum cleaner later. Scrubbing the place would be easier than asking the children to stop throwing snacks.

Brett gave her a shy smile and handed her the package. "This is for Max, but he seems otherwise occupied."

She cringed as a blizzard of pretzel crumbs flew through the air. And cringed again at the realization that Brett had stopped by only to drop off a present. How he'd even known it was Max's birthday she couldn't guess, but his generosity was counterproductive, raising expectations where she and Max both ought to have none.

However, she knew her manners. "Thank you," she said. "It wasn't necessary."

He shrugged, then ventured farther into the room. "Hey," he said, quietly but firmly enough to attract the children's attention. "No more throwing pretzels."

One little boy tested Brett by tossing the pretzel in his hand.

"I said no more." Brett lifted the bowl of pretzels out of the children's reach and placed it on a high shelf. This gesture was met with stunned silence.

Sharon held her breath, unsure whether he was going to yell at the children—or lead them in another game. He did neither. He simply met their stares.

She checked her watch again and cleared her throat. "I think it's time for everyone to say goodbye now,'' she announced, too bewildered by Brett's presence to sound pleased that the party was reaching its end. ''I've got goodie bags for all of you, so let's go upstairs.''

It took another ten minutes for the children to pair up with their mothers, receive their bags of treats and toys, recite the appropriate thank yous and bye-byes and clear out.

Deborah and Olivia lingered after all the other children and mothers were gone. Olivia and Max hunkered down to examine one of the presents he'd received at the party—a pair of plastic roller skates designed to clamp onto his shoes. The thought of her little boy, his chin and knees bearing fresh scars from his recent accident, roller skating petrified Sharon. But she had to let him learn to skate. Someday, heaven help her, he'd probably want to learn to ski, too.

''How are you doing?'' Deborah asked, stacking the empty paper coffee cups the other mothers had left in the living room. ''You want me to stick around?'' She shot a discreet glance in Brett's direction. He stood at the top of the stairs, staring down into the playroom with an expression bordering on horror.

''I'll be fine,'' she said, not sure she meant it.

''Okay.'' She handed the stack of cups to Sharon and called to her daughter. ''Livie? Time to go home.''

''It's a roller skate,'' Olivia announced.

''That's right.''

''I want a roller skate.''

''We'll see.'' Deborah exchanged a look with

Sharon, half sympathy and half exasperation. "It was a great party, really."

"Uh-huh." Sharon smiled wearily.

"I mean it. No tears, no bloodshed. You can't ask for more. Come on, sweetie," she called to Olivia. "It's time to go home."

Olivia took her mother's hand and gripped her goodie bag. "Is Daddy home?"

"He's coming over in a little while." Deborah peered over her shoulder. "Call me," she murmured, then shot Brett another look.

Before Sharon could respond, they were out the door. Max pushed his new roller skates across the floor as if they were toy cars. Brett still hovered at the top of the stairs.

She didn't know what to say. She was still holding the stack of cups, and disorder awaited her everywhere she looked, so she stated the obvious. "I've got some cleaning up to do."

"Can I give Max his present?"

"Of course." She felt out of whack, out of sync. She'd just endured ninety minutes of mayhem after two weeks of heartbreak. Her son was three years old. Two weeks ago, he could have died, but instead he'd just celebrated his third birthday.

And the man who'd rushed him to the hospital and gotten him the medical attention he'd needed, the man who believed the accident had been his fault, was now in her home.

She escaped into the kitchen—another scene of demolition. Let Brett do what he'd come to do, for whatever reason he'd come to do it. She was in no condition to figure out what he was up to.

She heard a blare of sound—Max's exuberant

hoot. "Wow! Mommy, Mommy, look!" he bellowed, clomping up the stairs and into the kitchen. She didn't want him to enter; the floor was covered with smashed bits of cake and gooey dribbles of melted ice cream. But she couldn't stand in the way of his excitement as he charged into the room, holding a bright red toy fire engine. "Look, Mommy! It makes noise!" He demonstrated by pressing a button, which caused a siren to sound. "And look at this!" Another button caused the red light on the plastic roof of the truck to flash. He pressed the siren button again and released a peal of laughter. "Look, Mommy!"

She forced a smile, but wondered why Brett would have bought such a clamorous toy for her son. Probably because he was planning to run away again, leaving her to suffer through the noise alone.

"Did you say thank-you to Brett?"

"Thank you," Max recited, even though Brett wasn't in the room. Then he dropped to his hands and knees and started to push the fire engine across the floor.

"Not in here, Max. The floor is filthy. Go play in the living room, honey."

"Okay." He pressed the siren button and grinned, as if the sound was his favorite lullaby. It echoed in Sharon's head, undermining any effect the aspirin might have had.

Brett took Max's place in the doorway. "Wow," he said, gaping at the torn napkins, the bent paper plates, the singed birthday candles on the counter by the sink, the soggy paper tablecloth with Happy Birthday printed on it in primary colors. "It looks like a war zone."

"That's what it feels like, too." She tossed all the plates into the center of the table and lifted the edges of the tablecloth, gathering it into one large, lumpy bundle of trash.

Brett picked a careful path through the crumbs, plastic forks and smears of icing until he reached the table. He helped Sharon lift the bundle of garbage from the table, then carried it to the trash can. His face was intent, his mouth set in a line of concentration. From the living room came the whine of the fire engine.

"Why are you here, Brett?" she asked.

He turned from the trash can, almost took a step and then caught himself and detoured around the small mound of cake he'd nearly ground with his shoe. He gazed at her, his face softening slightly, hinting at a smile. "The short answer is, I love you."

She sank into the nearest chair, momentarily overcome. She'd had two weeks without a word from him. He'd left her with nothing but his insistence that he had somehow caused Max's injuries and that she was better off without him. In the intervening time, she'd submitted her portfolio to the city's birthday committee, snapped countless portraits of anxious high school seniors, spent her evenings with Max and her nights alone, wondering why Brett's absence hurt so much, why she missed him so crazily, how he'd managed to insinuate himself so deeply into her heart.

She'd invited six of Max's classmates from the Children's Garden Preschool to his birthday party. She'd bought all these colorful plates and napkins, baked a cake and barely survived an hour and a half of pandemonium.

And now Brett was standing in her kitchen—actually, pulling the broom and dustpan from the closet and setting to work sweeping up the bits of food on the floor—and declaring that he loved her.

He'd claimed that was the short answer. "I think I need the long answer," she said.

He kept sweeping, dutifully cleaning up a mess others had made. "I missed you, Sharon. I missed..." He sighed, then knelt down and pried a sticky bit of frosting from the floor tiles. "I missed talking to you and watching you work and looking at you. And having sex with you. I just—I kept telling myself I was doing you a favor by staying out of your life. I thought it would be better for you." He smiled wryly. "But it didn't seem better for me."

"Because you missed having sex with me." Not that she'd minimize the importance of that. She'd missed having sex with him, too. She'd missed it a lot.

"I kept attending the Daddy School," he admitted, surprising her. "I couldn't seem to give that up. And that made me realize I couldn't give you up, either."

"Brett." She noticed dampness on the table from where spilled milk had seeped through the tablecloth. A discarded napkin lay within reach on the counter, and she used it to blot up the moisture. "It doesn't matter whether you can give me up or not. I'm a mother. I've got a son. That's not going to change."

"I know." He sighed again, apparently in resignation. "I don't like having Max in my face all the time. I don't like when he whines. I don't like having to deal with his diapers—or having to clean up after his party," he added, using the broom's bristles to create a rather impressive heap of crumbs and dirt at the center of the floor. "I bet you don't like those things, either—but they don't stop you from loving him."

"Of course I love him," Sharon confirmed. "I'm his mother. You don't have to love him, though. You're not his father."

"He needs a father." Brett propped the broom against the counter and stared directly at Sharon. "I lost my father. I know what that's like. Max needs a father."

"But you don't want to be somebody's dad," she reminded him.

"Why don't I?" He lifted the dustpan, fiddled with it for a moment and set it back down. "Because I don't want to get stuck with the hard parts of the job? No one wants to get stuck with that. Big deal. Not wanting to lose half my soul to a kid is normal. It makes me like a million other fathers. And mothers, too. None of us wants to do the hard stuff. But it needs to get done, so we do it." He reached for the broom again.

"How did you know it was Max's birthday?"

"I was here last week. You and Max weren't home, but your neighbor saw me. Deborah. She told me. Actually, it was her daughter who spilled the beans."

"Then why didn't you call? Why did you just show up without warning?"

He stopped sweeping and stared at her again. "Do you think this was an easy decision for me? Admitting that I love you enough to make room for Max in my heart?"

It must have been the toughest decision he'd ever faced. And he'd decided on her, on Max, on discarding everything he'd believed about his needs and the calm, peaceful, childless life he'd envisioned for himself.

Her headache vanished. The room suddenly seemed lighter, brighter—just as disastrously messy, but she didn't care. She rose and crossed the room to him, not caring if she stepped in fallen chunks of cake. "Put down the broom," she whispered, looping her arms around him, savoring the solid warmth of him, filling her lungs with his clean, male wonderfully familiar scent.

He smiled. "The place needs to be cleaned."

"I need to be kissed," she said, aware that a kiss was infinitely more imperative than a tidy kitchen.

Brett complied, letting the broom fall to the floor with a clatter. He kissed her, a hard deep possessive kiss. He'd obviously needed it as much as she did.

In the distance, she heard the wail of the toy fire engine's siren and the delighted laughter of her son. *Happy birthday, Max,* she thought. *Happy day for us all.*

EPILOGUE

"I CAN'T SEE!" Max complained. "Daddy, I can't see!"

Sharon was amazed at how easily Max had taken to calling Brett "Daddy." She was even more amazed at how readily Brett accepted his new title.

They stood, the three of them, on the sidewalk just outside the YMCA, watching a parade. Max wore the Red Sox cap Brett had bought for him to protect his face from the bright September sun. He'd changed so much in the past year, his face slimming, his body stretching, his vocabulary expanding almost weekly.

But he wasn't too big to sit on Brett's shoulders—and he wasn't too old to roar with delight when Brett swung him up onto those shoulders. Broad strong shoulders, the sort of shoulders that symbolized everything a father ought to be.

Sharon wished she could climb onto Brett's shoulders, too. She could see well enough through the two-deep crowd that lined the sidewalk, cheering and waving tiny American flags as the parade moved past them. A fife-and-drum corps clad in Colonial regalia strode by, drumming in crisp tempo while performing "Yankee Doodle" and other traditional marching songs. They were followed by a stagecoach pulled by a team of high-stepping horses—Max squealed with excitement when he saw the animals. It was followed by a caravan of classic antique cars, and then by the high school marching band, which blasted onlookers with a slightly out-of-tune rendition of a Sousa march. After the band the mayor cruised by, seated in an open convertible so he could wave to all his constituents. And then came the floats, representing just about every major retailer and social organization in Arlington.

They'd clearly all tried to outdo one another. The Garden Club's float was festooned in colorful spring blossoms. Holly's Department Store had a float featuring a rainbow theme, with a huge vat of chocolate coins covered in gold foil representing the pot of gold. Sales clerks on the float tossed coins to the crowds; Brett was able to snag a couple for Brett. The Preservation Society's float featured a reconstruction of the Old Town Hall, looking almost as rickety as the real thing.

"There's Evan's float," Brett murmured, pointing out the float sponsored by Champion Sports. The owner of the sporting-goods chain was one of Brett's poker buddies. Sharon had gotten to know him and his wife after meeting them at the wedding party she and Brett had hosted at Reynaud, the restaurant where they'd spent their first evening together, dancing and talking and beginning their long inexorable tumble into love.

"Baseball!" Max hollered, pointing to the float, which had been done up in a baseball theme. A mannequin in a Boston Red Sox uniform stood with a bat poised above his shoulder, while a mannequin in a New York Yankees uniform was arranged in a windup position, prepared to pitch. The depiction of baseball's fiercest rivalry, one whose fault line ran through Arlington, prompted cheers and jeers and good-natured heckling and bragging from the crowds at the corner of Hauser Boulevard and Dudley Road.

If Sharon could have climbed atop Brett's shoulders, she would have had a better vantage for taking photos. She supposed she could climb up onto the roof of the YMCA building—they might have a staircase leading up to the top—and shoot photos from there. But she didn't want to leave Brett and Max. And Brett would no doubt give her hell for standing on a roof.

She'd gotten a few good photos by darting among the throngs, breaking through to the curb for a moment and catching an image, a float, a smiling child or an elderly couple in folding lawn chairs, appealingly serene as they observed the parade. Those photos were for personal use, to preserve Max's memories of the parade. She didn't need to take photos of Arlington for any other purpose right now.

The commemorative books were everywhere. At least half the people crowding the sidewalk seemed to have one tucked under an arm or poking out of a tote bag. The vendors wheeling carts of souvenirs on the outer edges of the parade were hawking copies of the book along with pennants, miniature models of the Old Town Hall and other memorabilia. The cover of the commemorative book featured a photo she'd taken of the Old Town Hall at sunrise, when the pillared facade was glazed with the golden light of a new day.

She almost hadn't gotten the commission. A staff

photographer from the *Arlington Gazette* had also
been under serious consideration for the job, but the
committee had ultimately chosen Sharon. She should
have been thrilled, but instead she'd been suspicious.
"Did you pull strings for me?" she'd accused Brett.

"I swear, I didn't."

"But you knew people on the committee. That
friend of yours, Gail Murphy—"

"She wasn't the only person on the committee,"
he'd pointed out.

"But you knew her. You twisted her arm, didn't
you?"

He'd lifted the phone, punched in a number and
handed it to her. "Ask her yourself," he'd challenged.

Stunned, Sharon had stammered when a child had
answered. "I'm—I'd like to speak to Gail Murphy,
please." She'd glowered at Brett while the child hollered for his mother to pick up the phone, and he'd
shrugged innocently and wandered out of the
kitchen, leaving her to confront Gail alone.

Gail had reassured her that her talent, and not
Brett's connections, had decided the committee.
"Well, that's not exactly true," Gail had elaborated.
"The guy from the *Gazette* was very talented, too.
It was a tough call. But then someone brought in a
copy of Arlington Financial's annual report. It con-
tained the best photo of Brett any of us had ever seen.
We figured that if you could make Brett look that
comfortable in front of a camera, you must be some
kind of genius."

The photo he'd chosen for his firm's annual report
had been a good one, but not the best. The best she
kept framed and displayed on her desk at the studio.

It was the final photo she'd taken of him that first day, the candid one in which she'd captured a piece of his soul on film.

"That's about it, Max," Brett said, bending over so Max could slide off his shoulders and onto the sidewalk. The last of the floats had rolled past them, heading down Dudley. Max seemed generally satisfied with the pageantry—and with his loot: two foil-covered chocolate coins, a plastic whistle, a colorful Arlington pennant and an Arlington 300 button, which Brett had pinned to his baseball cap.

"That was a good parade," Max said solemnly.

"I thought it was pretty good, too," Brett agreed, holding Max's hand tightly as the crowd began to disperse.

"And now we're going to the carnival."

"The carnival is later this afternoon," Brett reminded him. "Right now, I think we need to get your mother a seat in the shade."

Sharon dismissed his concern with a shake of her head. "I'm fine, Brett."

"And my goal is to keep you that way. Why don't we go get something to drink."

"McDonald's?" Max asked. He pronounced it so clearly now.

Brett wrinkled his nose. No matter how Max pronounced it, Brett still didn't appreciate the noise level inside the eatery. "Why don't we stop in at my office," he suggested, instead. Arlington Financial's headquarters were just a block away. The building would be locked on a weekend, but as the owner of one of the companies it housed, Brett had a key.

Max let out a cheer. "I love your office!"

Brett and Sharon both laughed. She couldn't understand what Max found so exciting about Brett's office. Sure, he had lots of computers, and a very impressive photocopier. The carpets were soft, the ventilation system silent, and spinning around in Brett's swivel chair seemed to bring Max close to nirvana. But she suspected the office's strongest appeal, as far as Max was concerned, was its impeccable neatness. Nothing was ever out of place. No clutter obstructed the floors and tabletops. The place was more orderly than any room at home. When Brett had opened his house to Sharon and Max, he'd grudgingly opened it to all Max's toys, too. Max had exuberantly taken over the place, depositing his playthings throughout the house as if he were marking his territory.

Brett complained about the mess sometimes, and yelled at Max to clean up after himself. Max pouted but obeyed. "I am not going to do everything for him," Brett had explained to Sharon one time as they stood watching Max gather his stray toys from the den and lug them to his bedroom. "And I'm not going to let him turn the house into a place I don't feel at home in. I can be his father without giving up my own needs. I love him, but I'm not going to let him take over."

He loved her son. *Their* son. And he was holding his own with Max. He'd learned that being a father didn't mean losing himself.

Max skipped ahead of them down the sidewalk, then waited at the building doorway until they reached it. Brett unlocked the glass door and handed his key ring to Max, who liked to shake it and make the half-dozen keys on it jingle. He handed the key ring back to Brett once they were inside, because a greater temptation—the elevator button—awaited him there.

Once they arrived at Arlington Financial's empty suite of offices upstairs, Sharon sank onto the sofa in the waiting area. She was tired, and the summery heat, though not extreme, had gotten to her. "Put your feet up," Brett urged, pushing the coffee table closer to the sofa.

"My feet are fine," she assured him.

"Your feet are walking for two." He grinned when he said it, a lighthearted, almost boyish grin.

"What does *that* mean?" Max asked, sending Brett a challenging stare. Sharon found it fascinating that, although she saw a lot of Steve in Max, she was beginning to see Brett in him, too. He'd picked up some of Brett's attitudes, his gestures, his mannerisms. Whenever Max said something Brett had trouble believing, Brett stared at Max exactly the way Max was staring at him now.

"You know what it means," Brett said, vanishing into the small kitchenette. "It means your mom is going to have a baby."

"Not for another four months," she warned Max. She didn't want him to pester her constantly about when the new baby was going to make its appearance. Four months probably meant little to Max, though. He believed he was going to be getting a new sister or brother any day now.

"Is the baby inside your feet?" he asked.

"No," she said, sliding off her sandals and lifting her feet onto the table. "The baby is in here." She patted her swollen abdomen. In response, the fetus gave a little flutter.

"So what did Daddy mean?"

"He was just making a joke."

Max pondered this. Evidently, he didn't consider the joke funny. "Can I feel the baby?"

"Sure. It's moving around right now." She took Max's hand and pressed his palm gently to the taut swell under her blouse. His eyes grew round and his mouth spread in a smile as the fetus fluttered again.

"I'm going to be a brother," he said. "I'll be the big boy. I'll take good care of the baby."

She almost argued that he would not take care of the baby at all. She would never turn her son into a baby-sitter, a surrogate father for his sibling. She wouldn't dump responsibilities on him the way Brett's mother had. It was only when she'd assured Brett of this that he'd agreed, with some trepidation, to have a baby with her. She hadn't expected to conceive so fast, but she was thrilled that she had.

Surprisingly, so was Brett.

He emerged from the kitchenette carrying a fruit juice box for Max and bottles of water for Sharon and himself. When he saw her lounging on the couch, with Max's hand still pressed against her, holding the baby inside her, he smiled. Not a huge smile. Not a teary-eyed smile. Just a Brett smile—a contented smile, a smile that told her he was ready to love another child.

He settled on the sofa so that Max was trapped between them. Max hoisted himself onto the sofa, released Sharon's belly and grabbed his juice box. "What do you say?" Brett hinted.

"Thank you."

Brett nodded. "I heard you telling Mommy you're going to take good care of the baby when it comes."

"Yup." Max pulled the straw off his juice box and nodded earnestly at Brett.

"You don't have to do that, you know. It's my job and Mommy's to take care of the baby."

"Okay." Max sipped a bit of juice, then settled back into the cushions between his parents and shrugged, another gesture he'd picked up from watching Brett. "You and Mommy can take care of the baby, and I'll take care of you."

"You've already done that," Brett murmured, his eyes meeting Sharon's above Max's head. She saw no humor in his face, no irony. He'd meant every word. Max had taken care of him. He'd taught Brett more about growth and faith than she ever could teach him. Brett had known all his life how to be a dad. But Max had taught him how to love being one.

He'd taken very good care of Brett, indeed.

The Shannon Sisters

A Trilogy by C.J. Carmichael
The stories of three sisters from Alberta whose lives and loves are as rocky—and grand—as the mountains they grew up in.

A Second-Chance Proposal
A murder, a bride-to-be left at the altar, a reunion. Is Cathleen Shannon willing to take a second chance on the man involved in these?

A Convenient Proposal
Kelly Shannon feels guilty about what she's done, and Mick Mizzoni feels that he's his brother's keeper—a volatile situation, but maybe one with a convenient way out!

A Lasting Proposal
Maureen Shannon doesn't want risks in her life anymore. Not after everything she's lived through. But Jake Hartman might be proposing a sure thing....

On sale starting February 2002

Available wherever Harlequin books are sold.

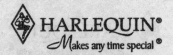

HARLEQUIN®
Makes any time special ®

Visit us at www.eHarlequin.com

HSRSS